My Best Friend's Ex

DARING DIVORCEES
BOOK TWO

SHANNYN SCHROEDER

Copyright © 2024 by Shannyn Schroeder

Cover created by Kari March Designs

This title was originally published by Entangled in 2019.

All rights reserved.

No part of this book may be reproduced in any form or by any electronic or mechanical means, including information storage and retrieval systems, without written permission from the author, except for the use of brief quotations in a book review.

ISBN: 978-1-950640-53-9

Chapter One

Trevor Booth brushed the rain from his hair as he walked into Sunny's Diner to meet his friends. While they didn't go to the divorce support group anymore, they still routinely met for coffee. His phone buzzed again. His ex, Lisa. It was her third text of the morning.

He stared at the screen as he neared the table.

"What's got you looking so serious?" Nina asked.

He glanced up before pulling a chair out to sit. Lisa wanted him to talk to their son.

"Trevor?"

"Huh?" He looked up again to find both Nina and Tess staring at him.

"What's wrong?"

"Lisa has been texting me since I got in the truck. Evan's acting up, and she wants me to talk to him."

"That's good, right? That she's asking for you to step in," Tess said.

"I suppose." He'd been feeling distant from his kids

lately, but it was normal. They were teenagers, and they lived with Lisa. His weekend visitation had been hit-or-miss. Part of him had wanted a more active role in their lives, though. This was his chance.

He glanced around to wave the waitress over to fill his coffee cup.

"What's Evan doing?" Nina asked.

"I don't really know. She said that he goes out without telling her where he is, and when she asks, he gets confrontational. They've been fighting a lot."

His phone buzzed again.

> Evan gets out of school at 3:30 if you want to pick him up.

Trevor sighed. Nothing like having his ex-wife passive-aggressively suggest how and when he should talk to Evan. He texted Lisa back to let her know he was working until five, but he'd call Evan and make plans for dinner.

> You could leave work early. You're the boss.

He scrubbed a hand over his face.

> And a conversation with Evan can wait a couple more hours.

> For sure today, though. Right?

> I promise.

He figured that would appease her, because she knew he made it a point to always follow through on a promise.

Lightning cracked outside. Rain pelted the plate glass windows of the diner, and he was glad his crew was working on an indoor job today.

> Thank you. I appreciate it. I'm at my wit's end with him.

> I'll see what I can do.

The waitress filled his cup, and he took a gulp. Then he turned his attention to the conversations going on around him. Tess was telling everyone about a weekend trip she and her boyfriend had taken with the kids to a water park.

Nina set her cup down. "Okay. Time for the rest of you to give us an update on the dating front."

A collective groan rumbled across the table. It had been months since Nina had issued a challenge to all of them to get back into the dating game. She passed a small flyer to each of them except Tess. "There's a singles mixer at this jazz club. I think we should all go."

Trevor read the flyer. He had no desire to meet a woman at a bar. He avoided even stepping foot in a bar. One of the perks of being a recovering alcoholic.

"There's not a drink minimum or anything," Nina said. Even though everyone in their group knew he was an alcoholic, it had always been Nina who was his biggest supporter.

"Even if I'm not expected to drink, picking up a woman in a bar isn't a good idea for me." He was fine being around people who drank. After being in AA for more than seven years, since a year after his divorce, he could function in most situations. He tended to use his alcoholism as a crutch to avoid interacting with people. He knew he did it, was aware it wasn't healthy, but as his sponsor often pointed out, he was a work in progress.

"I'm in," Evelyn said. She nudged Owen's elbow. "Let's do this."

They were best friends, having been a part of the divorce support group before the rest of them joined.

"Only if you come in separate cars and don't hang all over each other," Nina said.

"What are you talking about?" Owen asked.

Nina rolled her eyes. "How are you supposed to meet someone new if everyone thinks you're a couple?"

"No one thinks that."

"Keep telling yourself that," she countered. "Are any of you going to see Gabe soon?"

Evelyn laughed. "Why? You know he won't come with us."

She wasn't wrong. Gabe was more of a hermit than Trevor was. Trevor at least left the house every day to go to work. Gabe worked from his house. He'd never known anyone who disliked—no, distrusted—people more than Gabe did.

"Ugh. You guys are impossible."

"Maybe they're not ready to meet people," Tess offered.

"You didn't think you were ready, either, but when I prompted you to go out with Miles, look what happened."

"You have a point."

Trevor's phone rang. He glanced at the screen. Not a number he recognized, so he pushed it to voicemail. He tried not to interrupt time with his friends for a customer.

For the next half hour or so, they chatted and let Nina harass them about their dating lives. After he finished his second cup of coffee, he said his goodbyes and headed to his truck. Remembering the missed call, he pulled out his phone as he climbed behind the wheel. He clicked to the voicemail.

"Hello, Mr. Booth, I am calling from Rush Hospital. There's been an accident."

TREVOR NEEDED TO CHANGE POSITION, BUT HE COULDN'T. Trapped under the weight of his daughter's head on his lap and the grief surrounding both of his children, he couldn't force his body to move. So he sat on the couch for a few more minutes, guiltily soaking in the fact that his little girl—closer to woman than baby—had curled up and laid her head on his lap like she hadn't done since she was a toddler. Hannah slept silently while her older brother, Evan, snored in the chair beside them.

Trevor studied his kids. Hannah's long dark hair was spilling out of her ponytail. Evan sprawled in the chair, legs kicked out. He, too, no longer looked like a child. They seemed peaceful, though, so he wanted them to have this because when they awoke again, they would remember that their mother was dead and they were stuck with him.

While sitting in the near silence, he thought about the arrangements he still needed to make. He'd only made two phone calls from the hospital—one to Lisa's parents and one to her best friend, Callie. His former father-in-law had said he wanted to handle everything. The unspoken comment being that since the divorce, Trevor no longer had a claim to Lisa.

He'd shoved that aside, but now thoughts of Lisa and her parents were making him itchy. Easing Hannah's head off his leg, he stood and stretched. He scrubbed a hand over his face and walked through the house. He'd only been inside this place a handful of times. With the exception of the kids, he and Lisa had led very separate lives.

Not that it had been his choice, but he'd deserved it.

The walls needed to be patched and painted. A few pieces of trim were loose. The floor had seen better days. Why hadn't Lisa mentioned she needed work done? He would've taken care of all of this for her.

It was another reminder that she hadn't wanted him in her house.

In the kitchen, he got a glass of water with shaky hands. He gulped the liquid, knowing that tonight it wouldn't quench his thirst.

Before the glass was empty, the doorbell rang. *Fuck.* He'd hoped it would take them longer to get here from Indiana.

Trevor braced himself to face his former in-laws and opened the front door slightly. "The kids are asleep in the living room," he whispered before opening the door all the way.

Diane and Gordon looked older than he remembered, and their faces were ravaged with pain. Impeccably dressed in a black blouse and slacks, Diane strode into the house. Trevor briefly wondered if she'd changed into those clothes to show the world she was in mourning or if that was how she always dressed.

Gordon set a bag on the floor and shook Trevor's hand.

"I don't know what I'm supposed to say here," Trevor said, his voice scratchy.

"Not much to say."

In the living room, Diane stared at Hannah and Evan. "Why are they sleeping here? They belong in their beds. Crashing on uncomfortable furniture is the last thing their bodies need."

"They were exhausted and upset. We sat together until they passed out." He immediately regretted his choice of words, because it was too reminiscent of his drinking days. She shook her head and then knelt in front of the couch. "Hannah," she said softly, running a hand over his daughter's hair.

Hannah's eyes blinked open. "Grandma?"

"Yes, honey, I'm here."

Hannah sat up and looked around, like Dorothy after she'd returned home from Oz. Unfortunately, there wasn't a happy ending here. Her face crumpled, and Diane sat beside her and held her.

Evan woke and shifted. "Hi," he said, stretching his legs even more and throwing his arms over his head. At seventeen, he'd already mastered the manly way of hiding his emotions, and since he'd already cried with Trevor at the hospital, Trevor didn't expect to see much more from his son. Evan rubbed a hand over his head in a gesture Trevor had caught himself doing in uncomfortable situations.

"Have you eaten?" Diane asked.

"I ordered pizza earlier, but no one was particularly hungry," Trevor answered. He hated the constant implication that he couldn't care for his kids.

"Pizza?"

"We were a little busy today." Busy or not, it was usually pizza or some other takeout when he was with the kids, but he wouldn't admit that to Diane.

"How about I go in the kitchen and make something?"

"You don't have to do that, Grandma," Hannah said. "I'm still not hungry."

"Then let's get you to bed. The couch isn't a good place for you to sleep."

Hannah allowed her grandmother to usher her upstairs. Gordon, Trevor, and Evan all looked at one another. "Can I get you anything, Gordon?" Not that Trevor had any idea what he was offering.

Gordon shook his head. He had always been a man of few words.

"So, uh, I...about the arrangements. I have more phone calls to make to let people know. I wasn't sure..." Trevor swallowed hard. "I didn't know what you and Diane would want to handle, or what I should take care of."

"If you could make calls to her friends that would be helpful. Diane and I will handle the family calls."

"Okay. I'll do that now." He hitched a thumb over his shoulder toward the kitchen and gave Gordon a quick nod.

Outside on the back deck, Trevor leaned against the rail and then thought better of it. It wobbled under his weight. One more thing to add to the list of repairs. Then he pulled out his phone and made the most important call of the day.

It was evening, and Trevor hoped Karl would answer. Karl always did unless he was in a meeting.

"Hello."

"Hey, Karl."

"Trevor. What's up?"

Trevor sighed and sank to the stairs. "My ex died. I'm here with my kids and my former in-laws, and I haven't wanted a drink this bad in years."

"Talk to me."

CALLIE LARSON SAT IN THE BACK OF THE CAR DRIVING AWAY from O'Hare and rested her head against the cool glass of the window. Sights of the city flashed by as the car sped down the highway. She'd spent more time in the air than she had on the ground in the past thirty hours. The Philippines had never felt so far away. Just another dot on the map. Until today—yesterday. As soon as she'd received Trevor's message, she'd grabbed her things and gone straight to the airport, emailing her client on the way.

She'd never walked away from a job without finishing, but she couldn't think, much less shoot pictures.

Callie...It's Trevor. I hope you get this wherever you are. It's the only number I have. It's Lisa. She was in a car accident... She...she didn't make it.

The words echoed through her, and Callie's heart

lurched. Trevor's voice wasn't right, but she was torn between thinking he'd had a drink and thinking he was simply griefstricken. It was a rare occasion for her to pray, but on the entire flight, that's what she'd found herself doing. Hannah and Evan would need Trevor, and if he fucked up by falling off the wagon, she'd kill him.

She clung to the fact that Lisa had said he'd been sober for years, that he'd made amends as best he could. Lisa had forgiven him, even if she'd had no desire to reconcile.

My best friend is gone.

Callie had no idea how to come to terms with that. Trevor had called yesterday afternoon. By now, Lisa's parents would be there, trying to take over. She stared at the city skyline against the pinkish purple of the evening sky and thought of her friend. They'd left Indiana together two days after high school graduation, desperate to get away from their families. They'd had each other; they hadn't needed anyone else.

Now Callie had no one. The car turned down a side street. This had become Callie's favorite part of any trip. The feeling of returning home. But now, she had no idea how much longer this would be her home.

The car stopped, and the driver got out and opened the trunk. Callie jumped from the car. Although he was trying to be nice, she hated that drivers always wanted to take her bags. Her equipment was too expensive to entrust to just anyone. She reached into the trunk before he even touched a handle.

"I've got this, thanks." With her other hand, she pressed a ten-dollar bill into his palm. She swung her backpack over her shoulder and hefted the two equipment bags, leaving the trunk open for him to close.

For a full minute, Callie stood at the curb, staring at the house. She couldn't decide if she should go around back to the coach house where she lived or if she should go to the front door. She had a key, but using it suddenly seemed wrong. Lisa's family and her ex were inside that house.

But so were Lisa's kids. She straightened her tired body and forged ahead. She set a bag on the porch and rang the bell, which felt so foreign.

Trevor opened the door.

"Callie." His eyes widened in surprise. His eyes were clear, but he looked as exhausted as she felt. They also held a healthy amount of wariness. She hadn't seen him in years. The dark scruff on his jaw was now peppered with gray. But overall, he looked healthy. No alcoholic puffy red face. No sagging muscles. He was strong, broad.

"Hi."

He took a bag from her. "You should've called. I wasn't sure if you got my message." He looked at the other bags. "You didn't even go home first. I would've picked you up from the airport."

She smiled weakly. That was the Trevor she remembered from twenty years ago when she and Lisa had first met him. Always the helpful one. "I figured you'd be busy. Besides, I am home."

He shut the door behind them, his forehead crinkled. "Huh?"

"I rent the coach house out back." How did he not know that? Lisa had offered her the space four years ago.

"I didn't know. Lisa never said, and..." He shook his head. "I don't come here often."

That had been Lisa's doing. Callie filled her lungs. "Are they here yet?"

He nodded. She tucked her equipment bags into the front hall closet and walked into the living room.

"Who is it, Dad?" Hannah asked as she came from the kitchen. "Callie!" Her face lit up and she launched herself into Callie's arms, nearly knocking her over.

Callie held Hannah, who was looking more and more like her mother every day. She might've gotten her dad's dark hair, but she had Lisa's light blue eyes and fair skin.

"What's the commotion out here?" Diane said, wiping her hand on a towel. She saw Callie, and her lips flattened.

Yeah, no love lost there. Diane still blamed Callie for *making* Lisa run away, ever the bad influence that she was.

"Diane," she said with a nod of her head.

"Callie. What are you doing here?" The older woman, still thin, stood ramrod straight.

This would be good. If Trevor didn't know, neither did Diane. "I live here. In the coach house out back."

Diane's already-stony face became impenetrable. Callie withheld a snicker.

Hannah stepped back and took her hand. "Even if she didn't live here, Grandma, we want her here. *Mom* would've wanted her here. She's family."

Callie's throat closed. She couldn't swallow, could barely suck in a trickle of air. The teen was so much like Lisa. No one stood up for Callie the way Lisa always had. She squeezed Hannah's hand. "It's okay," she whispered. Looking at Diane and then Trevor, she added, "We're all adults. We know how to put our differences aside at a time like this."

She forced a smile she wasn't sure she'd ever feel again.

Diane, who would never let her manners be questioned, said with a tight smile of her own, "Of course. You look like you've been traveling. We've just had dinner. I'll warm some for you."

Trevor touched Hannah's shoulder. "Go help your grandma."

When they were gone, Trevor asked, "Can I get you anything? There's water or pop, but I haven't seen anything stronger."

So he'd looked. Callie tried to control her glare but failed. "There isn't anything stronger. After you..."

He stepped closer. "I wasn't looking to get drunk." He stared into her eyes. "Don't get me wrong, the urge was there. I lost my fucking wife, and the call of alcohol was strong. But I've come too far."

Callie nodded. His navy blue eyes were clear and sincere. She believed him, but she couldn't hide her wariness. "How are you holding up?" he asked.

"Okay." She shook her head. The gentleness of his tone crept over her, and tears threatened again. She'd never felt this alone. "I don't even know."

Trevor reached out tentatively and pulled her against his chest. In the warmth of his embrace with his soothing hand on her back, she released the tears and the grief she'd bottled since he'd first called her. Sobs racked her body, and Trevor simply held her tighter.

She didn't know how long they stood like that, but no one interrupted them. When she finally pulled away, Trevor's T-shirt was soaked. She wiped her face on her own sleeve and ran a hand down his torso. "Sorry about that."

"It's okay. We're all a mess. I know she was like a sister to you."

"I don't know what I'm going to do without her. She's been the one constant in my life since we were teenagers."

"Let's get you some food. You can tell me about your world travels."

Callie felt like she'd just slipped into the twilight zone. For years, she and Lisa and Trevor had been friends. She'd been slightly jealous of Lisa's relationship with Trevor. After all, they'd all met at the same time, and she and Trevor clicked in many of the same ways he and Lisa had. They'd never treated her like a third wheel, though. Even after Trevor and Lisa had married. But when he'd started drinking more and then they'd divorced, Callie had lost Trevor. She'd had to be there for Lisa.

Now his simple offer of conversation over dinner transported her to the past, and she realized her friend was back.

TREVOR STOOD OVER THE SINK AND WASHED DISHES JUST TO have something to do. Lisa had a dishwasher, and as far as he knew, it worked. But he needed to keep his hands busy. Diane and Gordon had moved into the small guest room yesterday, leaving Trevor to sleep on the couch. Diane had been right about the lack of comfort in sleeping there.

But there was nowhere else for him to sleep. He couldn't take Lisa's bed. He hadn't even been able to go into the room. He'd walked by, peeked in, and closed the door. Diane had decided what Lisa should be buried in tomorrow, just like she'd decided how the service would run and where they would eat after.

He didn't even know what he was still doing here. She acted as if he didn't exist. They didn't need him for anything.

At least when Callie had walked through the door, he'd been able to share some of the disdain Diane spread. Callie was probably the only person in the world Diane disliked as much as she did Trevor. In some ways, even more. If Callie hadn't convinced Lisa to move to Chicago with her, he never would've met her.

He dried the last dish and was at a loss for what to do next. The kids were up in their rooms. They, too, didn't seem to have a need for him.

When he turned, Diane and Gordon stood near the table. "We'd like to talk," Diane said.

"Okay."

"Outside might be better, so we have some privacy."

He tossed the towel on the counter and opened the back door, holding it for them. Diane walked down the stairs and sat on the old patio furniture that Trevor and Lisa had bought once his company started making money. Lisa had had dreams of big backyard barbecues with friends.

"We need to discuss the future," Diane began.

Trevor had expected a conversation about life insurance or handling Lisa's house, financial things they wanted to keep Trevor away from, but since he didn't consider a future anywhere with them, he was lost.

"The children need a stable environment."

Oh, fuck, no. "They have a stable environment."

Diane held up her hands, and for the first time since the divorce, her face softened. "We love our grandchildren. We just want what's best for them. Lisa's been their primary caregiver. She's done the day-to-day grind of parenting."

"I've taken care of my children."

"You've provided for them. You've always done that. Even when you were drinking. But children need more than financial security." She took a deep, wobbly breath. "They're all we have left of her. Parenting is difficult, and we don't want you to relapse."

"What exactly are you saying, Diane?"

"We'd like the children to come live with us." She reached over and patted his hand. "We know you love them. But are you prepared to take on everything? We're retired. We can give the children the attention they need."

Trevor swallowed. As much as his instinct wanted him to rage at her because they were his kids, deep down he knew she had a point. He'd never had to take care of the kids full-time. When they'd been little, Lisa had stayed at home while he'd worked. After the divorce, he'd seen the kids a time or two during the week and every other weekend. Recently, that had dropped off because they were teenagers. They'd wanted to hang out with friends.

So instead of yelling at his in-laws, he stood and said, "I'll think about it. But it's not a decision we're making without them. Their lives are here."

"Children are resilient. As a parent, it's your job to

make the best choices for them, even when they don't like it."

"I'm going back to my house for the night. Tell the kids to call if they need anything. I'll be back first thing in the morning." He grabbed his keys and hopped in his truck. For the past two days he'd been squeezing in going to his house to shower and change, but tonight, he'd sleep in his own bed. He needed the space to think.

For as angry as he wanted to be at Diane, she made valid points. What the hell did he know about being a full-time parent? Lisa had been an excellent mom. She'd always had her shit together, and he'd never bothered to learn any of it. He didn't have to; she'd had it covered.

Their kids were good people, and they were smart, in spite of all the ways Trevor might've fucked them up.

He was so bone-tired that he was grateful he'd bought his house in the same general neighborhood as Lisa's. At first, she'd thought he was trying to keep tabs on her, but he'd gotten the house because he wanted to be close to the kids. Lisa had come to like the idea because the kids could get to his house after school. He'd never had a reason to go to her house.

She'd spent years making sure he understood they were divorced, but until last year, he'd held out hope that they would get back together. And since then, he'd tried to move on with his life in ways he hadn't before. He'd started dating but had no one serious in his life. Dating was hard, and not just because so many people wanted to meet at a bar for drinks as a first date. Sometimes he felt too old for that kind of shit.

He was at the point that he could be around people who drank and be okay—until this week, anyway. Right now, he wasn't so sure that if someone offered him a beer he'd say no. But he also knew that he couldn't slip. Not now, with the kids counting on him.

He stripped on his way to the bathroom and took a long, hot shower. When he got out, someone was pounding on his door. His first thought was Evan and Hannah, but they had keys. So he wrapped a towel around his waist without drying and ran to the door.

Swinging the door wide without looking through the peephole, he was stunned to see Callie standing on his porch. Her hand was fisted and raised to knock again. Her eyes went wide.

"What's wrong? Are the kids okay?"

She blinked rapidly and opened her mouth. "Uh... they're asleep. I think." Her gaze coasted over him and he felt the sudden urge to cover himself.

Gripping the towel at his hip, he stepped back from the door. "Come in. I'll put on some clothes. Give me a minute."

Chapter Two

Callie needed a drink but knew Trevor wouldn't have any alcohol in his house. She felt like a crazed woman, pounding on his door, but after overhearing Diane, she couldn't let it go. She needed to talk to Trevor. She hadn't expected to catch him dripping wet and mostly naked.

She felt ashamed for checking out her dead best friend's ex-husband, but she was only human. Trevor had always been a good-looking guy, but he'd aged really well. The construction business kept his body built, and sobriety suited him. He had the bulky, toned muscle of a man who used his body every day. Unlike the gray she kept colored on her head, his sprinkling made him look more distinguished, sexy.

Callie laughed at her ridiculous thoughts. God, how she wished Lisa were here. She'd laugh with Callie and tell her that it was always okay to look as long as she didn't touch. Trevor was hers. Until he wasn't. Because he'd screwed up. Callie's laugh turned slightly maniacal.

Trevor came back into the room wearing low-slung sweatpants and a T-shirt. "Are you okay?"

She shook her head and took a deep breath. "Fuck no, I'm not okay. My best friend is dead, and you're thinking about letting her crazy-ass parents take her kids."

"And something about that was funny?"

"No." She rubbed a hand over her face. Jet lag was kicking her ass, so her filter was on the fritz. "I was laughing because you opened the door in a towel and I was thinking how good you look, which made me feel guilty because you're Lisa's husband—ex-husband. And then I thought about what she would say about all of it, and the whole conversation in my head was a little sick and twisted." After the words poured out, she inhaled deeply again.

"So it was basically laugh hysterically or cry."

"Pretty much."

"Come on. I'll make some coffee."

"Got any decaf? I'm wired enough as it is."

"Sure."

He led the way into the kitchen, and she sat at the small table. Only two chairs. For some reason, that made her sad. Which almost made her laugh again, because she didn't even have a table.

She sat in silence while he made coffee.

When the coffeepot began to sputter, he took the chair across from her. "Tell me why you're here. How did you even know where to find me?"

"I've always known where you live. Lisa told me."

"Yet she never mentioned that you live in her coach house." Callie shrugged. She knew Lisa tried to keep most of her life away from Trevor. She'd been too worried that she'd take him back. She'd believed Trevor was her true love, but they weren't good together. The only way to move on was to keep her distance. But saying any of that to Trevor right now seemed cruel. "I overheard Diane telling you that she wants to take the kids."

Trevor nodded. Then he rose and filled two cups of coffee. He set a mug in front of her and turned to the fridge. "All I have is milk. No cream."

"That's fine." She accepted the carton of milk and the sugar he offered. Did he remember how she took her coffee or was he just guessing? She stirred in the condiments. "You can't do it."

"What?"

"Let her have the kids. You know how Lisa felt about them. She would never want her parents to raise Evan and Hannah." Her voice cracked on the last part.

Trevor remained silent, turning his coffee cup in slow circles. Callie knew she needed to convince him. Tonight. She didn't know why it was imperative to have this discussion right now, but it was.

"How much did Lisa tell you about her childhood?" Callie asked.

"Most things, I think."

"Then you know how much she hated the way her parents raised her." She took a sip of coffee. "Her parents and mine were close. Best friends. That's why Lisa and I were so close. But our parents were controlling in ways that weren't normal. They told us how to dress, what to do, where to go. We made a pact when we were teenagers. No matter what, we'd look out for each other."

"I don't know anything about your parents, but Diane

and Gordon aren't monsters. It's not like Lisa cut them out of her life."

Like Callie had cut her parents from hers. She didn't know if Trevor was aware of that, but his comment carried the hint. "You're right. Lisa was always the good girl. She followed the rules, did what they wanted. The only time she ever went against their wishes was moving to Chicago with me." She drank more coffee. "Well, and when they demanded she move home with the kids after the divorce."

"What?"

"She never told you, huh? After the divorce, they reminded her that they told her not to move to Chicago. That she didn't have the capacity to make good choices, as evidenced by her marriage to you. She needed to come home so they could help her."

Trevor clamped his mouth shut. He took the news like a punch on that angled jaw.

"She didn't talk to them for a full two years after that. For all your faults, Trevor, she never thought of you as a mistake. You taught her to be strong. She always loved you. She had faith you were going to fix yourself and be a good father."

He rubbed roughly at his eyes. "You don't get it, Callie. I don't know what I'm doing with them. She took care of everything. I don't know how to do what she did."

"So you figure it out."

He huffed. "Easy for you to say."

"What's that supposed to mean?"

"It's easy to sit there and tell me what's best for my kids. How I should man up when you have no idea what it's like to be responsible for other people. The only person you have to worry about is yourself."

His words stung, but they were true. Except for Lisa. She'd always worried about Lisa and the kids. "You're right. I don't have kids. But I also know how important it is to do what's right. They're not my kids, but I love them. What's more, I know what Lisa would want."

"Christ, Callie. What if I fuck them up? She was born to be a mom. How do you know I'm what's best for them?"

She softened before continuing her argument. He was scared. "Let me ask you this—after the divorce, did she change her emergency contact information or the beneficiary of her life insurance policy?" Callie already knew the answer.

Trevor shook his head.

"That's because she trusted you."

"I don't deserve that trust. I can't do it."

"Yes, you can. You're not alone."

"The fuck I'm not. What? Are you offering to stay and help?" His laugh was bitter. "Going to finally hang up your passport?"

"Fuck you, Trevor. I travel for work. But I've been here. I've been a part of the kids' lives for years. More than just dropping in for birthdays and holidays. I'm one of the emergency contacts for school. Over the past year, I've probably had more dinners with them than you have."

As soon as she spoke those final words, she regretted them. His face fell. It didn't matter that she spoke the truth; she didn't have to be an asshole about it. "I'm sorry. I didn't mean it like that."

He waved a hand. "You're right. I didn't even know you were practically living with them. It kind of proves my point, though. I might not be the best thing for them."

"No matter what, you're their dad. They need you far more than they need Grandma and Grandpa. Even if they mean well, which I always doubt, they will crush the kids' spirit. Everything good that Lisa helped build in Hannah and Evan will fade."

"You grew up in that environment, and your spirit seems to be just fine."

"Because I fought them every step of the way and escaped the first chance I got." She'd attempted early on to reestablish a relationship with her parents after she'd moved. She'd believed they would treat her like an adult. Instead, they'd demanded she stop acting like a child and return home.

She tried a different tactic. "What about the message you're sending them? They just lost their mom. If you ship them off to Indiana, they'll feel like you don't want them."

"That's bullshit."

"How would you convince them otherwise?" Callie was clinging to anything she could. She had no legal claim to those kids, but she couldn't let Lisa down.

"I don't know what's right, but I want my kids to thrive. Like I told Diane, I won't make this decision without them."

Callie was glad he reiterated that and it hadn't been words thrown at his in-laws. She had little doubt that the kids would choose to stay here.

They sat in silence for a few minutes. Finally, Callie

said, "I really miss her. It's only been a couple of days, so maybe it's the idea that I can't just pick up the phone to hear her voice, but I miss her."

"I miss her, too." Trevor stared into her eyes, and she knew he'd been missing Lisa for a lot longer than two days.

His phone buzzed on the table. He glanced at the text and clicked the phone back to sleep.

"Girlfriend?"

He shook his head. "Nina. A friend, one from the group I have coffee with."

"From AA?"

"No. We met in a divorce support group. And we're just friends."

"No one special in your life?" She didn't know why she asked. She knew that Lisa had dated periodically over the past few years, but the kids had never mentioned any of Trevor's girlfriends. Part of Callie worried that he was still pining for Lisa.

He chuffed. "Dating sucks."

"Tell me about it."

"You can walk into any bar and have men talking to you within seconds."

"Been there, done that. It gets old." She smiled. "Like us."

"Why didn't you ever settle down and get married?"

She hated that question, so she offered her prepared answer. "Hard to have a lasting relationship when I travel. I've found most men don't trust that I can be faithful when I'm thousands of miles away." It was mostly true. She didn't need to mention that she'd thought she'd found her partner, once, someone who really understood her. But like everyone else, he'd made demands she couldn't live with. So she'd filled her schedule with so many jobs she wouldn't have time for a serious relationship.

THE ENTIRE DAY HAD BEEN BRUTAL. TREVOR HAD WOKEN UP early and gotten dressed for the service before heading back to Lisa's house. Diane had the kids up and ready, but they dragged their feet. The service had been everything Diane had wanted but had reminded him nothing of Lisa.

Callie's words from the previous night had started to sink in. He didn't speak at the service because he felt that it was no longer his place, but as everyone else stood and told stories about Lisa, Callie came to his side and took his hand.

The distance of the years and the alcohol-faded memories had made him forget what a good friend she'd been. Not just to Lisa, but to him as well.

The New Beginnings crew—man, he'd always hated that nickname—came to the service to support him even though they'd never met Lisa. They'd created a protective bubble around him, and for a few minutes, he could breathe.

But now the service was over, as well as the luncheon, and it was time to go home. He needed to talk to the kids about Diane's offer, but he had no idea where to start. So he drove back to Lisa's house in silence. Diane and Gordon's car was already in the driveway.

His fingers flexed on the steering wheel of his pickup truck. Callie slid him a look from the passenger seat. The kids seemed to take no notice of the additional tension. When he parked, they all continued to sit in silence, staring at the house. Hannah whispered, "It's weird not seeing her car here." Lisa's car had been totaled when she'd lost control in the rain.

After a deep breath, Trevor cut the engine and opened his door. Callie did the same.

On the curb, he said to her, "Thanks for your support today. I know I'm not your favorite person. It means a lot. Made it easier."

"Trevor, I don't hate you." She gave him a sad smile. "At first, part of me might've hated you a little. You hurt her. But you have your shit together. I don't have the energy to harbor bad feelings. Life's too short."

She blinked back tears, and Trevor had the urge to pull her to him to comfort her the way she had him, but the kids finally pushed the truck doors open and climbed out.

Diane stood in the doorway, arms crossed in her usual pose. "What are you waiting for?"

Hannah dragged her feet toward the front door. Callie stepped away to go through the backyard. Trevor and Evan followed Hannah, who froze at the top of the steps. Diane held the door open.

His daughter's shoulders hunched, and she turned back to Trevor. "I can't."

"You can't what, baby?"

"I can't go in. It's real now. She's never coming home." Her lips trembled.

Diane *tsked*. "It's your home. You spent the last two nights here without a problem."

Trevor grabbed Hannah by the shoulders. "What do you want?"

"Can we just go to your house?" Trevor looked at Evan, who shrugged, and then to Diane. Her eyes narrowed. He glanced at Callie, who had halted her progress to the coach house to watch the scene unfold.

"We can do whatever you want. Do you need to get some things, or do you have enough at my house?"

"I have enough. I'm just not ready."

"It's okay." He completely understood the concept of not being ready. He was unprepared for all of this.

With an arm around Hannah, he said, "Diane, the kids and I are going to spend the night at my house. I'll talk to you tomorrow."

"Trevor, we have things to deal with."

"I'm well aware. It'll keep." He asked Evan, "You need to get anything?"

Evan looked at his grandmother and then at Trevor. "I'm good."

While the kids didn't have duplicates of everything at his house, they each had a room and they kept clothes there so they wouldn't have to pack a bag whenever they came over. He'd tried to make his house as much a home as he could.

When he turned back to his truck, Callie was already moving away to go home. He considered inviting her, but that would just cause more trouble with Diane. The kids jumped back into the truck, this time with Evan in the front seat. Suddenly a million thoughts crashed into him. They had a few weeks left until the end of the school year.

He knew that even if the kids decided to go with Diane, they wouldn't go now. And next year Evan would be a senior. He wouldn't want to switch to a new school. Fuck. He'd called the school after the accident when he had to pull them out to go the hospital, but what now? Was he supposed to send them back on Monday? Should they stay home and grieve?

He needed to go back to work. His crew had been carrying the weight of the restaurant remodel for the last few days, and the customer was understanding, but he couldn't leave his life on hold.

He pulled up in front of his house. "I need to go to the store. There's not much to eat here."

Evan side-eyed him. "Grocery shopping in a suit? You might want to change."

"Good point. Then again, I look damn fine in a suit." Trevor chuckled.

Hannah jumped out of the truck. "That's false advertising. Some poor woman will look at you like that and start drooling only to be disappointed that your normal wardrobe is work boots and jeans."

"Point taken." The brief conversation eased his need to run. As soon as they were in the house, the kids disappeared into their rooms. That was where they normally went when they came over. How the hell was he supposed to know if this was okay?

He changed and then knocked on each of their doors to let them know he was leaving and to see if there was anything they wanted. They were both sitting in bed on their phones.

"I'm going to swing by the job site to make sure I'm still on track. Okay?"

Hannah looked up at him. "Okay. Don't forget to get stuff for dinner and lunch this week." Lunch? He had no idea what they ate for lunch. "Text me a list of what you need."

When he repeated himself for Evan, he got a wave. The boy didn't even look up from the phone. It irritated the hell out of him, but Trevor dismissed a lot of it as typical teenager crap.

There was so much for him to say that he was overwhelmed. For the moment, his kids were fine, and that was all that mattered, so conversations about what happened next could wait.

When he got to the job site, the guys were rolling up for the day.

His foreman, Jerry, met him outside. "What are you doing here?"

"Services are over. Kids are at my house, and I need food. I figured I'd stop by here and check things out."

"We're good. Everything's on schedule. Inspection on Monday will be a breeze."

"Thanks for keeping it on track. I'll be here for the inspection."

"I can handle it."

Trevor knew Jerry would be fine. He'd started years ago as Trevor's right hand. He could run the crew as well as Trevor. "I know. I need to be here. The superintendent will expect to see me."

"You're the boss."

"I'm going in. Enjoy your weekend."

"You, too." Jerry paused. "I mean..."

"I know what you mean."

Trevor walked into the closed restaurant. The electricians were already gone, and plumbers were finishing up, too. The superintendent, however, was nowhere to be seen. Trevor went to the back to check the kitchen. The room was in shambles, but the walls were all roughed-in, plumbing was in place. He saw nothing to raise concerns about passing inspection on Monday. Jerry was right. Everything was on schedule.

As he went back to his truck, Trevor looked up at the building. There had been a time not that long ago when he would have never considered taking on a job this size. Now it was routine.

By the time he got to the store, Hannah had sent him a long and detailed list of items to get. His cart was fuller than it had ever been in any store. Except a supply house, of course. Lisa had always told him that teenagers ate a lot. He'd seen it when they were with him, but he hadn't considered what it would be like to buy food for a whole week.

He looked at his cart again. Was this a whole week's worth of groceries?

As he stood in line to pay, his phone buzzed with another text. Damn. He didn't want to go back to find anything else.

> Is it okay if I invite Callie over?

Trevor stared at the text. Before he could respond, Hannah continued.

> She's sad, too, and probably all alone.

He sighed.

> Go ahead, but don't pressure her. She might not be up for it.

Sliding his phone back into his pocket, he began loading food onto the conveyor belt. Looked like Callie was going to be in his life again. He wasn't sure how to feel about that. She'd been a friend for many years, but Lisa got her in the divorce. Of course, Lisa and Callie had been childhood friends, but he'd met them both at the same time. Callie had meant a lot to him. In fact, in another life, he might've ended up married to her instead of Lisa. But in the beginning, in the crucial get-to-know-you phase, Callie was always taking off to travel. Lisa had been here.

Now Callie was back and his feelings were a bit muddled, but he didn't have time to sort out his emotions with everything else going on. He'd take whatever help she offered.

CALLIE STARED AT THE TEXT FROM HANNAH. HER INSTINCT was to accept the invitation. But they were at Trevor's house. Her phone buzzed with another text. This time Hannah sent Trevor's address. She debated asking if Trevor knew Hannah had invited her. She didn't want the kids to think there was any tension or bad feelings between her and Trevor, but she also didn't want to crash his house without his knowledge.

> Does your dad know you invited me?

> Yep. He's cool.

> Okay. I'll make dinner. Be there soon.

She left her house quietly so she wouldn't draw any attention. She stopped at the store and picked up ingredients for tacos. When she pulled up at Trevor's house, his truck wasn't outside, and she had the sneaking suspicion that she'd been lied to.

With groceries in hand, she went to the front door. Hannah answered.

"Where's your dad?"

"Grocery shopping. He has like nothing to eat here. What'd you bring?"

"Tacos."

"Thank God. I'm starving."

They went to the kitchen together, and Callie pulled food from the bags. She looked around the kitchen in a way she hadn't last night. It was a nice place. Not fancy, but clean lines, sturdy wood. So different from the lived-in feel of Lisa's house, where things were often falling apart.

Hannah helped without being asked. She grabbed a frying pan and pulled out a knife.

"How are you holding up?" Callie asked.

"Okay, I guess. It was too hard to be at home. She's all over the house." Hannah began chopping the onion. "And Grandma..."

Callie stiffened. "What about your grandma?"

"You know how she is."

Callie nodded but didn't comment. "You know what we need? Some music." She pulled out her phone and opened her music app.

"I have speakers. Hold on." Hannah ran out of the room, and Callie heard her thumping up the steps.

A moment later, she was back with two small speakers. She hooked them to the phone. Music filled the kitchen. The first song that shuffled through was "Born in the USA" by Springsteen. Callie dumped ground beef into the frying pan while singing.

They worked in silence as they added the onions and seasoning to the beef. The song switched to "Dancing Queen" by ABBA. Callie paused the song.

"Okay, you have to hear this. Your mother loved this song. Like completely adored it and would listen to it on loop for hours. Drove me crazy. We were tiny when the song released, but she found the album and fell in love. Your grandma hated it. To this day, I think she'd cringe if she heard it. She felt it was a bad influence on your mother." Callie left out the part where Diane had taken the cassette tape from Lisa. And how Callie had gotten her a new one that she'd kept hidden and only listened to on her Walkman.

"She almost never talked about what her life was like growing up."

"I guess I'll have to share all of her secrets then."

Hannah smiled, and Callie pressed the play button and turned the volume up. Then she and Hannah sang and danced in the kitchen while stirring the taco meat. They were having so much fun that they didn't hear Trevor come in.

When Callie spun in her dance, the sight of Trevor in

the doorway startled her, and she nearly dropped the spatula. The song wound down, so Callie lowered the volume again.

Trevor continued to stare at her.

"Sorry. We didn't hear you."

"Dad. Did you know that was one of Mom's favorite songs?"

Trevor's jaw muscle clenched, and he cleared his throat. "Yeah. I did. Can you get your brother to help you with the rest of the groceries?"

"Sure." Again the teen ran from the room.

Callie lowered the flame on the stove. "Hannah told me you knew she invited me."

"I did."

"Is something wrong?"

He shook his head. "When I came in…" He released a long, slow breath. "Seeing you dance around with Hannah to that song. I wasn't prepared."

"I'm sorry. I wasn't trying to upset you."

"No," he said quickly. "It was the look of happiness on Hannah's face. I wasn't sure I'd ever see that smile again." He neared and set a bag on the counter. "Thank you," he added quietly.

"I wasn't thinking. The song came on and you're right, I can't hear that song without thinking of Lisa, so I shared it with her daughter."

"I think we all need that reminder. She would want them to laugh."

"I agree." She turned back to dinner because if she didn't, she might start to cry again. After the service, she'd been afraid of being alone. For the first time in her life, she'd felt empty when she'd walked into her living room. Being here with Trevor and the kids eased that feeling.

"Hannah sent me to the store with a huge list. I got stuff for dinner."

"I told her I'd make dinner when she texted. Tacos."

"I didn't know you cook."

"I've picked up a few things here and there on my travels."

"I guess that beats my frozen pizza or sub sandwiches."

"Spoken like a true bachelor."

"Takes one to know one."

"True."

"Listen. I'm going to talk to the kids tonight about Diane's offer. Will you stay?"

She nodded. She was touched that he would ask. "Whatever you need."

The kids came in loaded with bags. They set everything on the kitchen table.

She handed the spatula to Trevor. "Here. Stir. Let's see what you bought."

The bags had lots of easy-to-prepare meals. Lunch meat. Bread. Peanut butter. Jelly. Cereal. Looked like he planned for the kids to stay here at his house. Callie wondered what that meant for her living situation. She'd have to talk to Trevor about that. If she needed to find an apartment, she'd have to start looking.

She took care of the refrigerated items since there was only one place to put them. The kids handled the nonperishables while they discussed the merits of the brands Trevor had bought. When the bags were empty, the kids moved to leave the room.

"Don't go far. Dinner will be ready in a few minutes," she said. She and Trevor prepared the rest of the meal, putting shells on the table along with chips and salsa and guacamole. She shredded some lettuce and chopped tomatoes while Trevor put the meat in a bowl for the table.

Callie loved the idea of a family-style meal. However, they didn't have enough chairs. "Do you have more chairs?"

"When the kids are here, we usually have pizza in the living room. Uh…"

"Don't worry. We can fill our plates here and take them in the other room."

"See? This is what I'm talking about. I can't even handle dinner."

She ran a hand down his arm. "You're doing fine."

"Not true, but thanks. I'll call the kids. You might want to make a plate before they come down. This'll be gone in a blink."

As if on cue, Callie's stomach rumbled. She hadn't eaten much at the luncheon after the service, so she was starving. She loaded a plate. Trevor's voice boomed in the other room. She munched on a chip while the kids and Trevor got their food.

When they were all settled in the living room, Trevor wasted no time in opening the discussion. "We need to talk about what happens next."

"What do you mean?" Evan asked. He crunched on a taco.

"Your grandparents made an offer, and I think you should know about it." At the mention of Diane and

Gordon, the kids froze. "They'd like you to come live with them."

Evan dropped his taco and Hannah put her plate on the floor in front of her. The kids looked at each other, and then turned to Trevor.

"Hell, no," Evan said at the same time Hannah asked, "Don't you want us?"

"Crap. No. I mean, yes. Fuck." He put his food down and wiped his hands on his jeans. "Your mom always knew what she was doing with you guys."

Callie snorted, and Trevor shot her a look.

"I have no idea how to do this. Your grandma brought up the idea that she'd like you to move in with them."

"That's bullshit. Next year is my senior year. All our friends are here."

Hannah's eyes became glassy, but she didn't talk.

"I'm not saying that you have to go. Or that I want you to go. I want you to know it's an option."

"So we can stay with you?" Hannah asked in a small voice.

"Of course."

"Then we're staying," she said emphatically. "Right?" she added with a look at her older brother.

"Yeah."

"Okay," Trevor said, the tight feeling in his chest loosening. He hadn't realized how much he'd wanted the kids to choose him.

Hannah smiled, and Evan returned his focus to his dinner.

Trevor picked up his plate. "Then the next thing we need to talk about is where we'll live. I can't afford to pay two mortgages."

Callie scooted forward on the couch. This wasn't her conversation to have, but the outcome would affect her.

"You guys can move in here permanently, and we can sell the other house."

Callie wasn't surprised that he led with that option. He'd said he'd slept on the couch at Lisa's. He obviously hadn't been comfortable sleeping in her room. She also knew that he'd intentionally purchased his house in the same neighborhood so it wouldn't interfere with the kids getting to and from school or their friends' from his house.

When no one said anything, he continued. "Or we can sell both houses and find something new. A fresh start."

"As long as I can bring all my stuff, I don't care which house we live in," Evan said.

"But what about Callie?" Hannah asked.

"Don't worry about me," she said.

Trevor looked at her. When their eyes met, it was like he hadn't even thought of her. And why would he? She wasn't his problem.

"Well, if we decide to sell that house, it'll take some time. It needs some work before it can even go on the market. I'm not going to throw Callie out on the street."

Callie smiled. "I can start looking for a place."

"Can't we stay there?" Hannah asked.

Trevor leaned back on the couch. He was trying to cover being uncomfortable. "I suppose we could. It still needs work, though."

"I think we should live there."

Callie set her plate on the coffee table. "Hannah, honey, don't worry about me. I'll be fine. It's not like I'll be homeless."

"But if we're here, you won't be with us."

Callie didn't know what to say. She'd never considered the impact her presence had on the kids.

"We have some time to think about it," Trevor said. "And no matter where Callie is living, she'll always be welcome to come over."

"It won't be the same," Hannah mumbled as she picked up her plate again.

They all dropped into silence, and it was killing Callie. "Well, I think the conversation has been heavy enough. Big decisions were made. Let's talk about something fun. What's going on with school?"

Evan popped the rest of his third taco in his mouth. "School's not fun."

"I think you and Dad should tell us some more fun stories about Mom." Hannah looked up at Evan. "Did you know Mom's favorite song was 'Dancing Queen'? And that Grandma hates it?"

"Now I know what to add to my playlist," Evan said.

Callie's eyes popped. "I didn't share that with you to use against your grandma."

Trevor laughed. "It might be fun to watch."

Callie couldn't hold back her own laugh. "You would think that, because she'd blame me."

"So what? You know you get off on being the troublemaker."

Absolutely not what gets me off. The flirtatious answer almost slipped past her lips, but Evan and Hannah were watching the interaction with rapt attention. Callie turned to them. "I am not a troublemaker."

"Really? What about the time you got us thrown out of Renaissance Faire?" Trevor prodded.

Evan shot out of his seat. "Wait. Don't say anything until I get back. I want to hear this."

"The juggler was wrong. He had no business getting us thrown out."

"Wait for me," Evan yelled.

Trevor had a glint in his eyes. She knew sharing this story was supposed to embarrass her, but if it made the kids smile and laugh and brought some joy in thinking about Lisa, she would do that all night.

Chapter Three

They shared a bunch of stories that were probably inappropriate for Trevor to be telling his teenage kids, the food was demolished, and the room was filled with laughter instead of crying. The kids dumped their plates in the sink and disappeared into their rooms again.

Trevor stood and reached for Callie's plate.

"I got it." She rose from the couch.

"You don't have to do that."

"I don't mind."

She followed him into the kitchen and for a brief minute, it all felt natural, which was weird because he hadn't laid eyes on Callie in years. He filled the sink while she wrapped up the little bit of food that was left over.

"Thanks for coming over tonight."

"I'm glad I was here. I think we all needed a night like this after the last few days."

He shoved his hands in the hot water. "About the house..."

"Trevor. It's okay. I get it. I'll be fine. Hannah will understand."

"For me, it's just about the house. That's where she moved on, you know? I don't have a place there."

"I know. She didn't make it easy for you."

"She shouldn't have. I didn't think about your role in this. Mostly because I didn't realize what a big part you've been playing in their lives."

Callie picked up a plate and rinsed it. "Like you said, no matter where I'm living, I'll still see them."

"But Hannah's right. It won't be the same." Trevor looked at her and saw Lisa's best friend, one she thought of as a sister. "I think Hannah might be using you to fill that void that I can't help with. You're a woman she trusts."

"It doesn't mean I need to live in her backyard."

Trevor felt trapped. He didn't want to live in Lisa's house, a place she'd filled with memories that had nothing to do with him. But he had this sudden revelation that his kids might need Callie. Hell, based on the last couple days, he needed her.

They finished the dishes, and Callie grabbed her purse. A stroke of panic hit him. He didn't want her to leave, but he pushed it back. "Thanks again for all your help."

"No problem. Let me know if you need anything."

"Well, if you're offering, you could swing by and let Diane know that the kids decided they want to stay with me."

She burst out laughing. "Hell no. I've held the sole responsibility for taking their girl from them. I'm not putting myself in the line of fire for taking their grandkids, too." Her laughter was like music. The sound brightened the room. She was so beautiful when she was laughing. Not that she wasn't always beautiful, but when she was smiling and laughing, she was magical. He wanted to lean in and pull her close.

Which was nothing he should be thinking about, so instead, he shrugged. "It was worth a shot since you were offering."

"Let me know when you plan to break the news."

"I won't need you to sit in on that."

She laughed again. "I want to know so I can make myself scarce, not so I can participate."

That made him smile. "When are you leaving town again?"

Her face shifted, masking the open happiness he'd just seen. "Not sure. I took off in the middle of a job when you called, so I might have to go back to the Philippines to finish up in a few days."

He nodded. He didn't even know why he'd asked. Having Callie here softened the blow of everything. In a way, it had been like old times, when they had been in their twenties and life had stretched out before them. She had been wild back then. And so much fun.

It had taken him years to understand how Lisa and Callie were friends. But they were so close, balancing each other out in ways that made them happy. There had been times that he'd been fiercely jealous of what they shared.

Now it felt ridiculous. Most people would go their whole lives without experiencing that kind of friendship.

Callie said goodbye and left.

From upstairs, music turned on. Loud. He moved to

the stairs to yell up and tell the offender to turn it down, and he paused because he realized it was "Dancing Queen." He'd never much liked that song, but he'd always put up with it for Lisa.

He went into his office and took out his calendar. He needed to get back to the jobs and plan how to move forward. The notes and updates Jerry had given him let him know that everything was on track, but seeing the site today had put his mind at ease. They had a few big jobs scheduled for the summer, which was bearing down on them quickly.

Damn. Summer was almost here. What the hell was he supposed to do with Hannah and Evan when they weren't in school? They were teenagers, so nothing? He'd never asked. They'd come to his house a weekend or two a month and he'd tried to see their sports and school activities, but he'd never tried to get a grasp on the day-to-day. When he'd spent time with the kids, he'd never worried about schedules. They'd been his for a few brief hours, and he'd let them do whatever they wanted.

He got out a fresh pad of paper and began making a list of things that needed to be fixed at Lisa's house. Even if they decided to sell, he would need to do some work. If they were moving in, it would be even more work. The layout of her house was similar to his, with one bedroom on the main floor and three upstairs. Maybe if he didn't try to sleep in her bedroom but moved into the guest room, he could live there.

It wasn't like she'd married someone else and built a life with that man in the house. It was simply what the house represented. She bought it because she knew she would never take Trevor back. He'd tried moving on, especially over the last year, when his friends had pushed him to start dating, but he'd had no success. He wanted to keep trying, but he wasn't sure how.

An hour later, he went up to check on the kids. Evan was sitting on his bed, computer on his lap, headphones on. Must be gaming time.

Trevor tapped the doorframe.

Evan looked up.

"Not too late with the games. Do you have what you need for school on Monday, or do we need to get more from the house?"

"You're gonna make us go to school?"

"Why wouldn't I?"

"Mom just died."

"I'm aware. But life keeps moving, man. You'll have work to catch up on so you're ready for finals. They have to be coming up soon."

Evan huffed. "No one's going to fail me. My mom died. That's like an automatic pass."

Trevor clenched his teeth and inhaled sharply through his nose before speaking. "Just because people are being compassionate doesn't mean you should take advantage of that kindness. Besides, we raised you to pull your own weight. Shit happens. It sucks that your mom died, but she'd come back to kick my ass if I let you skip school and bank on getting pity grades."

His son rolled his eyes.

"You know I'm right."

"Yeah. I can almost hear her nagging now."

They stared at each other for a painful moment, almost as if they really expected to hear Lisa's voice. Trevor knocked on the wood again. "Not too late."

"Define too late."

"Turn it off by midnight."

"Two thirty."

"Keep dreaming. You'll never get out of bed tomorrow."

"It's the weekend."

"Twelve thirty."

"One thirty."

"One." Trevor smiled, because he knew Evan had been angling for that all along.

TREVOR LEFT THE KIDS AT HIS HOUSE AND TOLD THEM TO eat without him. He was going to talk to Diane and Gordon. As much as he dreaded it, he needed to get it over with.

Hannah offered to tag along, but since his goal was to keep her relationship with her grandparents intact, he decided it wasn't a good idea. Diane's nasty attitude toward him was likely to be on full display, and his kids didn't need to witness that.

He parked in front of Lisa's house and cut the engine. It was hard to believe that a week ago he wouldn't even consider just strolling into her house. So much had changed so quickly. He didn't know what the fuck he was doing.

But his kids came first and if they wanted to stay with him, he'd figure it out. He climbed from the truck and used Hannah's keys to let himself in.

Gordon sat on the couch watching TV.

"Hi," Trevor said as awkwardly as he felt.

"Diane, Trevor's here," Gordon called.

Diane came down the steps. "I was going through some of Lisa's things. I didn't think you'd mind."

"That's fine. Take what you want." He crossed the room and sat across from Gordon. "I came to talk about the kids."

Diane settled next to her husband. Everything about the woman was sharp from the cut of her hair to the jut of her cheekbones on her thin face. Her eyes barely hid the disdain she had for him.

"I appreciate your offer, but the kids want to stay with me."

"This isn't about what the children want, Trevor. This is about making the best choice for them."

"All due respect, Diane, it *is* about what my kids want. They're not toddlers. Their lives are here. School, friends, sports."

"They can have all of that with us. And they'll have proper parental supervision."

Heat crept up his neck at her words. He kept his anger in check. "I *am* their parent."

"I know that." She inhaled deeply. "It's a lot of work staying on top of two teenagers. You have to work. You're running a business. I'm at home and can watch them."

You mean you can control them like you tried with Lisa. He barely kept the words from escaping.

"Look, Diane. I'm here as a courtesy to you. It's not open for debate. They're my kids and they're staying with me."

"And what happens when things get difficult? We

know how you handle it. How is that in the best interest of the children?"

He took another breath. "I'm far from perfect. I own my mistakes. If you want to hold my past against me, that's your choice. Lisa forgave me. My kids have forgiven me. We'll figure things out together."

She sniffed and he thought she might start crying. Gordon patted her hand.

Trevor stood. "Let me know when you're heading back home. I'll make sure the kids stop by to say goodbye."

He left without another word. Everything Diane said was true. He has no fucking clue what he was doing with the kids. But he loved them. He would do everything in his power to make them happy.

They'd had enough loss in their short lives. He had to make this work.

Outside, as he headed for his truck, he heard, "Psst."

He turned in a slow circle. Callie stood by the corner of the house in the shadows.

"What are you doing?" he asked.

She looked over her shoulder up at the living room windows and then ran across the lawn.

"Why are you lurking around like you're trying to sneak out of your house?"

"Diane makes me feel like a troubled teen all over again. How'd it go?"

He leaned against his truck. "About as well as expected."

"I didn't hear any yelling or objects being thrown, so I figured you were safe."

He smiled. "Were you going to come to my rescue?"

"Maybe." She returned a smile.

"Has she said anything to you?"

"Nope. Not that I've made my presence known. I'm doing my best to keep the peace for the kids."

"Speaking of, I should get home and make sure they ate."

"Thanks for doing this," she said.

"Doing what?"

"Handling Diane. Listening to the kids."

He wasn't sure how to take that. Did she think he'd actually ignore what the kids wanted? "I would never toss my kids aside."

"I didn't mean it like that. It's just...I know that it's gonna be hard for you to be a full-time parent. It'd be easy to send them off to Diane's. I'm glad they're staying."

"So am I."

"Good night."

"Thanks for checking on me. It's nice to know that after all these years, you'd have my back."

She walked backward toward the yard and raised her fists. "Against Diane? Always."

He watched her walk away. It was nice to have her back as a friend.

Monday morning, Trevor finally breathed easy. He got the kids off to school on time, even after some massive confusion about lunch. How the hell was he supposed to know they thought he would make lunch for them? Then he was on his way to Sunny's Diner to meet his friends.

He was the first to arrive, so he claimed their usual table and waved the waitress over to get a cup of coffee. As she poured, he saw Tess walking toward the door, so he turned over another cup and had the waitress fill that one, too.

Tess sat and smiled. "You're so good to me."

"I know."

"How are you holding up?"

He shrugged, unsure how to answer. "I talked to the kids Friday night. I told them that Diane wants them to come live in Indiana, but Hannah and Evan both want to stay with me."

"That's not surprising. Their lives are here." She sipped the coffee. "How did your in-laws take it?"

"Pretty much the same way they take everything when it comes to me—with barely restrained disgust."

"Ouch."

The door opened, and Nina and Gabe joined them. As Nina walked behind Trevor, she patted his shoulder and then squeezed before taking her seat.

"What's up?" Nina asked.

"I survived the weekend with the kids. I have to figure out what to do with Lisa's house. It needs work, which I'll take care of, but Hannah wants to live there instead of my house."

"Why? I thought your house was near the school and everything," Gabe asked.

"Mostly it's about Callie."

"Callie?" Tess asked.

Nina leaned forward to look around Trevor. "Lisa's friend."

Evelyn came sweeping into the restaurant. They all looked at her.

Gabe asked, "No Owen?"

"How should I know?" she responded, waving the waitress over.

They ignored that Evelyn knew Owen's schedule better than anyone.

"He's on at the firehouse," Trevor said.

Tess's brow furrowed as she turned the topic back to Trevor. "What does Callie have to do with the house?"

"She lives in the coach house. I think Hannah likes having her around." He took a drink. "And if I'm being honest, having her around these last few days has made things easier for me, too."

"I thought she didn't like you," Nina said.

He shrugged. "There was a time we were good friends. Then I fucked up everything in my life, and she'd been Lisa's friend first, so..."

They dropped into silence for a minute and enjoyed their coffee. "Callie helped me remember a lot of the good times with Lisa. We shared stories with the kids over dinner the other night. I kind of forgot what it's like to have someone who knows your history, who's been there. Someone who knew me before I broke my life."

Tess nodded, but he doubted anyone at the table truly understood that feeling. Sure, they'd all done their fair share of screwing up their lives during their marriages and subsequent divorces, but Trevor was pretty sure he held the title for ruining every good thing he'd had.

Gabe set down his cup. "Wait, we're talking about the hot chick from the funeral?"

Trevor choked on his coffee.

"Smooth, Gabe," Evelyn said.

"What? She is. Just wanted to verify who we're talking about."

"Uh-huh." Evelyn stared at Gabe. "Oh, God, did you ask her out?"

Gabe smiled crookedly, and Trevor's stomach sank. Gabe was a decent guy, but Trevor couldn't picture Callie with him. Callie was the kind of woman who needed to be out living life and interacting with other people. Gabe was basically a hermit. And if she was going to go all hermit-y, he should come before Gabe.

Where the hell did that thought come from?

"The thought crossed my mind, but I figured asking someone out during a funeral would be tacky."

"Smart move," Nina said.

"You're the one who's been telling me for almost a year that I need to get out and meet people."

"Not at a funeral, you freak."

Everyone at the table burst into laughter as Nina called Gabe names.

When their laughter subsided, Tess asked, "Do you have a plan for the kids?"

Trevor shook his head. Of course Tess would ask. She was the only other parent in the group of divorcées. "They're going to meet me at Lisa's after school to pack up more stuff to move into my house. Then I'll develop a plan to get the work done to get it on the market. Or move back in. Hell if I know."

"Not for the house, Trevor. For the kids."

"What do you mean?"

"I don't want to tell you what to do, but you've never been a full-time dad."

He knew Tess had his best interests at heart, so he believed she wouldn't say anything to hurt him. But her words were too close to what Diane had pointed out the other night. He nodded for her to continue.

"You need to set up the rules for them. You need to come up with a system."

Gabe leaned forward. "They're teenagers. They don't need or want constant supervision."

"But that's when they need it," Tess shot back. "They're used to having you for a few days at a time, and if they didn't clean their rooms or do the dishes, it was no big deal because they were going back to Lisa."

"I don't even know where to start. I left so much up to Lisa when they were little. She made the rules and enforced them. I followed along."

"If you know what the rules are, you're a step ahead of some parents. Think in terms of what expectations you have for them. And be realistic. If Lisa always made their lunches for school, is that something you're going to take on, or is that something they need to do? Or are you just going to give them money to buy lunch at school?"

"Where were you yesterday? None of this occurred to me. So although Hannah gave me a list of what to buy at the store, they both woke up for school this morning and looked for their lunches. How'd you know?"

"It's all the little things I do that William wouldn't think of because he's not there every day."

Trevor scrubbed a hand over his head. He'd never liked Tess's ex based on how he'd made Tess feel over the years, so knowing that he wasn't any better than William as a parent stung.

"Can you do me a favor?" he asked.

"Anything."

"Text me a list of all those things so I can talk to the kids."

"I won't know everything they have going on."

"I know, but if you give me a list, it'll be starting place." He drained his cup as the waitress swept by for refills. He needed to get to the job site, but he needed the extra caffeine more as his head felt like it might explode based on this conversation with Tess. He then texted the kids and told them to wait for him at home—Lisa's house—after school.

"I'll do it at lunch."

"No hot lunch date with Miles?" Nina asked.

Tess blushed. Over the past year, Tess and her boyfriend Miles spent many of their lunch hours together.

"He has a meeting," she replied.

For the rest of their time at the restaurant, Nina nagged both Gabe and Evelyn about their social lives. Trevor guessed he got a reprieve from the nagging because he just buried his ex-wife.

Last year, he'd still held out some hope that maybe he and Lisa might reconcile, and based on Nina's urging, he'd approached Lisa about it. She, of course, had shot him down, but it hadn't been as painful as he'd thought it would be.

We had our time, Trevor. I'm glad you're in a good place now. But it's time for both of us to move on. We'll always love each other. We have a family, but we can't be together.

When Lisa had spoken those words, it hadn't hurt. If he'd still been in love with her, it would've hurt. For the first time since his divorce, he'd gotten closure. He and Lisa had had their time. Their relationship was strong, and they were united for the kids. Trevor had asked a few women out and had dated, but nothing had developed further than a couple of movies or dinners.

Now, between the kids and having to sell a house, it looked like his pitiful dating life would be put on hold again. So much for moving forward. Being a dad had to come first.

At five-thirty, Trevor's phone buzzed with incoming texts. He slid the phone from his pocket. Hannah wanted to know where he was. She and Evan had been sitting at home waiting for him. Damn. He'd lost track of time on the site. He'd cut the other guys loose more than an hour ago, but since he'd gotten a late start, he'd stayed. He'd completely forgotten that the kids would be waiting for him.

He sent a quick text telling her to order a pizza for dinner and he'd be there soon. He rolled up his tools and locked up the site. He didn't have time to go to his house to shower, so it looked like he'd be sweaty and dirty while he talked to the kids. True to her word, Tess had sent him a list of things to go over with them.

And it was a hell of a long list.

Climbing into his truck, he thought about what to do. Hannah wanted Callie near. He understood, but he needed to be the parent now. He couldn't put Callie's needs above his and the kids'. He couldn't afford both mortgages, even with whatever she was paying in rent.

Assuming she was paying rent. Knowing Lisa, she

would've let Callie live there rent-free. He had no idea how to bring that subject up. Parking in front of the house, he cut the engine and sat for a minute to clear his head. His peace was short-lived, however, because a beater of a car squealed in behind him.

Pizza delivery.

Trevor got out of his truck and waved the driver over. "I'll take that."

The boy looked at the house and then back at Trevor, as if he wasn't sure he could trust Trevor not to steal someone's pizza. Trevor held up his wallet. "You could go to the door, but I'm sure no one inside has cash."

"Okay."

Trevor paid the kid and carried the pizza up the stairs. And knocked. How fucking crazy was it that he couldn't get into the house? Hannah opened the door and took the pizza from him.

"Thank God. I'm starving. You told us to meet you here after school."

"Yeah."

"We get out of school at three thirty."

He hadn't thought about that. "Sorry. I was caught up at work."

Evan came from the kitchen and grabbed a slice for each hand. Then he turned to leave.

"Hey, wait."

Evan turned.

"Have a seat. We need to figure out what we're doing." Evan plopped on one of the armchairs.

Hannah sank to the couch. "I thought we already did that."

"So did I. But this morning was a cruel reminder that I have no idea what I'm doing."

"Should I go get Callie?"

"No. This isn't about the house. This is about us."

"But...she's family."

Trevor sat on the arm of the empty chair. He rubbed a hand over his head. Fine sawdust rained down, so he stopped and refocused. "It's not Callie's job to make decisions for you guys. That's on me. And you. We have to figure out how to function."

Pulling his phone from his pocket, he said, "Tess sent me a list of things we should talk about."

"So Tess can tell you what to do, but not Callie? She's been here. Tess doesn't even know us." The attitude was something he'd never seen in Hannah before, and it startled him. He took a breath so he wouldn't snap at her and then spoke. "Tess isn't telling me what to do. I asked her to send me a list of all the mom things she does because I have no clue. Last I checked, Callie's not a mom, either."

Hannah didn't respond. She simply ate more of her pizza. Evan still hadn't commented. He was busy going in for another slice.

Looking back at his phone, Trevor continued. "For instance, this morning, you guys expected me to have lunch made for you. I'd assumed that since you're not toddlers, you'd make your own."

Hannah's lip trembled. "We know how. It's just that Mom..."

Trevor closed his eyes. He was completely fucking this up. "I know. I'm not saying you have to. But no one told me. I need to figure out a schedule, and we need to decide what we're all going to be responsible for. As much as I'd like to say that I can do what your mom did, it would be a flat-out lie."

"If you got me a car, I could drive us to school. Then you wouldn't have to worry about getting us there," Evan offered. Of course he'd try to get a car out of this. He'd been asking for one for almost a year.

"We'll see. Let me get things with the house settled and maybe we can get you something. But if we do, you'll have to chip in with everything like driving your sister to practice and going to the store if we need it."

"I can do that."

"Let's talk school first. What do I need to know?"

"I know." Hannah jumped up and ran to the kitchen. A moment later, she returned carrying a calendar. "Mom keeps everything on here. We can use this." She handed Trevor the calendar.

He took a minute to look at it. Lisa, as always, had everything organized. Finals were marked later in the month. Marching band camp for Hannah. He flipped through. Lisa had things marked all the way through the rest of the year. ACT test for Evan, the start of school, a college fair. It took all of thirty seconds to start to feel overwhelmed all over again.

"It's not that bad, Dad," Hannah reassured him.

Noise from the other side of the house caught his attention, and he looked up to see Callie standing in the doorway to the kitchen. "Hey, guys. I saw the light on, so I came over. Am I interrupting?"

Trevor shook his head. "We're still figuring things out." He pointed at the pizza. "Help yourself."

She grabbed a piece and came closer. "Whatcha

looking at?" She angled her head and then laughed. "The master calendar."

"It's not funny. Do you see this? Who can keep track of all of this?"

Callie edged around his legs and sat on the chair beside him. "I think that's kind of the purpose of the calendar. To keep track."

She leaned closer, and Trevor caught a whiff of her perfume or something. It was light and summery. He wanted to take a deeper breath, then suddenly realized how wrong that was. He shifted away.

Callie gave him a confused look.

"I haven't been home to shower yet."

She moved into his space and sniffed. With a smirk, she said, "Not too bad."

CALLIE HAD NO IDEA WHAT SHE WAS DOING. WAS SHE flirting with her best friend's ex-husband? It was all kinds of wrong. She'd come over to the house when she saw the light on because she was lonely. A soul-deep loneliness that she wasn't sure how to handle. Then when she saw Trevor sitting here looking all confused and vulnerable, she wanted to get closer.

So she made a joke, but in truth, he smelled good. Like a hardworking man and sawdust.

Hannah tossed a crust back in the box and said, "Mom kept the calendar so she would know where we needed to be and other things she needed to remember. She has marching band camp listed so she remembers that she has to get me to school on those days. Just a dropoff."

"What about this ACT test for you?" Trevor asked Evan.

"I took it already. Mom wanted me to take it again. I don't want to. You can take it off the calendar."

"Why did she want you to take it again?" Callie asked.

"My score kinda sucked."

"Well, taking it again might be a good idea then. You should know what you need to get for the colleges you're looking at," she explained.

"I'm not going to college."

Trevor's face shot up from studying the page in front of him. "What are you talking about? Of course you're going to college."

"No, I'm not. School is stupid. I hate it. Why would I sign on for four more years?"

"Because that's how you go places in life."

Callie watched as Trevor became agitated, and his reaction caused a similar response in Evan.

"I'm not going to college just so I can pretend I'm going to get some great job when in reality, I'm gonna be stuck with a hundred grand in debt."

"You don't need to worry about debt. Let me worry about what it'll cost. You need a degree."

Evan lifted a shoulder. "You didn't."

Callie looked from father to son, both of them ready to boil. She laid a hand over Trevor's. "Maybe he has a point."

"What?" Trevor stood.

"College isn't for everyone, and it would be a waste of money if it's not something he wants."

"Yes," Evan said, with a fist in the air.

Whatever she'd expected, it wasn't this. Trevor's eyes flashed, and his jaw clenched. "Can I see you in the kitchen for a minute?"

She nodded and stood. Following him out of the room, she felt like she was headed to a firing squad. Trevor walked until he was near the back door before he wheeled on her.

"How could you?"

"What?" She honestly didn't see anything wrong with what she'd said.

"You completely undermined me as his father. He needs college. It's something Lisa and I always expected of them."

"But he's almost an adult. He has to start making his own decisions."

"He's a child. Allowing him to make a stupid choice makes me stupid. It's my job to help him get where he needs to go in life."

"Trevor, you can't make him want college."

"I don't give a fuck if he wants it. He needs it."

She sighed. There was no getting through to him. "I think you should at least listen to his reasons for not wanting to go."

"I didn't ask you what you think. Just because you felt the need to buck against everything your parents ever expected of you doesn't mean every kid should. They're *my* kids."

His words were like a slap to her face. Her throat constricted, but she wouldn't give him the satisfaction of knowing. She swallowed hard and lowered her voice. "Seriously? I'm well aware that they're your kids. That doesn't mean I don't love them and have their best interests in mind."

Then she turned and slipped out the back door. Stomping across the grass to get to her house, she allowed the anger to wash over her. How dare he? Of course she believed college was important, but it only mattered to people who wanted jobs that required a degree. Whatever.

Inside her cozy house, she opened a bottle of water and checked her email. She had proposals out and was waiting to hear back, but she'd been neglecting her work since the funeral. In fact, most days she could barely get out of bed. But after tonight, a trip to the other side of the world sounded pretty damn good.

And as luck would have it, the client whose shoot she'd left because of Lisa's death had sent a message. They loved the work she'd completed and wanted her to come back to the Philippines for more photographs. She reread the email slowly. They wanted her to travel to smaller villages and shoot so they could create brochures that exhibited the local cultural experience.

Callie loved those jobs the most. Where she could just let loose with her camera and shoot anything and everything that interested her. She replied, saying that she'd be there in a couple of days. With the time difference, she expected a quick response, so she kept her phone nearby. Email was great for the initial contact, but she preferred to speak with the people hiring her to get a real sense of what they wanted.

She logged onto her favorite travel site to book her flight. As she worked, she saw the glow of the light in Lisa's kitchen. Part of her wanted to go back and hang out with the kids because she always missed them when she was gone, but the rest of her knew that if she walked back into that house, she and Trevor would fight. It might even get ugly. What he'd said hurt her, and she wasn't going to just forget it.

They were all grieving and out of sorts, but that didn't give him the right to treat her like she was a stranger who didn't know the kids or what Lisa would want for them. Before she could get too wrapped up in her anger and hurt, her phone rang. It was Jasmine, the woman who had booked her for the job in the Philippines.

"Magandang umaga, Jasmine. It's good to hear from you." Callie only spoke English fluently, but she'd traveled enough that she had a collection of phrases in many languages.

"I'm sorry to hear of your loss."

"Thank you." Condolences from strangers were the hardest thing about losing someone. They didn't know Lisa, had no idea what her death meant, so going through the motions poked at her. She knew they were being kind, but it felt phony.

"Are you sure you're ready to get back to work?"

"More than I thought. Let's talk about this project. What are your goals?"

As Jasmine explained what kinds of photos they wanted, Callie took meticulous notes about where she'd be going so she could plan ahead. She was so caught up in the information that she didn't notice when all the lights turned off at Lisa's and she was alone again.

Chapter Four

Trevor felt like an ass, and for the past week, he'd been kicking himself for the way he'd spoken to Callie. He'd felt blindsided by the whole conversation with Evan. Of course he and Lisa wanted the kids to go to college. It was part of why he'd busted his ass for years. They wanted Hannah and Evan to have a better life than they'd had. Wasn't that what every parent wanted?

But he'd had no business talking to Callie like that. He knew that she wanted him to look at the big picture. If nothing else, Callie always had the kids' backs. He couldn't fault her for that.

And now he couldn't even apologize. She hadn't answered her phone, and although he'd knocked on her door every day, she hadn't opened it. After the third day, he gave up and assumed she'd left town again. She had mentioned that she might have to finish the job she left. He kind of thought she would've said something before leaving, though.

He and the kids had fallen into a rhythm. Hannah

decided she wanted to take over dinner, for which Trevor was grateful because in general, he didn't cook. He knew how to, but when it had been just him, it had seemed like a waste. Hannah found some recipes, and he and Evan had become her guinea pigs. In trade, Evan took over making lunches for both of them, as long as Trevor reminded him at night.

That boy never got out of bed early, and he couldn't remember to do anything without about ten reminders. Trevor couldn't imagine what he planned on doing, if not college. They'd completely tabled the conversation after that night.

They all continued living at his house, but Hannah insisted that she wanted to move back to Lisa's. Trevor left his job every night and went to Lisa's to do a little work before heading home and collapsing. It might not be a great routine, but it was a routine.

He had cut out some busted drywall so he could patch a hole Evan had made a couple years ago. Back then, Lisa had mentioned that Evan was angry and acting out, but she hadn't told him Evan had thrown things and busted holes in the walls. Evan copped to it as soon as Trevor brought it up. As he measured the hole, the doorbell rang.

Who the hell would come here? The only person who ever came by was Callie, and she had a key.

He went to the front door and found a delivery guy on the porch. "Can I help you?"

"I have your dinner."

"I didn't order anything." But he could smell onion rings and French fries, so he considered paying for it because his stomach growled.

"The name is Callie?"

She must be back. "Yeah, I'll take it. What do I owe you?" Trevor pulled out his wallet and paid the teenager. He took the bag of food out the back door and through the yard. He knocked on Callie's door and waited.

"Coming. Give me a minute."

He heard scrambling inside a moment before the door swung open. She answered with her eyes down while digging in her purse.

She stood just inside the door, her honey-blonde hair dripping on a silky robe. The tanned skin of her legs caught his eye, but he forced his gaze up.

"Man, you guys made great time. I wasn't expecting you..." She trailed off as she realized it was Trevor.

"Your dinner came to the front door. I almost kept it, but I figured that would be another dick move."

"Another?" she asked with a raised brow.

"I've been trying to reach you all week to apologize. I didn't know if you were avoiding me or what."

"I left for a job. But I would've avoided you."

He held out the bag of food. "I'm sorry. I shouldn't have talked to you like that."

She studied him for a minute, then nodded. "Are the kids here?"

"They're at home." He paused and then added, "My house."

"You want to join me?"

"I can't take your dinner."

She took the bag from him and opened it. "There's plenty. I always overbuy my first night back in town. I think I'm hungrier than I am because I've missed good Chicago food."

The smell of hot dogs and fries wafted out. "You sure?"

"Come on." She angled her head and walked away from the door. She set the bag on the kitchen counter.

As she moved through the small house, the short robe drew his attention again. Correction—her legs caught his focus. The entire length of them was completely visible, and if she bent at the waist, he was sure he'd find out whether she had anything on underneath. His dick twitched in response to where his thoughts were headed. His mouth dried, and he swallowed hard.

"I'll be right back. Go ahead and take the food out."

He watched her disappear around the corner and shook his head. He should not be noticing Callie's legs or anything else for that matter. She was Lisa's best friend. What the hell was wrong with him?

The stress must've been getting to him. It'd been a while since he'd been with a woman, and without a doubt, Callie was attractive. And showing a lot of tanned skin. He bit down hard. Then he turned toward the sink to wash up before eating. He needed to clear his head.

Callie came back in, and he was almost afraid to turn around. She grabbed the bag from the counter next to his arm and he caught a whiff of some fruity shampoo or something. She'd changed into a T-shirt and long shorts and looked totally comfortable. A sick part of him regretted that she'd covered up. He wanted to smack himself upside the head for his thoughts. "Better hurry or I'll eat all the onion rings."

He slowly dried his hands before turning to follow her. He took a couple cans of pop from the fridge. She sat on the floor in front of her couch, food spread out on a trunk used as a coffee table. Trevor lowered himself to the floor. As soon as his ass made contact, he had the thought that he might not be able to get up again.

She set a hot dog in front of him.

"What hot dog stand delivers?"

"A lot of them use a delivery service. One of the perks of living in a big city."

"I had no idea." He unwrapped the dog, but before he lifted it for a bite, he said, "I really am sorry for what I said to you."

She lifted a shoulder but didn't look at him. "You weren't wrong. They're not my kids."

Hearing her say it didn't sound any better. "That was pointing out the obvious just to be a dick. I'm sorry."

He took a bite of the hot dog, and his mouth watered. He was hungrier than he thought.

They ate in silence for a few minutes. When he balled up the wax paper, he added, "I was caught off guard when Evan said he didn't want to go to college. I didn't know what to say."

Callie wiped her lips with a napkin. "He and Lisa fought about it. I'm surprised he never mentioned it to you. He was sure you'd be on his side."

"Why the hell would he think that?"

"Because you didn't need college to be successful."

"I don't want him to have to bust his ass every day like I do."

"So maybe let him see what it's like."

"Huh?"

"It's almost summer. Put him to work with you. He'll

either discover that he loves working with his hands, or he'll rethink college." She picked up a fry, dragged it through ketchup, and popped it in her mouth.

"What if it doesn't work?"

"Then he'll have to figure it out. He has a point. College isn't for everyone. That has nothing to do with my relationship with my parents, who, for the record, did want me to go to college. While I did, it was on my terms." She drank from the can of pop.

Trevor's throat was dry, so he did the same. "Everything I said was out of line, I get it."

She nudged him with her shoulder. "I'm just giving you a hard time."

"I'm out of my depth with them, and you made an easy target." He sighed.

"You need to figure out how to deal with them, Trevor. Lisa's gone. She doesn't get a voice anymore. As sucky as it is, it's all you."

He released a heavy breath. He didn't need the reminder. "What are you doing here without the kids anyway?"

"Repairing the house."

"Have you decided to sell?"

He shook his head. "Hannah still wants to stay."

"It's *your* call."

"They've lost enough, haven't they? If staying here will bring them some comfort, I can suck it up."

Leaning close with a smile, she said, "I'm not that bad to have as a neighbor. I try to keep the wild parties to Saturday nights."

"It's not you. I look at that house and all I see is the

place where she moved on without me. Like, she probably had men in that bedroom."

"Oh my God. Are you still hung up on her?"

"No. I just…" He didn't know how to explain it. "We were over. But we still had a history. I don't want to think about her screwing some other guy."

He tried to ignore the voice in his head that wondered why Callie would care if he were still hung up on Lisa. Her tone sounded almost jealous, and he knew that made no sense.

Callie sat and stared at him, as if she was searching for the truth. Then she nodded. "If it'll make you feel any better, I don't think she ever brought any guy home." She sipped her pop. "Don't get me wrong. She dated and definitely moved on, but she didn't do it here."

A whole bag of mixed emotions smacked him. He'd known Lisa had begun dating over the last few years, but he didn't need Callie to remind him of it. At the same time, he was glad that it hadn't happened here. He finished his drink and stood. "I'm gonna get back to work. Thanks for dinner."

"What are you thanking me for? You paid for it."

He smiled. Forging this new friendship with Callie felt good. He liked having her in his corner. He looked around the room. "Do you need any work done here?"

"Like what?" She stood now, too, and followed his gaze.

"Anything broken?"

She shook her head. "I don't need much. There are times when I'm working and I'm lucky to have a real bathroom. Living here is pretty much a luxury."

He huffed. The house was small and cute, but far from luxurious. "Well, let me know if anything needs to be replaced. Lisa didn't keep up on any of the maintenance."

"Will do." She gathered their trash and headed to the kitchen. "What are you going to do about Evan?"

"I think you're right about him getting a job. Whether it's with me or somewhere else, he might need a taste of the real world."

He walked past Callie. With his hand on the doorknob, he added, "Thanks for your help with them. I'll try to do a better job listening."

"Thanks."

"Next time, maybe don't be so quick to run away."

"I didn't run away."

"Sure you did, Callie. It's what you do. That's not a dig, just reality." He opened the door. "Have a good night."

TREVOR PULLED UP TO THE HOUSE AND HONKED THE HORN. He'd already texted Evan and told him to be ready. A minute later, Evan came through the door and climbed into the truck.

"Where are we going?"

"You'll see."

Evan narrowed his eyes. "I can't tell if that's a good you'll see or a bad one."

Trevor smiled. "It's good."

He followed the GPS to get to the house in Melrose

Park, a suburb not too far, at least distance-wise. It was rush hour, so no matter which route he took, they were going to be stuck in traffic. Trevor tapped his fingers on the wheel. The guy selling the car said he had a few prospective buyers. No wonder—it was a great price. So unless there was something horribly wrong with it, it would sell fast.

"Where are we?"

"We're almost there." Trevor had considered just buying the car and having Owen or Tess drive it home for him, but he decided that Evan should be part of the decision.

He parked in front of the address and texted the owner. A man came from the house and Trevor opened the truck door.

"We're here to look at a car he's selling."

Evan's eyes lit up. "Really?"

"Rein it in. First, I don't know if it's in good shape. Second, if he knows you're super excited, he might not want to negotiate."

Evan schooled his features. "Okay."

"Let's go."

They climbed from the truck and Trevor introduced himself and Evan to the car owner. "Hi, I'm Trevor."

"John."

They shook hands and John walked them over to the small SUV. There were some scratches and dings.

"Why are you selling?"

"We got this for my daughter, but she just graduated and bought herself something new." He handed Trevor the keys. "It runs well. I've kept up on the maintenance."

"Can we take it for a drive?"

"Be my guest."

Trevor got behind the wheel and Evan sat in the passenger seat. He started the engine and looked at John. "You want to come with?"

"Nah. I'll wait here. Your truck is worth more than that. I'm sure you're coming back."

That was pretty trusting. Trevor eased out from the curb and listened to the engine as he drove around the block and onto the busy street. He punched the gas and the car took off. He tapped the brakes.

"What do you think?"

"It's a car and it runs. I love it."

Trevor laughed. "Let me check under the hood when we get back. I want to make sure there's nothing obviously wrong."

"But then we can get it tonight?"

"Yeah."

Evan did a fist pump.

"Like I said, there are going to be rules for this. You need to take care of the car. And you'll have to get a part-time job to pay for gas and insurance. I'll cover you for now, but insurance for a teenage boy is expensive."

"Okay. I'll get a job."

"And you'll have to help with driving your sister."

"Okay."

He circled back around and parked. Then he popped the hood. He checked all the fluids, showing Evan what he was doing and explaining why. For the first time in a long time, Evan paid total attention.

Trevor imagined spending long summer nights

working on the car and teaching Evan valuable skills. He might finally have a way to connect with his son.

Just as he slammed the hood shut, another car parked in front of him.

John tilted his chin. "Looks like the other buyer is here."

Evan's eyes filled with worry, as Trevor looked over his shoulder. A woman stepped from the car.

"Hey, John, let's talk price." Trevor pulled cash from his pocket. "My son likes the car, but we both know it's overpriced. If you shave three hundred off, I'll drive it home now."

"Deal." John looked at the woman. "Sorry. The car is sold."

"Oh, man. This is the third time I've shown up minutes too late."

"Sorry," Trevor said.

"I get it. Tough market." She turned and got back in her car.

"Let me go in and get the title."

Trevor handed Evan the truck keys. "You drive the truck home. I'll drive this. I'll call and get insurance on it and get plates tomorrow."

"Does that mean I can't drive it tomorrow?"

"Maybe tomorrow night if I get it registered after work. Insurance is just a quick phone call to my agent."

"Okay."

He looked a little disappointed, but Trevor felt better taking the car on a longer test drive. He didn't want Evan driving it until he knew it was safe.

"I'll finish up here and see you at home. Drive safe."

Evan turned toward the truck and then came back. "Thanks, Dad. This is really cool."

An hour and a half later, he was back at home and Hannah met him at the door.

"So does this mean that when I turn sixteen, I get a car, too?"

"First, Evan is seventeen. Second, you haven't even taken driver's ed yet. And third, you guys can share a car."

"Hmph."

"I'm going to try and get everything settled with the car tomorrow so that you and Evan can get to school on your own. I'm going to get some stuff fixed up on the other house so we can move everything there."

"Fix up what?"

"There are some repairs that your mom should have taken care of. The bathroom needs some help."

"Are you doing anything to my room?"

"Not unless there's something wrong with it."

She hefted a sigh. "Thank God. My room is perfect. I finally got it just the way I want it."

Trevor looked at her and almost asked what made it perfect, but he thought better of it. Given the state of everything else—and the lack of maintenance—he had the sudden thought that she'd spray-painted the walls or glued something to the ceiling. It could be a problem for a different day.

Evan came downstairs. "Can I show Hannah the car?"

"Sure. No driving it anywhere yet." He tossed him the keys.

"I know." Nudging Hannah's shoulder, he said, "Come on."

They headed outside and from the front door, Trevor could see Evan pointing things out to his sister.

For the first time since Lisa's death, he felt like maybe he could do this. It wouldn't be easy, but they really could figure it out.

CALLIE HEARD BANGING AND HAMMERING AND DRILLING coming from Lisa's house again. It was the third time this week. Trevor was killing himself over there every night after working all day. She hadn't seen the kids at all. None of it could be considered healthy.

This coming from the queen of unhealthy parent-child relationships. She walked across the yard and looked up at the house. Windows were open, which would explain why she'd heard his noise. Lights blazed in almost every room.

What the hell was he doing? He'd originally made it sound like he was going to slap some paint on the walls and patch some holes. Nothing should be this noisy. Although she had her key, she pounded on the back door to get his attention. She waited and a minute later, the door swung open. Trevor stood in the kitchen in a sweat-soaked T-shirt and dusty jeans.

"What are you doing?" she asked.

"Working on the house. I thought it would be good for the kids to be back here before school let out. To be in their rooms to study and stuff." He stepped back, so she followed him in.

He grabbed a bottle of water from the fridge and twisted off the cap. Then he drank it all in long gulps. Callie watched his throat work. It reminded her of an old Diet Coke commercial where a bunch of women in an office gathered around to watch the construction worker on break.

I am so bad.

After tossing the bottle in the recycling bin, he asked, "Is there a problem?"

"You tell me. You've been here every night after work. Have you even seen the kids?"

"I see them every morning before school. I see them when I go home." His blue eyes darkened to a stormy color as he looked at her. "What are you getting at?"

"It looks like you're avoiding them."

"I'm working to make everything better for them, not avoiding them. I can't be everywhere at once. If I'm not here, this doesn't get done."

"Maybe they could help. Or at least come here for dinner. Something." She knew she was treading dangerously close to none-of-her-business territory, but she couldn't ignore it.

Trevor turned and walked away. *What the hell?* She stomped after him into the living room and then into the bathroom in the hall. The entire room had been demolished.

"I thought you said you had some simple repair work to do. Paint and trim."

"That was before I discovered a leak in the wall. With mold growing behind it. Since I had to tear out the drywall, I figured I might as well just replace everything and update it. All of the pipes were bad. In this bathroom and the one upstairs." He turned to look at her. "I don't want them living in this. And I don't want them here when I'm cursing at their mother for having problems like this and being too stubborn to call me to ask for help."

"I didn't know."

"You're quick to assume I'm shirking my fatherly duties. I check in on them after school. Once I get the worst of this done, the rest will go faster."

A stab of guilt hit her. She had assumed the worst of him, and it wasn't fair. She'd told him she'd be here to help, to support him and the kids. She'd yet to do anything but offer unwanted advice. "Tell me how I can help."

He looked her up and down, from the spaghetti-strap tank top down to her canvas sneakers. She felt his gaze along every inch. Then he snorted.

"What?"

"You're not exactly dressed for construction work."

"I think I'll be fine. It's not like I'm going to be running a jackhammer. I can carry things to the garbage. I can help hold...things." She pointed ineffectively at the tools and materials lying around.

"I'm fine, Callie. Go home."

She planted her fists on her hips. "No. I told you that I'd be here for you and the kids. Let me help."

He sighed and rubbed a hand across his jaw. The rasp of the stubble sounded through the small room. "Fine. You're gonna get dirty."

"Dirt doesn't scare me. Bring it on."

He stepped closer and reached around her. Heat radiated from his body, and the smell of a construction site seemed to be his signature scent. His arm brushed hers as he slid back and handed her a pair of gloves and goggles.

"What are these for?"

"Safety first." Then he walked around her and out the door.

"Coming?" he called without turning back.

She scurried after him. "Where are we going?" He was already up the steps when she asked. At the top of the stairs, her jaw dropped. There was a stack of broken drywall sitting in piles from the bathroom all the way out to the hall.

Trevor pointed at the pile. "That needs to go out." Then he crossed his arms as if he expected her to balk at a little manual labor.

"I didn't see a dumpster. Where am I putting it? The regular garbage can can't hold all this."

"There are construction debris bags sitting beside your place. Fill them as much as you can and I'll drag them to the alley." He moved toward the stairs again.

"Where are you going?"

"Back down to the other bathroom to start drywalling."

"I thought you said it needed new pipes."

"Done."

"Already? You've only been at this a few days."

"I'm good like that."

Their eyes locked, and something zipped between them that felt a little too much like flirting. Her heart thumped, and she blinked rapidly.

"Well," she said to break whatever trance had sucked them in, "I'll get to work."

"Yell if you need anything." He turned and headed down the stairs.

Maybe the whole trance thing was on her. Her loneliness combined with friendly teasing allowed her brain to play with her. Of course Trevor wouldn't flirt with her. He'd been married to her best friend.

She tugged on the gloves. They were about three sizes too big. Who the hell had a hand that big?

Her libido answered, *I bet Trevor does, and I know what that means.*

Giving herself a mental slap and making a note to get back on Tinder, she turned to look at the pile of drywall. With a grunt, she hefted the first piece and carried it downstairs. Just like Trevor said, there were two giant bags sitting on the lawn with drywall already in them. She added her piece to the pile and went back for more.

On her second trip, the back door and screen were wide open. As she neared the door, Trevor came through holding two full sheets of new drywall against his shoulder. She shifted to the side, putting her back to the wall to make sure he had enough room to pass. He smiled as he did.

She glanced down at her small piece of broken drywall. Then back to his bulging biceps as he turned the corner to get into the bathroom. He thought she was cute. Well, so what if she couldn't balance building materials? She had other skills. She tossed her piece on the pile and returned to the bathroom.

Below her, she heard the sound of a drill. And music. Nothing she knew, but at least it was more pleasant than silence. Every now and then, she and Trevor would pass while working—her getting rid of the old, him bringing in the new. It was quite metaphorical. If her muscles weren't screaming at her, she might think about grabbing her camera and taking a few shots.

By the time she had all of the big pieces hauled out, she was dying of thirst. A beer sounded great. She rarely drank beer, but she felt it was appropriate since she was doing construction work. She hopped down the last step and neared the bathroom before she realized that she'd almost approached Trevor and asked him if he wanted to grab a beer with her.

What the hell is wrong with me? The man was an alcoholic.

She sighed and went to the kitchen to grab a bottle of water. Taking one for Trevor, she went back to the bathroom. His deep voice carried over the sound of the drill. Was he singing?

Silently edging closer, she peeked around the corner of the door. Trevor's phone sat on the toilet tank playing some twangy country song about a guy whose girl broke up with him and he was moving on. It was kind of pop-y and cute and absolutely nothing she ever would've imagined Trevor singing.

When they'd been young and he'd been in a band, this song was the opposite of what they'd played. He'd been all edgy and hard rock. Too bad he tried to live that lifestyle, too. But it had been more than the band and the bars. Lisa thought if he gave that up, he'd be sober. It had taken losing her and his family for him to see that his life had spiraled out of control.

When he bent to get some more screws, she knocked on the doorframe to distract herself from checking out his ass. He started and looked over his shoulder at her.

She smiled and waved the water bottle at him. "Thought you might be thirsty."

He straightened and took it. "Thanks."

As he twisted off the cap, she said, "Cute song you were singing."

He raised an eyebrow at her and started glugging the water down like he had in the kitchen. To occupy herself, she opened her bottle and drank. It was time to update her dating profiles. She hadn't dated a blue-collar guy since her early twenties. She'd forgotten how hot they were.

ME: GLOBE-TROTTING PHOTOGRAPHER

YOU: BLUE-COLLAR GUY GOOD WITH HIS HANDS

Trevor snapped his fingers in front of her face. She blinked and looked up at him.

"Where'd you go?" he asked. "You looked like you were about to—"

Rather than finishing, he stepped away and took another swig of water.

"What did I look like?" Somehow she felt like she was poking a bear but couldn't help herself.

"You really want to know?"

She nodded and gulped water.

"You looked ready to hump the sink."

She snorted and choked on her water. She had been thinking about humping, but not the damn sink. He leaned his ass against the vanity and crossed his arms while waiting for her to finish choke-laughing.

After taking a deep breath, she said, "My mind wandered, but rest assured, while it's been a while since I've hooked up with someone, your bathroom fixtures are safe."

Color rose in his cheeks. He probably didn't think she'd answer so honestly, but she was too old to put up any kind of pretense. By the time she'd reached thirty, she'd stopped playing games. Once she'd crossed the line over forty, she'd decided to own it. She was a healthy woman who enjoyed sex. She had no reason to deny it.

Of course, she also had no desire to admit to Trevor that it had been him she was thinking about.

"Anyway," she continued, "the pile upstairs is gone. Is there something here I can help with?" She took a moment now to actually look at the progress he'd made. In the hour that she'd been hauling garbage, he'd managed to get walls back in place. "Wow."

"What?"

"You really are fast. When I saw this room with no walls, I thought for sure you'd be in here for days getting drywall up."

The corners of his mouth lifted. "There's still a long way to go, but getting the walls back up is a good feeling. Progress in a positive direction."

Callie nodded. Progress in a positive direction. She needed to find some of that for herself. Which started with her finding some other guy to ogle.

Putting the cap back on her bottle, she said, "If you don't need me, I'm going home. I need a shower and ibuprofen."

Trevor's face sobered and he reached out. "Did you hurt yourself?"

"No. I'm fine. Muscles will be sore tomorrow, that's all."

"You sure?"

"Yep. And if the ibuprofen doesn't work, I'll just have

to call Sven the Swedish masseur to come take care of me." She winked and backed out of the room.

"Sven, huh?"

"Leave my fantasies to me."

Trevor watched Callie sashay out of the small bathroom, covered in dust and with dirt smeared on her cheek. Her ponytail flopped crookedly, but she was cute. When she'd offered help, he'd imagined her hightailing it back to her place, but she'd stuck it out. He tossed his empty water bottle on the pile of trash.

He didn't know what was going on between them, but it was making him uncomfortable. In more ways than one. He shifted his dick in his jeans. Callie had always been Lisa's hot friend. Not that Lisa wasn't beautiful. But Callie was alluring in an untouchable way.

And he hadn't been imagining her staring at him tonight. Even if she was horny, she'd never once looked at him like that. He should've kept his mouth shut instead of egging her on, but he liked her straightforward attitude. About everything. She seemed much less untouchable these days.

It was getting late, and if he wanted to make sure the kids finished their homework, he needed to get home. He flicked off the light and went upstairs to see if Callie had moved everything. The pile was gone, so the room was ready for new drywall. Then he could bring in his taper by the end of the week.

He looked down the dark hall. The door to Lisa's bedroom remained closed. He knew he had to clean it out, get rid of all her things, but he hadn't been able to make himself do it. Hannah had asked Diane to leave it, so Lisa's mother had only taken a few items and left the rest. No one had been in the room since. The kids might want something, and he had no idea what should be saved. They couldn't leave it as a shrine. Fuck. There was just too much.

He left the house and hit a drive-through on the way to his house. When he walked through the door, the living room was dark and silent. So much like it always was when he came home. But now it was supposed to be different. The kids were here, living with him. Shouldn't there be some sign of them?

He tossed his keys and food on the table and trudged up the stairs. Both of the kids had their bedroom doors closed. Not much of a family vibe they had going on. He knocked on Hannah's door and waited for her to acknowledge him. He didn't want to see anything he shouldn't.

"What's up, Dad?"

"You guys eat dinner?"

"Yep. Sloppy joe and fries. There might be some left on the stove. But I'm not sure."

"That's okay. I'm good." He paused, trying to think of what else to say. "How was school?"

"Okay."

"Homework?"

"Done."

He looked at her for a minute before realizing he had nothing else. He had no idea how to engage his daughter in conversation. "I was just at the house. I should have the bathrooms up and running by the end of the week. But, uh, we need to sort out your mom's stuff."

Hannah's head snapped up.

"We need to clean out her bedroom. Decide what to keep and what to donate."

She nodded slowly.

"Do you want to be there? Or should I try to do it before you move back in?"

"I think I want to help."

"Okay." He tapped the doorframe. "Don't stay up too late."

"I won't. Thanks, Dad."

He nodded, but he had no clue what she was thanking him for. He went to Evan's room, knocked, and swung the door open. "Hey, man, homework finished?"

"Yeah."

Trevor entered the room and leaned against the desk. "I've been thinking about what you said about college."

Evan looked at him with guarded eyes. "Yeah?"

"What do you think about working with me for the summer?"

"For real?"

"I think having experience of a real job might help you decide if that's what you want."

"What about football?"

"What about it?"

"I'll have camp."

"We'll work around it."

Evan nodded.

"You don't have to, you know. If you'd prefer to get a job doing something else, that's fine, too."

"No. Working with you sounds cool. Remember when we built the deck on the back of the house?"

Trevor smiled. Of course he remembered. Evan had been getting into trouble at school, and Lisa told Trevor to come up with a way to talk to him. They'd talked while putting a deck on the back of his house.

"That was fun," Evan said.

"You acted like it was torture."

Evan chuckled. "That's because I was pissed off. But the actual building? I liked that a lot."

"Why didn't you ever tell me? I would've let you work with me more."

Evan shrugged.

Trevor hated that teenage shrug. It said nothing and so much all at the same time. He'd prefer the actual words. Instead of pushing, he said, "We'll go this weekend and get you some boots and work jeans."

"Do I get my own tools, too?"

"We'll get you started. Then see how it goes."

"Cool."

"See you in the morning."

"'Night."

Trevor pushed back toward his room. Maybe Callie was onto something. He'd been looking for a way to connect with Evan for a long time. It had never occurred to him that his son might like to build as much as he did. As he looked back down the dark hallway, he realized that she'd been right about something else, too. He had been immersing himself in work as a means of avoidance.

It wasn't that he didn't want to spend time with the kids. He loved them more than anything. Work was how he'd always taken care of them. He provided financially, and Lisa had done everything else. Yeah, it was unfair and he definitely recognized that now. But there was no turning back.

It was time to rebuild his family in a new way, a way that would work for all of them. As he stripped off his dusty, sweaty clothes, he wondered how Callie fit into the dynamics of the new family.

Chapter Five

Callie spent the next few nights crashing Trevor's work party. She had no idea what she was doing since she'd never worked construction, but deep down, she knew what he was doing wasn't healthy. She at least had seen the kids stop by and hang out for a while. But their lives shouldn't consist of passing moments.

How could Trevor not see how important it was to spend time with the kids without it being work? Life was too short.

She texted Hannah and Evan and told them to come to the house tonight because they were going to do something fun. Now she just needed to convince Trevor to join them.

Her greatest fear was that he'd continue to choose work over family time.

She knocked on the back door even though she knew he wouldn't answer. He just left the door unlocked for her to come in. She entered the kitchen and stopped. She heard none of the usual racket. Trevor's truck was out front, so he had to be there.

"Trevor?"

"Upstairs," he called.

She climbed the stairs and realized that Lisa's bedroom door was open. She didn't think anyone had stepped foot in there since the funeral. Callie eased into the room.

Trevor sat on the corner of the bed flipping through a book. It took a minute for Callie to recognize it was the scrapbook that Lisa kept of Callie's work. Lisa had been so proud of her.

"Hey," she said.

Trevor looked up. "You're really fucking amazing. I had no idea."

"Thanks." She glanced around the room. Very little had been moved, but someone had gone through Lisa's things.

Trevor followed her gaze. "Hannah and Evan took what they wanted. I guess the rest is up to me. I don't know what to do with it."

"Would you like me to clear it out?" she offered.

"Damn. I'm sorry. I should've asked if you wanted any of her things. I've been so busy trying to fix the bathrooms and keep up with the kids I hadn't considered. You're welcome to anything you want, Callie." He closed the book he held.

Callie nodded, feeling a little overwhelmed by Trevor's compliment as well as being in her best friend's space. "I'll take care of it for you. Do you think her mom might want anything?"

"She took some stuff after the funeral, but I'll text her

and ask." He stood and tossed the book on the mattress. "Are you sure you're up for that?"

"Yeah. It needs to be done. Leaving it like this isn't good for anyone."

"I know. I'm trying."

"I know you are. I wasn't criticizing." She shook her head. She hadn't prepared for this. "I came over to tell you to pack up your tools. You're done for today."

He cocked an eyebrow.

"The kids are on their way here, and we're going out." He looked down at his dirty work clothes.

"Hannah is bringing you fresh things."

"There's no shower. Bathrooms are torn apart."

"You can use my shower."

He stared at her.

"They need this, Trevor. Hell, you need this. Take a break. Have fun with us."

"What kind of fun are you dragging me to?"

"Cosmic bowling."

"I hate bowling."

"You don't hate bowling. You're just not good at it. It's one sport where it's completely acceptable to suck."

"Sport?"

"I use the term loosely." She took his hand and felt an odd comfort in the touch. "Come on. How can you refuse crappy pizza and the chance to humiliate me?"

He sighed. "Fine."

"Yay!" She gave a little jump. She tugged his hand. "Go shower. I'll bring your clothes as soon as the kids get here."

She had thought for sure it would be harder to

convince him. She'd been ready to pull out every guilt trip she could think of. But he'd relented pretty easily. Now she just had to pray the night would be as much fun as she hoped. "Clean towels are in the cabinet next to the tub," she called from the top of the stairs.

"Got it," he answered. Then she heard the back door open.

She turned off the light in Lisa's room and checked out the bathroom on her way out. The man was a machine. The room was back to looking like an actual room. He had the drywall done and taped. He hadn't been kidding when he said he wanted the kids to be able to move back soon.

A few minutes later, the front door opened, and Hannah and Evan came in. As soon as she saw them, she was glad that Trevor was pushing so hard to have them back here. She missed them. "Hey, guys. Who's ready for some fun?"

Evan closed the door. "What are we doing?"

"Ugh. You sound so much like your dad. Trust me."

"Where is he?" Hannah asked. "I have his clothes." She lifted a plastic bag.

"He's showering at my place. I'll take them over and tell him to hurry." Callie took the bag.

Evan plopped on the couch and stared at his phone. Hannah went to the bathroom to see the progress. "It's almost done," she said.

"Yep. Your dad is fast. I'll be back in a minute." She moved through the house and out the back door. In her house, as she neared her bathroom, the water shut off.

Callie froze. She had a sudden image of Trevor buck

naked and dripping wet. She shook her head. Her thoughts were so many levels of inappropriate. She needed to get it under control. She tapped on the door.

It swung open, and Trevor stood in front of her with a towel wrapped around his waist.

She smiled. "We need to stop meeting like this." She thrust the bag at him. "Hurry up. We're all ready to go."

"Bossy."

"You know it." Then she spun and went back to the kids before her mind had the chance to do any more indecent wandering.

Trevor had no idea why he'd let Callie talk him into this. He had a lot of work to do. And a night at a bowling alley where there would surely be a group getting drunk was not how he wanted to spend time.

But there he was, driving all of them to the bowling alley in Evan's beat-up old car that Trevor had just bought. Although they would all fit in the truck, he had it filled with tools and didn't want to take it where someone might be tempted to break into it. The directions Callie had given him put them driving a lot farther than necessary. He could've found three closer alleys. But she seemed to have her heart set on this one.

Hannah chatted with Callie about her day at school, and Trevor realized he never got that kind of rundown from her. *How does Callie manage to do that?*

He parked the car and checked out the parking lot.

The building looked newish. Not quite the dive he'd expected. They all stepped from the car, and Callie stopped in front of him and Evan.

Holding out her hand she said, "Phones."

"Huh?"

"Give me your phones. We're spending the night together. No phones."

"You're not taking Hannah's phone," Evan said. "Because her nose isn't constantly in it."

"Here, Callie," Hannah said with a bright smile and handed over her phone.

"Suck-up."

Hannah simply stuck her tongue out at her brother. Evan gave Callie his phone, and she dropped it in her purse. Then she wiggled her fingers at Trevor.

"I'm not a kid."

"I know that. But the most important people in your life are right here. Who else might call who is more important?"

She had him there. He slapped his phone in her palm. She gave him a huge smile in return. Her grin was bright and shot straight through him, making him feel light.

"Let's go." She spun on her heel and put an arm around Hannah. "We should play girls against guys. I think we can kick their butts."

Trevor's long stride easily caught up to them. "Care to place a wager on that?"

Callie shot him a look from the corner of her eye. "Like what?"

"Losers have to cook dinner for a week," Hannah announced.

"That's bogus," Evan said. "That's not punishment for you. You cook anyway."

"Fine, if we win, you guys have to cook dinner. What do you want if you win?"

Callie held up a hand. "Hold on. Are you sure it's not punishment for us to have to eat food they cook?"

Hannah burst out laughing.

Trevor nudged Callie's shoulder. "Funny. I'm not totally inept in the kitchen."

Evan reached the door first and held it open for all of them. "Can I make her do my homework if we win?" he asked as Trevor passed.

"Nope. Nice try, though."

"You'll have to do our laundry," Trevor suggested. "For a month."

Hannah wrinkled her nose. "Your clothes are gross."

He lifted a shoulder. "Then I guess you better win."

His daughter gave him a look that was so much like her mother that he almost tripped on his own feet. Her eyes lit with the idea of taking his challenge.

"You'll be sorry," she said.

They got shoes and were assigned two lanes. The room was dark, black lights glowing. Many lanes were filled with families, and the *crack* of bowling balls against pins filled the air, quickly followed by cheering.

Trevor looked around as Callie led them to their lanes, carrying their shoes. He saw a counter for food but didn't see any pitchers of beer. Although he'd never been a bowler, he'd been bowling enough in his life that he knew it was one of those activities that drew drinkers. Like any other sport.

They sat on plastic chairs and changed their shoes.

"You guys go pick out your balls. I'll order pizza," Callie said.

"I'll get that," Trevor said, standing awkwardly in the funny-looking shoes.

"I got it. You set up the computer." She smiled and pointed at the screen.

The kids took off to go find the right-size balls. Trevor entered their names in the computer and tried not to be irritated that Callie didn't trust him to order pizza. What did she think, that he'd sneak in a beer or two while waiting?

When the computer was ready, he grabbed a ball, and the kids returned. Callie sat on a chair next to him while Hannah and Evan took their first turns.

"I could've gotten the pizza," he said, more sharply than he'd intended.

"I know. I thought it would be more efficient to each take a job. And that" —she pointed to the screen— "is a task I always screw up. I don't have the patience for pressing the buttons to get the names in."

"Oh."

"What's going on?"

"Nothing." He watched as Evan's ball dragged in the gutter. He turned to face Callie. "I thought you didn't want me near the bar because you thought I'd drink." He paused and then added, "I can be around alcohol without drinking."

She smiled at him, her teeth glowing eerily in the black light. "Well, there's no worry about that here. They don't sell alcohol."

"What?"

"It's a dry bowling alley."

Trevor blinked and processed her words. He wasn't sure how to feel about it. Did she think he was that much of a risk, or was she being considerate? He had no idea how to handle this woman. She was infuriating one minute and amusing the next.

Hannah yelped as she knocked pins down.

Callie pointed down the lane. "Looks like you're in trouble."

She winked at him with a smirk, and Trevor knew that he was indeed in trouble.

For the next two hours, they laughed and bowled horribly. Callie danced and cheered like she was in a championship game. She did nothing halfway. She was all in, all the time. No matter what it was—something vital or inconsequential. Callie loved it all.

Her spirit was infectious. He found himself laughing and teasing while they played. After the first game—where the guys won—they decided to switch it up and play adults against kids, with no stakes. Callie had tried for double or nothing, but he knew enough to get out while ahead.

By the time they were leaving, Trevor felt about a million pounds lighter. After he changed, he took everyone's shoes to return to the counter. The old-timer manning the register took the shoes.

"You have a lovely family there."

Trevor looked over his shoulder to where Callie and the kids were still rehashing the finer points of their games. "Yeah, I do. Thanks."

Callie sat in Evan's car beside Trevor on the ride back to her house. Her cheeks and stomach hurt from so much laughing. Based on the constant chattering between Evan and Hannah, and the fact that although she'd returned their phones, they weren't using them, the night had been the success she'd hoped for. Lisa might not have done a regular family night out, but she'd had a daily routine that Callie could count on. She missed dropping in on them whenever she felt lonely.

With Trevor working so many hours, she knew he wasn't spending much time with the kids. Accusing him of avoiding them wasn't very nice, but his actions still felt like it. Pushing him to do this had been good for all of them.

Especially her. She loved being part of a family.

Trevor pulled up in front of the house. Turning in his seat, he said to Evan, "Take your sister straight home. Finish homework. I'll be there soon."

Evan nodded and pushed out of the back door. Callie opened her door and stepped out. Before Evan moved to the driver's side, she snagged him for a hug. "I'm glad you came out with us."

He returned her hug with a muffled, "I didn't think I had a choice."

She laughed. "You didn't really, but you could've been an ass about it."

"It was fun. Thanks, Callie." He went around and

climbed in behind the wheel, readjusting the seat to accommodate his shorter legs.

Hannah came to her side and hugged her. "We should do this again. We need a rematch. I can't believe they beat us."

"Next time we'll have to pick something they suck at."

"Good luck with that," Trevor said from behind her. "I'm good at everything."

Hannah sat in the car and waved to her dad.

Callie and Trevor silently watched the car pull away. The air between them was charged, but she didn't understand what was causing the tension. It had been a good night.

"Thanks for making me go out with them."

"They needed it," she said, then added quietly, "So did I." She turned to walk up the gangway toward the backyard.

Trevor followed.

"Where are you going?" she asked, afraid that he planned to do more work on the house instead of going home.

"I'm walking you to your door. Making sure you get home safely."

She chuckled. "It's not like this is a dangerous neighborhood."

He shrugged. He obviously had something else on his mind, so she let him walk beside her to figure out what he wanted to say. At her door, she slowly took out her keys. He still said nothing.

"So, this is me," she said, cheerfully jingling her keys.

He stood close and then leaned against the doorjamb. "Why did you pick that bowling alley?"

She could've played it off, but she knew what he was asking. "I had to search around to find a place that doesn't serve alcohol. That was the only alley in the area."

"I'm capable of being around alcohol." His voice was tight, his shoulders tense.

She patted his chest. "I wasn't worried about you going on a bender with your kids. But I have no idea how difficult it is for you. You have this immense wall up, and you let nothing through. I chose to play it safe. I wanted tonight to be fun, not stressful."

She let her hand slide away from him. He released a slow breath. His eyes softened and darkened simultaneously.

He licked his lips and stared at her. This suddenly felt like a date—an awkward first date between two virgin teenagers. "This is weird," he whispered.

She smiled. "I was just thinking the same thing. Why?"

"Why, what?"

"Why is it so weird all of a sudden?"

"I don't know. Maybe because everything is so different. We used to be friends. But that was before. With Lisa. Now Lisa's gone, and I have the kids."

She nodded at the accurate assessment. "Life changes. Doesn't explain the weird, though, does it?"

She wondered if he felt the same buzz of attraction that she did. The force that made her want to lean closer, put her hand on his chest again, absorb whatever comfort he offered.

"I think we need to learn how to be friends now, not the friends we used to be," he offered. "It's a weird position to be in."

That certainly cleared up her blurred ideas. While

she'd been inappropriately ogling him, he'd been trying to figure out how to friend-zone her.

"I think we're doing a pretty good job, Trevor. I'm glad you want to be friends. I like being part of this." She pointed toward the house. "With the kids."

"You'll always have a place with the kids, Callie." He shoved his hands into the front pockets of his worn jeans. "With all of us. You're family."

Her throat tightened, but she smiled. "Thanks."

"I wouldn't have made it these last few weeks without you."

"Sure you would've. You've got your friends. They seemed very protective and helpful when I met them."

The corner of his mouth lifted. "Yeah, but they have their own lives."

"Are you implying that I don't have a life?" She gave his shoulder a little shove.

"That's not what I meant. Man, you make it hard."

She giggled. "That's what he said."

His eyes widened and he stared at her. "Did you just make a *that's what he said* joke?"

"I'm sorry, did I offend the frail sensibilities of a construction worker?"

A slow smile crept across his face. "You're definitely full of surprises." He pushed away from the wall. "Good night, Callie."

She unlocked the door and went inside, still feeling confused about her feelings for Trevor.

Trevor spent the next week killing himself working around the clock to finish the bathrooms so the kids could move home. He spent every waking hour on the job or on the house.

He did his best to convince himself it wasn't because he was avoiding Callie. He'd almost kissed her after bowling. She'd been honest and straight with him. She pushed him to be better, but she didn't ignore his problems, either.

And she made sex jokes to keep things light.

Now the house was done and all he needed to do was pack everything he owned, move in, and then sell his house. Piece of cake.

Yeah, right.

Lucky for him, he had great friends. Nina was coming over to help him pack. Then Owen was bringing a bunch of firefighters over this weekend to move him. All it would cost him was some pizza and beer.

He stood in the middle of the living room with a stack of empty boxes, unsure where to start. At least he didn't own a lot of crap. A knock sounded on the open front door.

"Hey," Nina called. She came in.

Trevor did a double-take. She wore jeans and a snug T-shirt with gym shoes. Her usually perfectly styled hair was up in a ponytail.

Her eyes widened. "Something wrong?"

"Uh, no. I don't think I've ever seen you wear jeans."

In fact, Nina was always dressed to impress. She was an event planner who worked with high-end clients. Her wardrobe probably cost as much as his truck.

"Did you think I would wear my Jimmy Choos to pack boxes?"

He only knew she was referring to shoes because he'd suffered through an entire breakfast listening to Nina and Evelyn discuss designer footwear.

She clapped her hands. "Where do you want me to start?"

"This is gonna sound stupid, but I don't even know. Lisa's house is full."

Nina stepped closer and touched his hand. "If you're going to live there, you need to start thinking about it as your house, not Lisa's."

He nodded. She was right, but he had no idea how to start.

"Let's make two piles: one to move, one to donate." She turned in a circle. "You probably want your books. And obviously clothes. Why don't I start there? You can go around and put a sticky note or something on the things that you want."

Trevor couldn't stop the smile. He'd never seen Nina at work, but here she was, completely in her element. Over the last year or so, he'd seen her become bolder, less of the mousy companion they were used to. The bossiness suited her.

She grabbed a box and began packing books. The kids were upstairs packing their things. Tonight they'd be back home for good. He'd get his clothes there today and move the rest this weekend. After rummaging around, he found a pad of sticky notes. He put one on his recliner. He eyed the couch. Nah, Lisa's was better. His lamp? Maybe.

As he worked his way around the room, Hannah came thudding down the stairs.

"You can't be done already," he said.

"Nope. Need another box." She stared at Nina. "Hi."

"Hannah, you remember Nina, don't you?"

"Sure." She turned to Trevor. "Is Callie coming?"

"No. Why?"

Hannah lifted a shoulder. "Just figured she'd be here. She's with us all the time." Picking up an empty box, she asked, "Do you want me to call her? You have a lot to do here."

"Nah, we got this. I'm going to donate a bunch since we won't need two of everything at the other house." *Other house* was better than *Lisa's house*. A step in the right direction.

"Okay." Then she sprinted back up the stairs.

Trevor surveyed the room. He thought he had everything marked. He felt Nina staring at him. "What? Did I manage to screw up your sticky note system?"

"What's up with Callie?"

"What do you mean?"

She abandoned the box of books and stepped close. Lowering her voice, she said, "Did you not get the distinct impression that Hannah was...protective?"

Trevor stared at her. Sometimes she was harder to understand than his teenage daughter.

Nina continued, "She doesn't want me here. That's why she wants to call Callie."

"Callie's important to them, especially Hannah. She's

been a huge help." He took his pad of notes and walked to his bedroom. He didn't want to think about what Nina was implying.

Nina followed with an empty box. "So there's nothing between you and Callie?" she asked as she began opening his dresser drawers and stacking clothes in the box.

"We're friends."

Nina pinned him with a look and an arched brow. "What kind of friends?"

"No benefits involved." Even if the thought had crossed his mind on more than one occasion.

"So she's just not into you, huh?" Nina teased.

"Women find me irresistible. Alcoholic single dad with two teenagers. Every woman's dream."

Nina tossed T-shirts on the pile. "You're a catch." She sighed. "All joking aside, any drinking issues?"

"I'm good. There have been days, you know, but I haven't gotten as far as walking into a liquor store or bar, so that's good."

"If you ever need someone to go to a meeting with you, you know where to find me."

"Thanks. I've been talking to my sponsor a few times a week."

"Meetings?"

"No time. Between figuring things out with the kids and fixing up the house, I've been exhausted."

"Tiring yourself out shouldn't take the place of the program."

"I don't need the lecture."

"No lecture. I worry about you."

He filled a box with the junk that had collected on his

dresser. He stuck a note on the furniture. "I appreciate your concern but I'm okay."

Hannah appeared in the doorway again. "I'm done. What's with the sticky notes?"

"Nina suggested I mark what's coming with me so the rest can be donated." He moved to the closet and pulled out his guitar.

"You still have that?" Hannah asked.

"Of course."

She sat on the corner of the bed.

"I have a picture of us that Mom gave me. It's me sitting on your lap while you played."

She used to do that all the time when she was little. "Can you teach me?"

He smiled. "I don't think you can sit on my lap for lessons. I haven't played in years. We can get you lessons if you want."

Her face fell a little, and he knew he'd screwed up again. "I can try. I don't know much about teaching it. That's all."

"Okay," she said. "You need help here?"

"No, we have it. There's not much."

She looked to Nina and back to him.

Evan stuck his head in the room. "I'm gonna head home, okay?"

"Did you load your boxes in your car?" Evan sighed. "I will."

"Take anything Hannah needs, too. You guys can head home if you want. I'm going to finish this."

"I can't haul all of her stuff. I don't drive a moving van."

"Ha ha," Hannah said as she shoved past him. "See you at home."

Home. Huh. He hadn't had a real home with his kids in a long time.

Right after they left, his phone buzzed. He fished it from his pocket. A text from Callie.

> Need help?

> No. Kids are on their way home with some of their stuff. Dinner?

> Sounds good.

He looked over his shoulder at Nina. "You want to come to the house for dinner with us? Callie's cooking or ordering."

"As much as I'd love to watch the friends with no benefits in action, I have some work to do at home."

"I'm never going to hear the end of it, am I?"

"Not until I get some good details."

"No details to give."

"Not yet."

He shook his head and went back to his phone, which had continued buzzing in his hand. Callie had fired off text after text asking about dinner choices and what time he'd be there.

> And what about dessert?

He smiled and looked over the mess of his room.

> Get whatever you want. I'll be there within an hour.

"Do you need some privacy with your phone?"

"No." He scooped the few items from his closet and shoved them, hangers and all, into the box on the bed. "We can donate everything in the kitchen."

"Do you want me to call someone to come do a pickup?"

"I can handle it. If you have a specific charity you like, give me the information."

"Sure." She taped up a box and marked the side.

As if he couldn't figure out that all of his boxes would be going to his bedroom.

His bedroom. His house. His family. He was really doing this.

And this time, he'd get it right.

Chapter Six

Callie moved through Lisa's house as comfortably as she did her own. The kids had gotten home a few minutes ago, and Hannah joined her in the kitchen. Hannah wanted to learn how to cook on the grill, so they made a quick trip to the grocery store to buy some burgers and hot dogs.

Then they started the grill. She tossed the patties on and closed the lid.

Standing close, Hannah asked, "So now we just stand here?"

"No. We can have a seat and wait till it's time to flip them." Callie dragged a chair close to the one she was near and patted it.

Hannah took the seat. "Where are you going next?"

"I'm not sure. I have a few proposals out for jobs."

"Far?"

Callie leaned back and rested her head on the chair to look up at the evening sky. "I think I'd like to go to England this summer. I haven't been there in a few years."

"What's it like?"

"Wet. It really does rain a lot there. But it's beautiful. And London is bustling and amazing."

"What's your favorite part?"

Callie didn't even hesitate. "Men with accents."

"I meant the sights." Hannah giggled.

A throat cleared behind them, and Callie angled her head to see Trevor. "Hey."

"Hey. So all of your globe-trotting is to find men with accents, huh?"

She smiled. "Accents are pretty sexy."

"You have some shrimp on the barbie?" he asked in the most awful Australian accent.

Callie and Hannah doubled over in laughter. "That was horrendous," Callie said.

Trevor came closer and shrugged. Lifting the lid on the grill, he took the spatula and flipped a burger. "I tried."

Hannah stood and took the spatula from him. "I'm learning."

She awkwardly flipped a burger, stepping back when the flames flared up. Looking up at Trevor, she said, "Don't worry. You have other good qualities."

"Yeah?"

"Yeah." Her smile was bright.

Callie's throat tightened. Damn it. Playful teasing should not make her teary-eyed. But it felt so good to see Trevor smile. Like for right now, the weight of the world wasn't on his shoulders. She knew it wouldn't last, so she drank it in.

When Lisa had died, she'd thought her whole world would fall apart. This felt normal to her, even without

Lisa here. Trevor stood close and watched as Hannah handled the burgers. Then she added a few hot dogs.

"I'm gonna be like *the* cook. I'll amaze people with my skills when I get to college. No cold pizza for me."

"Don't get too excited," Callie said. "I doubt there are any dorms that will let you have a grill. Open flames and drunk college kids don't mix well."

Hannah turned to face Callie, giving her a stern look. "I'm not going to be a drunk college student."

Callie huffed. "We'll see." When Hannah's eyes widened, Callie got the hint. She didn't like Callie mentioning getting drunk in front of Trevor. How could she explain to Hannah that they couldn't pretend? "Even if you're not, plenty of others will be."

She stood. "I'm going to make a salad to go with dinner. You guys need anything else here?"

"We have it," Trevor said, oblivious to his daughter's silent communication. Over his shoulder, his eyes met hers. "Thanks, Callie."

"No problem," she said with a smile.

They ate dinner together as a family around the dining room table. They laughed and joked, and the kids talked about school. Finals were two weeks away. Trevor sat silently while Callie asked questions about their classes and what kind of tests they'd have to take. Evan, of course, just grumbled about how stupid tests were.

It all felt normal. They'd had dinner together like this so often over the years that there was no awkwardness. But shouldn't things have been different with Trevor there? They'd barely spoken over the last couple of weeks. He worked a lot, and he'd said he didn't need her help.

She'd been surprised when he answered her text

tonight. She'd half expected him to pretend he hadn't gotten it.

After they'd cleaned up dinner, Trevor told the kids to go unpack the stuff they'd brought from his house.

Callie saw her chance to talk to him when he grabbed a box from the living room floor and took it to the guest room. She took another and followed.

"So this is where you're moving in?"

He jolted at her voice. "I think it's best. This isn't Lisa's space. I can make it mine. Plus it gives me some privacy."

She set the box she carried on the bed. "I'll finish clearing out Lisa's room this week. I got caught up in some work." And clearing out her best friend's stuff was harder than she'd thought it would be.

"Thanks." He ripped open the box and starting hanging things in the closet.

She looked in the box she had. More clothes. "Are you bringing your dresser or are you using this one?"

"I'm bringing my furniture this weekend." He looked at what she was doing. "You don't have to do that."

"I know I don't have to. I want to help." She wanted to make sure they really were okay. "Maybe since this is for the dresser, just slide it into the closet for now."

"Yeah." He took the box from her, his fingers brushing hers. Then he shifted away fast.

"What about the other boxes?"

"I have some books." He pointed to the bookcase in the corner. "That fit in my truck, so I brought it over with this trip. You can put those away."

"Sure. Any specific order?"

His face filled with confusion. She explained. "Alphabetical by author? By genre?"

"However they fit."

"You're such a dude."

"Nice of you to notice."

He smiled at her, and whatever doubts she had fell away. She went to the living room and returned with a box of books. Not that he had it labeled. She basically lifted and shook. He joined her by the bookcase and they emptied the boxes and talked about work. He was telling her about the restaurant job he was finishing up.

Evan stuck his head in the room and said, "Hey, Dad. I'm gonna go hang with friends."

"Not too late."

"I know." He smirked. "Not bad for an old man. You got hot chicks helping you pack and unpack."

Trevor cringed. "Evan."

Callie touched his arm. "I don't mind being referred to as a hot chick." She winked at Evan.

"See ya," he called as he left.

"So who's the other hot chick?" she asked.

"Nina helped me figure out what needed to move and what I'll donate. And like I said, she's a friend."

"Like I'm a friend."

He stared into her eyes, holding the gaze a beat longer than normal. "Not quite," he said quietly.

Her heart thudded, and the rest of the world fell away. A book slipped from her hand. The *thump* of it hitting the floor broke the moment.

When they finished the books, there wasn't much left to do. The rest would wait until the weekend.

"I guess I'll head home," she said.

"Actually," he started, "are you going to be around for a bit?"

She nodded.

"I think I'm going to hit a meeting. Nina reminded me that I need to make time for that, so since it's still early, I'd like to go. Will you be home in case Hannah needs something?"

"Sure." She liked that he turned to her to help with the kids.

"I'll only be an hour or so."

"Take your time." She brushed her hands on her shorts. "I'll let Hannah know she can come over if she wants."

"Thanks."

She walked to the door and then turned. "I like this new version of Trevor. I liked you twenty years ago. You were a hell of a lot of fun. But this grown-up version? I like him more."

He stood still. No response.

She added, "Except maybe you could smile more. I promise it won't kill you."

His somber expression cracked, and he laughed. "I'll keep that in mind."

He was still laughing as she ran upstairs to talk to Hannah. It was a good sound.

As the school year came to a close and finals neared, Trevor realized the house and the kids were a little crazy. Books and notes filled the dining room table and Hannah was little more than a ball of stress. Every time he suggested she take a break, that she didn't need to kill herself over a test, she reminded him that she needed good grades to get into college.

He stared at the huge calendar on the wall. He had a basement remodel that he was starting this week. Hannah had a band concert Thursday night, and she was supposed to start driver's ed on Monday. Evan had nothing on the calendar other than finals. He told Trevor he was fine, and Trevor didn't want to nag, but he saw no way around it. Evan needed a high school diploma.

His son breezed into the kitchen and opened the refrigerator.

"What are you studying for tonight?" Trevor asked.

Evan laughed. "I'm not."

Trevor crossed his arms and took a deep breath. He'd been doing a lot of counting the last few weeks. "This is not negotiable. I need to see you studying. No studying, no car, no friends."

"Come on. Finals aren't until next week!"

"Then you have plenty of time to study."

"I'll study the night before."

Trevor shook his head. "I get that you don't think school is important. Your grades reflect that. I understand that you don't want college. But blowing off finals and getting sucky grades limits your options. That's all I want you to understand. Keep your options open."

"And if I don't, you're gonna make me?"

"Yep."

"Fine." Evan turned and stomped away.

"Down here. Bring your books here so I can watch you study. No phone," Trevor called after him.

"Hannah's taking over the whole table."

"She'll make room." Trevor turned to where Hannah was working with earbuds in. He had no doubt she'd heard the entire exchange, but he touched her shoulder to get her attention.

Tugging an earbud out, she said, "What?"

"Your brother is coming down here to study. How about we do a guitar lesson?"

"Now?"

Trevor was glad he'd thought of it. It would give Hannah a break and allow Evan to study in peace.

"Sure."

"Yeah," she answered as she slammed her book shut.

"Clear a spot for Evan and go grab my guitar from the front closet. We'll play in my room." That way he could keep an eye on Evan *and* teach Hannah.

In the kitchen, he made notes about what he needed to load on the truck for the basement job tomorrow. They were doing demo for the next couple of days. It would be messy, exhausting work.

A few minutes later, Evan came back and plopped down at the dining room table. He set a book in front of him but made no move to open it.

"What are you working on?"

"American history. It blows. What do I need to know any of this for?"

Trevor almost shrugged but realized it would be too close to agreeing with Evan, and he'd learned his lesson there. "Sometimes you have to do things you don't like. It's part of life. I'm going to be in my room with Hannah. Holler if you need any help."

Evan flipped the cover open on the book. Trevor remembered those days. They were fucking miserable.

He'd hated school, too. He never needed a damn thing he learned in history class. But before he opened his mouth to commiserate with his son, he left the room to hang out with Hannah.

She was sitting on his bed, holding the guitar on her lap. She randomly strummed the strings. When she looked up, pure joy reflected in her eyes. His girl loved music. He wished he'd thought of this before.

"Ready?"

"Yep. Where do I start?"

"Let's keep it simple. Move forward so your feet are flat on the floor." He moved to position the guitar on her lap. "We'll do some basic fingering techniques, but it takes some getting used to. Your fingers will hurt."

"Yeah, yeah. Tell me what to do." She stared at him with a broad smile.

He moved her fingers into position for a D chord and told her to strum. Then he fixed the pressure and the strings and had her try again.

Nothing fazed her. She took correction and didn't complain about repeating things. While she strummed, he peered out to make sure Evan was still at the table at least pretending to study.

CALLIE LET HERSELF IN THROUGH THE BACK DOOR AND SAW Evan sitting at the dining room table surrounded by a mountain of books. She wasn't sure why she'd decided to come over, but lately sitting at home alone felt stifling. Yet when she walked into the house, she felt content.

Evan looked up with a scowl when she came in. "Problem?"

"School sucks."

"Sometimes, yeah."

A guitar strummed unevenly in the other room. When she looked in that direction, Evan said, "Hannah and Dad."

Callie took a seat next to Evan. "Anything I can help with?"

"I doubt it. I have to memorize all of these dates and people from World War II. When am I ever going to use this information?"

"You might not, but learning it makes you an informed citizen. Next year, you'll be old enough to vote. You help decide what happens in our country. To not know where we came from could easily lead to us making the same mistakes again. That's true of anything in life."

He snorted. "You sound like Mom."

"She was a smart woman." She pulled the text closer. "Look. I'm not going to convince you that this is interesting or even necessary, but I can offer you some tips to remember it."

"Yeah?"

"I have a horrible memory. Your mom used to make me flashcards for everything when we were in high school."

"That worked?"

Callie laughed. "No, but when I took the information and related it to something I liked, it was easier to remember."

"Huh?" Callie bit her lip and thought. She wasn't a teacher or a mom. She didn't really know how to do this. "Okay. This is war. How many video games do you play that are some version of war?"

"A lot, I guess."

"Imagine World War II as a video game. Put the people and dates and vocabulary into places that make sense to you. Make up a story or draw a map. You can do this." She closed the book. "Work from your notes."

Evan didn't look completely convinced, but he opened his notebook and folder and pulled out study guides and notes.

She looked at some of the information. "Here. Let me give you an example. The Battle of the Bulge was really important. I like art. So I'd represent that battle with a picture." She took a piece of paper and sketched a fat man. She labeled the countries around him and added some funny details.

"That's ridiculous."

She smiled. "Yeah, but if I'm sitting down to take a test, all I have to do is remember this picture. Easier than flash cards."

"I guess you've got a point." He flipped through his notes. "I don't know how to do that."

"You don't need to draw. Your video games have stories. Make up a hero. Or use a real one. Give him a mission. The mission stats are the facts and details you need to remember."

"Huh. That kind of makes sense."

Callie smiled. She stopped short of giving herself a pat on the back, but she felt good. While Evan hunched over a paper and began making his own study guide, Callie went to go see Hannah and Trevor. Just as she neared his bedroom, the playing began again, but this time it was smooth and good. She recognized the opening strains of "Sweet Child o' Mine."

She waited outside the door and listened. It had been years since she'd heard Trevor play. The song transported her back twenty years to many of the dive bars Trevor's band had played at. Her weekends had been filled with hanging out with Lisa and Trevor and the band. Even after Evan was born, Callie sometimes went to the bar to hang out, but things had started to fall apart by then.

Trevor had spent more time drinking than he had with his family. Lisa had been overwhelmed with having a baby. As things got worse between Trevor and Lisa, Callie had felt torn. She'd loved them both. So she'd thrown herself into her career.

As the song played on, she found herself being drawn closer until she was in the doorway, watching Trevor play. She was struck by an image of him onstage in a smoky bar, staring down at the crowd, a huge grin on his face. He loved playing. Hannah stared at him with adoring eyes, a clone of her mother.

Damn. She wanted this. This sense of family.

Holy crap. Where did that come from?

When he strummed the last chord, Callie automatically clapped. Trevor's head snapped up.

"Hey," he said.

"I forgot how good you are."

He shrugged, obviously uncomfortable with her praise.

"I didn't," Hannah said. "I remember him playing when we were little."

"You were too young, so you don't remember the rock days," Callie said. "They played a lot of Guns N' Roses. Oh, and the hair bands."

"Hair bands?" Hannah asked.

"Dudes from the '80s. Big hair. Hard rock. Love ballads. Poison. Mötley Crüe. And of course, Guns N' Roses."

"How could we go wrong with Guns N' Roses? Best of both worlds. We played rock and still wooed women." He winked at Hannah. "It's how I got your mom."

"Why'd you stop playing?"

Trevor swallowed and then stood. "Got busy with work. Didn't have time."

Hannah took his answer in stride, but Callie knew better. Lisa had demanded he stop playing with the band or she'd leave him. He'd quit for her, but leaving the band hadn't curtailed his drinking, which had continued to get worse.

"Who's up for ice cream sundaes?" Callie asked.

"If you're making them and cleaning up, sure," Trevor answered with a smile.

Hannah raced from the room to gather ingredients.

Callie turned to follow, but Trevor touched her hand to stop her.

"Thanks for that."

"What?"

"Not calling me out to Hannah."

Callie's heart hurt for him. "She knows you're an alcoholic. She also knows you're recovering. Give her credit. She loves you."

"Yeah, but no parent wants to admit to all of his failings to his kids." He shook his head. "I know they'll figure it out by the time they're grown, but if I can hold on to this a little longer, I will."

Part of her understood, but she still felt like he was selling himself short. He was building a new life with his kids. That alone was something to be proud of. Hell, it was more than she'd done with her life.

Trevor gave her hand a squeeze before releasing it. Then she went to have ice cream.

Chapter Seven

Callie stood in the middle of Lisa's bedroom, and a pang of guilt stabbed her. She'd cleared out everything for Trevor. He'd told her to take her time sorting through Lisa's things. He'd moved the bed out and brought up the one from the guest room so he could have his own bed downstairs. Other than that, he said the room wouldn't be used for anything.

But the stuff needed to go. She had the clothes packed and in her car, ready for donating. The makeup and lotions were tossed in the trash. She'd taken a few more items that she thought Evan and Hannah might like to have and put them in their rooms.

She was down to the final box, and she wasn't sure what to do. It contained Lisa's memories of her relationship with Trevor. Callie couldn't throw it out, but she didn't think the kids should have it unless Trevor said it was okay. This was exactly the kind of stuff a grieving spouse didn't want to go through.

Sitting on the bed, she opened the box and began to

look at the collection. It felt voyeuristic, but Callie couldn't stop herself. She opened cards and letters from Trevor to Lisa. He'd personalized every single card. No matter how sappy or sentimental the verse inside, he always added his own words. Callie's heart filled with love for her friends as well as a bit of jealousy over what she'd never been lucky enough to experience.

The opening and closing door downstairs startled her. She'd wanted to get everything done before Hannah and Evan came home. She'd thought she had the time. "Hello?" she called.

She walked into the hall and looked downstairs to see Trevor walking through the living room peeling off a wet shirt.

Once it was over his head, he looked up and saw her staring. "Hey, sorry. I didn't know you were here."

"No problem. I'm just finishing up in Lisa's room."

"Thanks. I need to change. One of the new laborers had a hard time understanding the concept of making sure the water was turned off." He held up his dripping shirt. "I'll be out of your hair in a few."

"Actually, if you have a few minutes, I have stuff for you to look at so I know what to do with it."

He nodded and disappeared around the corner toward his room. She pretended not to stare at his back. And his arms. And all the muscle created from hard work. With a deep breath, she went back to the guest room.

She gathered the letters and cards. She put them back in the box while she waited for Trevor to come up. Hopefully, with a shirt on. A minute later he was in the room. "Wow. You cleared out everything?"

"Yeah. I have a few boxes in my car to drop off. And then there's this." She tapped the box.

He sat beside her and waited for an explanation.

"It has your wedding album and letters and cards. Little mementos of your relationship with Lisa."

He blew out a breath and pulled the box closer. He looked inside, pulled out a little teddy bear. "I can't believe she kept this." He held it up. "I won this at a neighborhood carnival on one of our first dates. She teased me about not winning her one of the big prizes."

Callie's heart squeezed again, and she stood to give Trevor privacy. He reached out and took her hand.

Pulling her back to the bed, he whispered, "Please stay." She sat next to him and watched as he pulled out a stack of letters. He looked at a couple of cards and moved them aside.

"Why the hell did she keep all of this?" "Because they were fond memories. You were in love and had a good relationship for a long time."

"But I ruined it. I thought she would've burned everything."

"She loved you. You weren't a monster."

He grunted.

Callie stood and moved in front of him. "I don't think I need to tell you that alcoholism is a disease. You know that. But you were never a monster."

"Don't make excuses for me."

"Don't make Lisa out to be a saint. It took both of you to mess up your marriage." She reached into the box. "There are pages and pages of proof that you are a good man."

"Maybe at one time."

"You are now." She dropped the letters back and touched his jaw. The sadness she saw on his face broke her. He had no faith in himself. She lowered and pressed her lips to his. She meant to offer him reassurance, but at the contact, her system buzzed to life. She stroked his lips with hers. When he opened, she kissed him in earnest, stroking her tongue along his, tasting the coffee he'd undoubtedly had with his lunch.

The kiss was slow, spreading warmth through her body. His hand in her hair brought her back to reality, and she jerked back.

Touching her lips, she stared at him with wide eyes. From behind her fingers, she mumbled, "I'm so sorry. I don't know what I was thinking."

She backed away and then sprinted down the stairs. Trevor called her name, but she didn't stop. She ran to her car and started the engine. In the rearview mirror, she saw the boxes of Lisa's clothes. Guilt swamped her. She'd kissed her best friend's ex-husband. What the hell was wrong with her?

"I'm sorry, Lisa," she said as she pulled away from the house. The problem was that she was sorry she'd crossed that line with Trevor, but she couldn't say she regretted it.

Trevor stood, allowing envelopes to fall from his lap. "Callie," he called, but she didn't even slow. By the time he got to the front door, she was pulling away from the curb. *What the hell was that?*

The last five minutes of his life were a mind fuck. He returned to the bedroom and scooped up the things he'd dropped and shoved them all back into the box. Callie had been right. These were happy memories of an earlier part of his life.

It was time to move on. One day, his kids might want to look through this, but he didn't need to. He closed the box and tucked it on the shelf in the back of the closet. Then he turned and stared at the bed where Callie had kissed him. He took a minute to try to process it. He could still smell her lotion or perfume lingering in the air. The feel of her silky hair between his fingers and her slick tongue on his.

He should feel bad, but he didn't. If he really took stock of how he was feeling in this moment, he'd have to admit he was doing pretty damn good. He and Callie were both single adults. While he could admit that the when and where of the kiss might have been weird, the kiss itself had felt right.

Going back downstairs, he took out his phone and called Callie. It went to voicemail. He didn't know what to say, so he hung up. They'd need to talk about this, but it wasn't something to be covered in a message.

Hours later, Trevor was back in his driveway, but there was no sign of Callie's car. He let himself into the house and yelled for the kids.

Hannah stuck her head around the corner from the kitchen. "Dinner is almost ready."

Trevor made his way to the kitchen. "Smells good. What is it?"

"Chicken on the grill and fried potatoes," she said, pride spilling across her face.

"You cooked on the grill by yourself?"

She rolled her eyes. "Callie showed me how. I'm not an idiot. I'm fifteen. If you trust me to cook on the stove, you can trust me to cook on the grill."

She was right, but he didn't want to admit it. It would be too close to admitting she was growing up. "Is Callie coming for dinner?"

"No. She stopped by and asked about finals, but she said she was meeting friends for dinner."

He nodded and hoped Callie really did have plans and wasn't just avoiding him. When Hannah left the room to call Evan, he snapped a picture of the grilled chicken and sent it to Callie with the message,

> Thanks for teaching Hannah how to work the grill.

Bubbles popped on his screen immediately.

> No problem.

At least she wasn't totally avoiding him.

> We should probably talk.

No immediate bubbles this time. Evan stomped down the stairs, and both kids surrounded him and began filling their plates. Trevor helped himself and as he sat to eat, his phone buzzed with a message.

> I'm sorry.

Trevor stared at the phone a minute. Then he stood and told the kids, "I'll be right back."

He hated the thought of Callie being upset or worrying about the kiss, so when he got to the back patio, he called her.

She answered on the second ring. "Hi."

"Got a minute?"

"Yeah."

"You don't have anything to be sorry for."

"I shouldn't have kissed you. Especially while we were in Lisa's bedroom. Looking over all the good memories the two of you shared. It was a bad move. I don't know what I was thinking. We should probably forget it happened."

She was rambling, but Trevor heard the real worry. He didn't want to forget the kiss, but he wouldn't push her into something she didn't want. "It's your call, Callie. We did nothing wrong."

"It's complicated. You have a whole new life you're figuring out."

She was right, but her answers didn't sit well with him. "I don't want to screw this up," she whispered, so quiet he almost missed it.

"We're not going anywhere." He knew then that she was afraid of messing up this shaky new family dynamic every bit as much as he was. "Enjoy your night with your friends. See you tomorrow?"

"Sure."

He disconnected, not feeling any better.

Back at the dinner table, Hannah said, "Grandma called today."

"Yeah?" Trevor prompted as he cut into his chicken.

"She wants us to come visit when school is over."

Trevor set his silverware down and looked at the kids.

"I think it'll be fun. And it's a good idea. They really miss Mom."

Trevor glanced at Evan. "You okay with that?"

"Sure. As long as it's only for a week or whatever. You said I could work with you this summer."

"I have plenty of work for you. I'll have to look at my schedule and see when I can drive you down."

"She said she'd come and get us," Hannah said.

"What about your band camp?"

"We have two weeks off after school lets out before it starts."

Trevor nodded and dug into his dinner. Hannah was turning into a really good cook. He'd miss her cooking while she was gone. He'd quickly gotten used to her meals. "Okay. But maybe you can make some extra dinners and stick them in the freezer," he said with a smile.

Hannah rolled her eyes again. "How did you manage to live years on your own without me cooking for you?"

"If you don't want me to get spoiled, don't be so good at this."

"She's not good at everything. Remember the roast thing?" Evan began making gagging noises.

"Everyone is entitled to a few mistakes," Hannah rebutted.

Trevor sat back and enjoyed the sounds of his kids and wondered how he'd lived so long without them on a daily basis.

For the next week, Callie and Trevor fell into a routine of spending every evening together with the kids. They had dinner and helped the kids study for upcoming finals, and then they watched TV together. Every night when she went back to her place, her chest tightened. She hated walking away from the house.

She'd lived alone for decades. It was how she'd chosen to live. But lately, it was different. She'd been feeling lonely, and she didn't like it. The kids were gearing up for finals, which meant a crazier-than-usual schedule. Tonight, as they settled in to watch a zombie show, Hannah flounced on the loveseat across from where Callie and Trevor sat.

"Dad, would you please tell Evan that he has to drive me to school tomorrow?"

"Dude, you know that's the deal with getting the car."

"She has a first-period test tomorrow. I don't have to be there until eleven. That's not fair."

Trevor looked back and forth between the kids. "I'll drop you off."

"Don't you have breakfast with your friends?" Callie asked.

"I can skip."

"I'll take her to school. Go hang out with your friends."

"You sure?" Trevor asked.

"I'm always here to help out. No big deal." She leaned over to Hannah. "Just knock when you're ready to go. If we leave early enough, we can have time to stop for doughnuts."

Hannah's face brightened. "Thanks."

Evan said, "Bring some back for me?"

Trevor smiled. "I think that's Callie's payback for someone who doesn't want to get up early."

Callie shoved Trevor's leg. "I said nothing like that. Of course I'll bring some back. I don't play favorites."

They all laughed and started the show, talking over one another to guess what would happen next. Callie felt so at home, it was a constant reminder that she'd made the right decision in telling Trevor that they should forget they kissed.

Except when he smiled like he was now, like he had no cares in the world, she wanted to sit on his lap and toy with his mouth and share in that joy. But she ignored all of those feelings for the safe ones.

After the show ended, she went home. She opened the door and was met with a wall of heat. What the heck? She walked to the other end of the little house and checked her air conditioner. She had one big window unit that did a decent job of cooling the whole place. Except right now, it wasn't running. She turned all the dials and even took to smacking it.

It was good and dead. Damn. Going from room to room, she opened all the windows and prayed for a cross breeze. She took a cool shower, but by the time she crawled into bed, her skin felt clammy again. She lay on the mattress and tossed and turned. But sleep wouldn't come.

It made no sense, really. She'd traveled all over the world and had slept in many uncomfortable places. She'd lived in heat and rain and humidity, and she'd always managed to sleep. Something about being in her own bed messed with her sense of everything. She was supposed to be comfortable here. It was one of the reasons that she loved coming home.

After an hour of tossing and turning, she grabbed her pillow and phone and went back to the house. She had her key, but she didn't want to just walk in without warning. Standing at the back door, she texted Trevor.

> Still up?

> Yeah. What'd you need?

> My AC went out. Can I sleep in the guest room?

While she waited for an answer, the door in front of her opened and Trevor almost crashed into her. He was shirtless, wearing low-slung sleep pants. Seeing him like that reminded her of the kiss she was supposed to forget. "You have a key," he said.

"I know. But I didn't want to just stroll in. You're entitled to some privacy. What if you were walking around naked or something?"

His chuckle was low and made her skin tingle. "I have kids. Privacy went out the window when they were born. Besides, so what if I was walking around naked?"

Her skin flushed warm as she tried not to picture him naked.

He stepped back from the door to allow her to come in. The cool air washed over her skin, and her nipples hardened. *Totally just from the air-conditioning.* She hugged her pillow to her chest. "Thanks. I'll go get a new unit tomorrow."

"You can stay as long as you want. We have the space." He closed and locked the door behind her. "You need anything for the bed?"

She smiled and knew it was a little too brightly. "Nope. I have my pillow. The blanket on the bed will be fine. Thanks again."

Why was she acting so goofy? When Lisa had been alive, Callie had spent the night all the time. Then again, she'd never planted a kiss on Lisa.

Trevor smiled and shook his head. "Good night, Callie." Then he walked back to his room, safely on the first floor away from her rambling and uncontrollable lips.

CALLIE SLEPT SOUNDLY, AND WITH THE EXCEPTION OF mildly erotic dreams that she knew she shouldn't have had, she woke well-rested. Trevor was already gone by the time she rose to go back to her place and dress. She knocked on Hannah's door before leaving to make sure she was awake.

At her house, she dressed quickly. The humidity hadn't lessened overnight. The air was thick with moisture. It was uncomfortable for her, but she worried about her equipment. Throwing things in a bag, she took them back to Trevor's.

Trevor's.

Huh. That was a first. She hadn't thought of it as Lisa's house. And it felt good. While she waited in the kitchen for Hannah to get ready, she searched online for a new window air conditioner. The prices made her choke. The unit she was using had been in storage when she'd moved in, so she hadn't needed to buy one. It was probably really old, but it had worked fine.

The prices angered her because she knew that the current heat wave allowed stores to jack up the prices because people were desperate. Maybe Trevor knew someone who could get her a deal. She made a note to text him about it later.

Hannah came down with a bag much smaller than her usual backpack.

"Traveling light today?"

"I only have two exams."

"How are you getting home?" Callie asked.

Hannah shrugged. "Probably the bus. Unless I wait for Evan to finish his test, but that means I'll be hanging at school for at least an extra hour."

Callie grabbed her keys. "Call me when you're done. I'm working from home."

"Thanks. Mom never picked me up in the middle of the day."

"She had to work."

"I know. But it's nice having you around."

"I like being around."

TREVOR SAT AT SUNNY'S DINER DRINKING COFFEE WITH HIS friends. He'd already assured them all that things were going well with the kids. His house was on the market, and with a little luck, it would sell soon.

"How are things with Callie?" Nina asked.

"Fine," he answered stiffly and gave her a warning look.

But Nina wasn't about to let a look stifle her. "Just fine? Nothing going on?"

He sighed. "We're friends. She's helping me with the kids. Would you ask me questions like this if it were Tess helping me?"

Tess smiled and set down her cup. "We've never had any chemistry. From what we all saw, you and Callie have it in spades."

He didn't know what to say to that, so he drank more coffee.

"Don't mess things up," Tess said. "The kids depend on her and if she leaves, they'll be devastated."

"She wouldn't leave the kids." He was a hundred percent sure about that. He saw the love she had for them every day.

Nina shifted in her seat. "So does that mean you're pursuing something?"

"I don't know what I'm doing." He looked around the table at his friends. These people had his back. They had for years. If anyone could help him navigate the muddied waters of his current situation, it would be them. "She kissed me."

"And?" Evelyn asked, leaning forward, suddenly interested in the conversation at his end of the table.

"Then she said we should forget it happened."

Owen scoffed. "Dude. Are you so out of practice you don't know how to kiss?"

He shot Owen a dirty look. "I can kiss just fine. It was a damn good kiss."

"But it's complicated," Tess supplied.

"Understatement of the year."

"What are you going to do?" Nina asked.

"Hell if I know." As if on cue, his phone buzzed with a text from Callie. She wanted to know about an air conditioner. His friends' staring distracted him, so he couldn't quite grasp what she wanted.

"Ooo...That's Callie, isn't it?" Evelyn sang.

He nodded. "Her AC went out last night." He looked back at his screen. Callie continued in another text that he actually had to scroll through. She wrote a text the same way she talked, and it made him dizzy.

He stood and tossed some bills on the table. "I need to take care of this."

Tess reached out and touched his arm. "Call if you need anything."

"And have juicier details for breakfast next time," Evelyn called after him as he walked out the door.

Instead of reading the long text, he called Callie.

"Hello."

"What do you need to know about the AC?"

She sighed. "Didn't you read my text?"

"No. It would take you a minute to explain this, but probably five for me to wade through that thing you call a text. By the way, a text is supposed to be short."

"Whatever."

He could picture her wrinkling her nose and sticking her tongue out at him, and he smiled as if she were standing in front of him.

"I looked online before leaving the house this morning, and after dropping Hannah off, I went to two different stores. These people are crazy with what they want to charge. I thought maybe you might know someone who could get me a deal."

At least she hadn't wasted her money.

"I don't know if I can get one cheap. I'll look around."

"The weather says it's going to stay in the nineties all week. It's not dropping, so I kind of need to get one now."

"No, you don't. It doesn't make sense to get screwed on the price because they have you over a barrel. Just stay at the house."

"That's a generous offer, but I need to work."

"So?"

"My darkroom is in my spare room."

He hadn't thought about her developing her pictures. He hadn't walked through the coach house when he'd been there. "I didn't know you developed pictures."

"Most of what I do for jobs is digital, but sometimes, I want the feel of film, you know?"

No, he had no idea, but she was passionate about it. "Set up in the basement. It's cool and dark down there."

"I can't take over your space, Trevor."

He sighed again and rubbed a hand over his face. "You're picking up my kids and dropping them off. Helping with homework. The least I can do is make sure you're comfortable. Use whatever space you need."

"But—"

"But nothing. Let me do this for you. It'll give me time to look around and decide whether it makes more sense to get another window unit or invest in forced heat and air for the coach house."

"Are you sure?"

"Yes."

"Okay. Just so I can finish the job I'm working on now. A couple days—tops."

"Like I said last night, stay as long as you need." His offer was heartfelt, but in the back of his mind, he knew he was only adding to the complexity of their situation.

"Thanks again."

"It's the least I can do." He drove to the job. Even though he'd be spending his day in a space that was dungeon-like, he whistled as he entered the job site. Complicated or not, he liked having Callie in his life.

THEY MADE IT. THE BOOTHS HAD BEEN BORDERLINE homicidal for the last week. The kids had been uptight about finals. Trevor's job had hit snags. Callie had done her best to stop anyone from lashing out unnecessarily.

But they'd done it. They ordered in for a celebratory dinner. Callie sat at the table and listened to the kids laugh while Trevor tried to nag them about packing for their trip to see their grandparents. Callie couldn't imagine them being gone. Granted, it was only going to be a week, and she'd often traveled for at least that long. But it was different when she was the one being left behind.

Although she had work to do and jobs to pitch, she hadn't had much free time since Lisa's death. She and Trevor had become close. Every night after the kids went to bed, they stayed up and watched TV or talked about their days. She loved hearing the crazy stories from Trevor's job sites. She'd thought about asking if she could tag along one day to take pictures. She had little doubt she could find a fascinating story.

Trevor waved a hand in front of her face. "Where'd you go?"

She blinked. "Sorry. Just thinking." She pointed at Hannah and Evan. "With them gone, it'll be so quiet. And the free time…"

"I didn't even think about those perks," Trevor continued, picking up on her teasing tone. "I could walk around naked all the time."

Evan groaned, and Hannah said, "Eww, gross."

Callie and Trevor laughed.

But the image stayed in her head. The reality of the kids' leaving tugged at her. Not only would she miss them, she'd miss this—the whole family experience.

And her alone time with Trevor.

Maybe the kids' being gone was a blessing. She wouldn't feel obligated to be here, so she could go out, meet people, socialize with someone other than Trevor, who was not her husband. Or boyfriend. Or anything, really.

The kids rambled on about what they might get to do at their grandparents' house, and Trevor just nodded at their excitement.

"Not to burst your bubble, guys, but I grew up there. Although things have probably changed, it's about as boring as it gets. The town has one movie theater and a couple of restaurants. There's not much to do for fun."

Hannah sighed with a sweet smile on her face. "But

Grandma and Grandpa moved farther out from town. They're surrounded by farms."

"Ugh. That's even worse." Callie hated that damn town. It was so confining.

Hannah laughed again. "That's because you don't like the peace and quiet of nature."

She opened her mouth to argue, but the girl was right. If Callie had her choice of assignments, she always chose urban areas. "Well, I hope you have a great time."

She stood and began cleaning their dinner mess. Trevor told the kids to go pack. Evan and Hannah ran upstairs, arguing over how much they could take.

Trevor joined Callie at the sink where she washed dishes. "You don't have to do that. Evan will be back."

She shrugged. "I don't mind."

He leaned against the counter and studied her. "What're you thinking about? Something's been bugging you all night."

"I don't know. My life feels a little unsettled right now."

"Work?"

"That's part of it. It's like I've gotten used to the routine of being here with you and the kids, and I've done some local work, but I need to pitch new ideas and get steady work. But at the same time, they're going to be gone and it messes with the routine I've had since..."

She realized she was babbling and clamped her mouth shut. Resting her forearms on the edge of the sink, she leaned forward and prayed for clarity. Which was not likely to come as long as Trevor was standing so close and had been talking about walking around naked. *Lord, what is wrong with me?*

His hand landed on her shoulder, and he squeezed before rubbing her back. "I'm a shitty friend."

She looked at him over her shoulder. "Huh?"

"I've been leaning on you so much, and I never stopped to even ask how you were doing, how you're holding up. I'm sorry."

"You have nothing to apologize for. We've been leaning on each other. Lisa's death just has me thinking about my life and where I want to go from here. Being with the kids is a reminder of things I've missed out on."

"Regrets?"

"Not really. I never thought of myself as mother material. The crying and diapers and sticky fingers. Not my thing." She straightened and turned so she stood hip to hip with Trevor. "But the good parts. Like dinner tonight. The bickering banter and teasing. The family thing. I never considered it. At bare minimum, I took it for granted."

"You have family here. Always."

She appreciated his words, but she still felt itchy. "It's more than that. It's having someone to lean on, share my life with. I've been traveling and moving around for so long. When I came back, Lisa was my family connection. But these past weeks, hanging out with you, talking about our days... It's been a reminder of what I don't have."

Trevor didn't say anything, but he wrapped his heavy arm around her shoulders and pulled her close. It wasn't sexual or flirtatious, but it made her blood race all the same.

"We're packed, Dad," Hannah yelled from the top of the stairs. "Can we go for ice cream?"

Trevor moved away from her slowly, allowing his arm

to caress the entire span of her shoulders. "What do you say? Ice cream?" he asked her.

"Who can say no to double chocolate fudge brownie?"

His face contorted. "How do you still have your teeth? Mine hurt just thinking about how sweet that is."

"You don't know what you're missing." She winked and pushed off the counter.

The look he gave seared into her, letting her know that he'd been thinking about what he'd been missing, too.

Chapter Eight

Trevor was late to work the following morning because he waited until Diane showed up to get the kids. Callie was conveniently gone. He double-checked to make sure Evan and Hannah had everything they needed, and he offered Diane some cash, which she brushed off. By the time they were in the car, he needed another cup of coffee.

The basement job was running behind because the plumber hadn't passed his inspection. Now that they were approved, everything rested on his shoulders to get them caught up. As if it were his fault they were behind. Jerry had been on site to accept the drywall delivery, and by the time Trevor walked into the basement, the crew had an entire wall done.

"How's it going?" he asked his foreman.

"Fine," Jerry answered gruffly.

Trevor raised an eyebrow. Jerry tilted his chin toward the door, and Trevor walked out with him.

"What's the problem?"

Jerry stood close and spoke with a low voice. "The new guys are working out okay, but this homeowner is killing me. He's been down here three times checking our progress. He doesn't understand why it's taking so long."

Trevor shook his head. There wasn't much you could do with a customer like that. "Let's get out of here, so we don't need to put up with him."

"Crap," Jerry muttered.

"What?" Trevor followed Jerry's gaze to the window above them, where the curtain fluttered.

"He's probably going to complain that he's paying us to stand around and talk."

"I'll handle him."

Jerry was an excellent employee and had worked for Trevor for years. He could run the job as well as Trevor, but he sucked at dealing with people. The man liked to work with wood and drywall. Social interactions with customers rarely went well.

They turned toward the basement stairs again. "Realistically, you think we could have this done by the weekend? If I give him a deadline, it'll be easier to keep him off our backs."

They took stock of what they needed to do. If they rocked out the drywall and spent the next two days taping and painting, they'd be ready for trim this weekend. But Trevor couldn't ask the guys to work their weekend away, and there wasn't room in the budget to pay them overtime.

Normally, Trevor liked to put in weekend hours by himself. It helped structure his time, and he liked the solitude. Lately, though, he hadn't been logging the hours, not during the week or on the weekends. Time with his family had taken precedence over work.

It was the first time in many, many years that was true.

With the kids gone until Sunday, though, he could put a dent in the trim Friday night and Saturday. Then he thought of Callie.

The woman made his head spin. He didn't understand what was brewing between them. They'd hit a solid stride as friends, but there was a constant undercurrent. Sexual tension? Attraction? He didn't know what to call it, but it was getting worse. Or stronger.

Fuck.

Thinking about Callie kept him hard in ways no one had in a long time. It didn't help that for the past week, they'd shared the same living space. Her scent was everywhere. He couldn't escape it, other than to sit in his room. Even then, he still had thoughts of her in her skimpy shorts and tank top. And being alone with those images didn't relieve the hard-on situation.

Not knowing what to do about Callie was a problem for later. Right now, he needed to drywall the hell out of this basement so he could move on to more lucrative jobs. He turned to the work that always occupied his hands and soothed his mind.

By the time he got home, he was covered in a fine white dust and his clothes were glued to his body. But the drywall was up. He walked into the house and was met with eerie silence. He'd lived alone in his house for years, but now he suddenly missed the regular noise of his kids.

"Callie?" he called, because despite teasing Hannah, he didn't really plan to walk around naked if Callie was there. No one answered. He left his boots near the door and peeled off his shirt on the way to the bathroom.

He felt a million times better after his shower. After pulling on a pair of shorts, he gathered his dirty clothes and took them to the basement. As soon as he opened the basement door he remembered telling Callie she could use the space for a darkroom, so he called out again. Still no answer, so he ventured down to the washing machine. He got his clothes started, and on his way back toward the stairs, he looked around.

Callie hadn't brought in much. She had some trays spread out on a cheap folding table. Bottles of chemicals sat off to the side. Then she had a clothesline hung up, just like in the movies. He couldn't help but see what she'd been developing. She had shots of the kids and some random pictures of flowers. The last few, though, took him by surprise.

She'd taken pictures of him working on the bathrooms here in the house. How had he not known she'd done that? Some photos were crisp, clear, and bright enough that he could use them in a brochure. Then she had a couple of him in black and white. It had been early on in the project, maybe even the first day she'd helped him.

"Hey." Her voice carried quietly across the basement.

"What's this?"

She squinted at him in confusion. "It's what I do."

"How were you so sneaky that I didn't even know you were taking pictures of me?"

"I've learned to be stealthy. The best way to get a natural shot is to take it when the subject is unaware. That's when he's at his most vulnerable." Her cheeks flushed, and she pushed past him. "This was just for fun. I had a few frames left on the roll, and I needed to use it up. You weren't supposed to see them."

"Your work is really good. Not that my opinion means much."

"Thanks," she said, not making eye contact as she tugged the photos off the line and stacked them up. "If it's okay with you, I'll leave this stuff here until after I get the new AC unit."

"I told you that's fine. You ready for dinner?"

"Uh…" She stared at his bare chest and dragged her eyes up to his face.

How was he supposed to ignore such blatant attraction?

"I figured you'd want your space to be alone," she mumbled.

He crossed his arms. "You're here, so I'm not alone."

"I planned to head back to my place."

"Why? It's gotta be a hundred degrees in there."

"The kids are gone for the week, and I thought you'd appreciate your freedom." She shifted, clearly uncomfortable.

He shook his head. "Callie, I don't know how else to say this. I thought I was being clear. I like you being in my space."

She slowly licked her lips, and he followed the line of her tongue. She might not have meant to tease, but every nerve in his body perked up.

He stepped closer. She backed up until she bumped the table. Trevor caged her in with his arms. He kept his body back, lowering his face so they were eye to eye.

"What are you doing?" she whispered.

"Something we both want. Something we'd both enjoy."

She gulped as he moved closer. He waited to give her a chance to push him away, tell him no, refuse in some way. But she didn't.

He brushed his lips against hers. He took his time kissing her softly, exploring her taste, her texture, her desires. With each swipe of his lips or tongue, his body inched forward, longing to press against her, feel her soft body. But he held back, leaving her space.

Her participation was slow, but once their tongues touched, she angled her head to deepen the kiss, and her hands became busy stroking his shoulders and neck and chest. There was nothing hurried about their interaction.

It was the best fucking kiss he'd had in years.

Callie finally pressed against his shoulder and pulled away from him. Their chests were heaving, and she looked up at him with heavy eyelids.

"Holy cow," she said.

He straightened. "That's the best you've got?"

She just stared, her eyes now wide. She licked her damn lips again, but he knew that she'd be tasting him this time.

"Come on," he said. "Let's get some dinner. I think Hannah left stuff in the fridge."

He didn't touch her as he turned away. Looking over his shoulder, he said, "Coming?"

"In a minute."

"Then we can watch a good movie for a change. If Hannah makes me watch another sappy movie, I might cry."

He jogged up the stairs, leaving Callie to consider his kiss and where else it could lead.

Callie's head was spinning. How could Trevor initiate a kiss like that in the basement and now sit next to her on the couch, watching one of the *Die Hard* movies, acting as if nothing had changed?

He sprawled over his side of the couch, still wearing nothing but a pair of shorts. He should be a little more courteous to her. Seeing him sit like that made her want to crawl over him and have a repeat performance. And maybe more. She stole glances at him and tried to process what was happening between them. But she came up with nothing.

When the credits started to roll, he turned off the TV and then stood. "I'm heading to bed. I have a ton of estimates to do tomorrow."

She stood and stretched, wondering if he was extending an invitation.

He slid an arm around her waist and kissed the side of her head. "Good night. See you tomorrow."

Then he slipped past her.

Wait. What?

"That's it?" she asked.

He turned back and looked at her. "What do you mean?"

"You planted a hell of a kiss on me downstairs, and now nothing. Shouldn't we at least address that?"

He came back toward her, looking like an animal stalking its next meal. His eyes darkened as he neared.

Her pulse thundered.

"You seemed a little skittish after the kiss. Make no mistake. I want to do that again, and I have every intention of doing so, but I thought you needed some time to wrap your head around it."

She swallowed hard and tried to focus. What answer had she been looking for? She'd half expected him to back off the way she had the first time their lips had touched, to tell her he shouldn't have and they shouldn't. But he made no such move.

She was glad.

"This is weird, isn't it?"

"Not how I would describe it." He reached out and pushed her hair from her shoulder, his fingers caressing her skin. "Fucking hot. Memorable." He licked his lips. "Delicious."

She began breathing fast again.

"Not weird, though," he continued.

"But—"

"Sleep on it, Callie. If you never want to kiss me again, say the word." Then he walked to his room and closed the door.

She stood in the living room and considered everything. They had some hot chemistry. There was no denying that. They had a long history, not all of it good. But the bulk of the bad revolved around his drinking and his relationship with Lisa, both of which were gone.

Over the last month, they'd become more than friends. In many ways, they did everything a couple did, except sleep together.

Maybe that was her problem. She hadn't been on a date since coming back to Chicago. Although she'd been meaning to update her dating profiles, she hadn't done anything. She'd been using Trevor to fill that void in her life. He'd taken care of those empty, lonely spaces, and now he'd offered to satisfy the last area.

She turned off the lights and went upstairs to the spare room. Using her phone while she lay in bed, she logged into her profiles and updated them one by one. Her picture was old, but she liked it. Did she need something sexier?

After fluffing her hair, she looked at herself in the camera. No makeup and the lighting wasn't great. She snapped a couple shots. Then sighed. She was too old for this shit. She decided to leave her picture the same.

Satisfied that her profile was good enough—and really, how good did it have to be?—she scrolled through her prospects. Moments later, she had a ping. Craig had sent her a message.

> Hi – I love your profile pic. You like to travel?

She typed her response.

> Yeah, but I travel mostly for work.

> What kind of work?

Points to Craig for not immediately asking to hook up or sending a dick pic.

> I'm a photographer. How about you?

> Insurance agent. Not too exciting, I know.

> We all need to pay the bills.

They continued to chat for a while, even though it was getting late. In between messages, Callie scrolled back to check out Craig's profile. He lived in the suburbs, but not too far. He listed his hobby as craft beer. Was that some way of saying getting drunk was his hobby?

He asked for her number to be able to text. They continued the conversation via text, and Callie had fun. They joked about work and the weather, of all things. Then he asked if he could take her out to dinner tomorrow.

Just like that. A real date. She agreed and said good night. As she turned off the light, she thought about her date. It was a good move. Testing the waters would help her get her head straight about Trevor.

TREVOR WENT TO WORK IN THE MORNING WITH A SMILE ON his face. While he generally enjoyed his job, he rarely walked around with a grin. But his night with Callie had been better than normal. While he always enjoyed his time with her, their kiss had been hot. She wanted more with him; she just had to come to terms with it.

He brewed a pot of coffee for her before he left because he knew she liked to have a cup before she did anything else with her day. He drove to the suburbs to get to his first appointment. He pulled up at the house for the estimate.

Given that they weren't out of the basement job yet, he normally wouldn't look to book another residential job, but since this was a deck job, he wanted to look. Decks were easy money, and it was something he could put Evan on without too much hassle.

He preferred commercial work, but depending on the job, he'd have an issue with Evan working. It would only take one superintendent asking Evan how old he was to cause trouble. Plus, being out in the sun building with wood was how he'd spent all his summers as a teenager. It would give Evan a taste of the good and bad of manual labor.

He rang the bell, and a woman answered the door wearing workout gear. "Hi," he said. "I'm Trevor from Booth Construction to give you an estimate for a deck."

"Of course." She cracked the screen door open a few inches and pointed to the corner of the house. "If you just go around back, I'll meet you there."

"Okay." Trevor inhaled deeply. He understood people not wanting him in the house if he was doing outside work, but this woman looked afraid to open the damn door. He walked around back. The yard was huge with a neatly manicured lawn, the grass a bright green. A garden ran along the fence on one side. Attached to the back of the house was the ugliest deck he'd seen in a while. No one had taken care of it.

He stepped up and felt the lumber give far more than it should. The wood was spongy. He grabbed the rail and shook. As he suspected, it wobbled.

The patio door opened, and the woman came out.

"Sorry about that," she said. "My dog is an escape artist. As soon as the door opens, he shoots through."

He nodded. At least she wasn't afraid of him. "Is it a big dog?"

"Not yet. She's a Lab puppy." She looked at the deck. "As you can see, it's in bad shape."

"Yeah, it is. What were you looking for?"

She handed him a piece of paper. On it was a computer-generated sketch of a deck. She'd obviously gone to the home improvement store and had this done.

He took a moment to study the drawing. "I assume you need me to do the demo. Will you need me to haul away the debris, or will the village pick it up?"

"I honestly don't know. It might be better if you just got rid of it. My neighbors can be picky."

He snapped a picture of the sketch and emailed it to himself. "Will you be ordering the material and having it delivered, or is that something you want me to provide?"

"We'll order it. If you can just make sure the list is accurate, we'll have it delivered. We're looking for you to bid for doing the labor."

"Okay. I'll take a few measurements to make sure this is accurate, and I'll have the estimate ready for you by tomorrow."

"Excellent. You have my email address?"

He nodded.

"I'll be inside if you need anything else."

He walked to her with his hand extended. "Nice to meet you, Ms. Wilson."

"Rebecca, please."

"Rebecca. I'll be in touch."

She went back into the house, leaving Trevor to take

his measurements. Everything on the drawing matched exactly, which was a good sign. An even better sign that Rebecca gave him the information he needed and then went back in the house. Hopefully, the rest of his estimates would go as smoothly.

After logging about a hundred miles driving to and from estimates, he was more than ready to go home. Yet another reason he preferred commercial work. For those jobs, he usually received a print and could do the estimate from the comfort of his house.

The heat wave still hadn't broken, so his shirt was stuck to his back even with the AC blasting in the truck. Of course, it didn't help that he kept thinking about Callie, which kept him hot. He stopped to get an iced coffee, and after parking the truck, he texted Callie.

> Dinner tonight?

He immediately added,

> I'm thinking ice cream.

> For dinner?

> I'm an adult. I can have ice cream for dinner.

> I'm gonna tell the kids.

> You wouldn't rat me out. What kind do you want?

> As much as I'd love to join your night of no adulting, I can't. I have a date.

Wait. What? She has a date? The air in the cab of the truck thickened with the heat. What was he supposed to say to that? He filled his lungs with the oppressive, moist air. He'd told her to think about them. Callie had a habit of running when things got hard. He'd let her run to figure out what she wanted.

> Okay. Have fun.

He grabbed his drink and stopped at the grocery store on the way home to pick up some double chocolate fudge brownie ice cream. Just in case.

CALLIE TOOK A COOL SHOWER AND STOOD IN HER bathroom applying makeup. Nerves fluttered in her gut. It was at times like these that she would've gone to Lisa for advice or a pep talk. She had no one who lived nearby that she could go to. Picking up her phone, she went to social media and posted that she had first-date jitters.

Her online friends would get it. Within moments she had her pep talk. People chimed in with well wishes and warnings. Others offered to be her emergency call should she need an escape. Whoever said online friends weren't real friends had no idea. She slipped into her favorite summer dress and sandals.

Craig had suggested going out to dinner but hadn't said where, so she wasn't quite sure how dressed up to get. Glancing in the mirror, she liked what she saw. This dress had always made her feel confident because she knew she looked good in it. For some reason, tonight she needed the added boost.

At seven on the nose, a knock sounded. She appreciated a man who showed up on time. She shoved her phone and keys into her purse and opened the door.

Craig stood at the threshold, hand tucked into his pants pockets. He wore a crisp button-down but no jacket. He looked pretty much the same as his profile picture, which was a relief because she'd been afraid that some seventy-year-old dude might show up. But unlike in his photo, he had a beard. Kind of. It was more like a wannabe beard. Just a tuft of fur jutting out from his chin.

"Hi," she said.

"Hi. You look beautiful. Your profile picture doesn't do you justice." He leaned in and kissed her cheek.

The fur tickled. And not in a good way.

"Am I dressed okay? I wasn't sure about where we're going."

"What you're wearing is fine. We're going to Tucker's. It's one of my favorite places. They have a great variety of craft beer."

"I'm not really a beer drinker." Even before she'd started practically living with Trevor, she'd rarely drunk. Pulling the door closed behind her, she smiled. She walked ahead of Craig through the yard, and movement in the kitchen caught her eye. Was that Trevor spying? Oh, she was totally going to call him on that later. She smirked all the way to street.

Craig hit his key fob, and the lights of a BMW lit up. It sat in front of the house, facing the wrong way in front of a fire hydrant. *I guess Craig's too special to park like everyone else.*

He opened the door for her. "Sorry," he said. "I normally don't park like a jerk, but this car is my baby. I wasn't sure if you'd be ready, so I wanted her to be in the shade."

Callie had no freaking clue what to say, so she just smiled and climbed in. While Craig walked around the car, she scanned her memory for which friends said they could bail her out. You know, just in case.

At the restaurant, which was a glorified bar, they ordered burgers, and he insisted on getting some samples of craft beer for them. He wasn't horrible. Just horribly boring. All he'd done from the moment they were seated was talk about craft beer.

She initially reminded him that she didn't drink beer. But it didn't dissuade him. It was as though he thought he was going to convert her.

When the samples arrived, she tried to be polite. She lifted one of the mini glasses and sipped.

"No. You have to get the full experience. This one is hoppy with hints of nutmeg. Press your nose into the glass and get a real feel."

She gave a perfunctory sniff and sipped again. It wasn't any better the second time. It tasted like some third-grader's science experiment. She pushed the glass toward him. "Not for me."

"Okay. Try this one."

"Should I cleanse my palate first?" she asked.

"Your taste was really small, so you're probably fine."

Her sarcasm had been completely lost on him. "I'm sorry. I don't enjoy beer. And this tastes funky."

"No need to apologize, we just haven't found what works for you yet."

He really didn't get it. She was beginning to regret not meeting him here so she could drive herself home. She waved the waitress over and ordered a Coke.

"That's not a good way to cleanse your palate."

"I'm not cleansing my palate. I'm drinking pop with my burger." She picked up her burger and took a big bite so she wouldn't have to talk to him anymore, which was just fine for Craig, because he continued to fill the air.

He talked about his first batch of homebrew. Callie just kept shoving food in her mouth so she wouldn't have to do anything other than smile or nod. The food was decent but she couldn't help but think she would've enjoyed ice cream more. It didn't help that Craig's damn beard thing kept distracting her. It was like he'd bitten into a gerbil.

She'd never had a huge preference for or against facial hair. Some guys wore it well. Like Trevor with his constant I'm-too-lazy-to-shave scruff. But Craig looked ridiculous with that thing sticking out of his chin.

Then he dripped ketchup onto it and just kept talking. She made a point of wiping her own mouth a couple of times hoping he'd get the hint, but he didn't. She ate in record time, and as soon as she swallowed the last bite, she set her napkin down.

"I hate to rush, but I have a long day tomorrow. I should be getting home."

"Sure. No problem." After finally wiping his faux beard, he paid the check, waving off her offer to pay half.

They drove back to her place in blissful silence. Craig parked a few houses down, on the right side of the street and not in front of a hydrant. He cut the ignition and said, "I'll walk you home."

She stepped from the car and waited while he reached into the back seat. He came around the car holding an insulated lunch box.

When he saw her looking, he said, "I have a surprise for you."

Callie tensed every muscle in her face to stop the cringe. Surprises were supposed to be good, and there was nothing about this situation that was.

They walked toward the house, and Callie scanned for lights. It looked like the kitchen light was on. Maybe Trevor was there, ready to spy again. Then he could interrupt. If only she could be so lucky. But she saw no movement.

At her door, she faced Craig. "Thanks for tonight."

"It doesn't have to be over yet." He lifted his lunch box. "I brought you samples of my latest brew. It's rich with notes of chocolate and chili peppers. I thought we could share." He looked at her with wide eyes. Then he added, "Just a drink. I don't expect to sleep with you after our first date."

As if. "It was thoughtful of you to want to share, but like I said at the restaurant, I don't like beer. Especially craft beer." *Definitely when created by a craft beer guy who doesn't listen.*

"Maybe you would if you'd give it a chance."

He leaned forward as if to kiss her, and all Callie saw was the furry chin approaching. She pressed her back into the door and held up a hand to stop him. "I don't think this will work. You're obviously passionate about craft beer, and I'm not into it."

He eased away at the same time her door opened and she fell into a hard chest.

"Hi, Callie." Trevor's hands landed on her hips to steady her. "I'm sorry. Am I interrupting?"

"Trevor," she said. Damn. Why was she so breathy? "What are you doing here?" *Thank God you're here.*

He flicked a thumb over his shoulder. "I got you a new air conditioner, so I installed it."

"Thanks." She looked up at him and prayed he could read her face and not leave.

Smiling, he said, "If you want, I can run you through how it works."

Turning back to Craig, she said, "Thanks again for tonight. Good luck." She waved and backed into her house.

Craig nodded and moved back down the gangway.

Trevor closed the door, grin still in place. "Good date?"

"Craft beer guy out there didn't talk about anything but beer. He really wanted to convince me that craft beer is where it's at."

"Maybe it is."

"Please. I manage to be here with you all the time without drinking anything, much less some brew a guy concocted in his closet. We also don't need to discuss drinking."

"Well, I am an alcoholic, so that might be an inappropriate conversation." He walked toward her, and she backed up until she bumped the counter. He huffed and reached past her into the freezer. He pulled out a pint of ice cream. "Should've chosen dinner with me."

He'd bought her ice cream. Even after she'd blown him off for a date with Craig. Even after she wanted to ignore the chemistry they shared. He'd even gotten her favorite flavor. She addressed the unspoken issue. "This is weird because you're Lisa's husband."

He held out the pint, and she shook her head. He put it back in the freezer.

"I *was* her husband. I haven't been in almost a decade. And she's gone. We're not hurting her. Lisa and I led our own lives. This isn't weird for me at all. If it's too weird for you, I understand. Sorry I pushed."

He was such a good guy. She knew that if she told him to back away, he would honor her decision. He'd move on and date other women, bring them home to meet his kids. That thought burned in her gut. She didn't want some other woman in his life. She swallowed hard and stared into his eyes. "Here's the thing. My mind keeps telling me that it should be weird. That you're off-limits. But while we were kissing? Weird was the last thing on my mind."

He shifted closer still, pushing his hand into her hair. The rough denim of his work jeans scraped against her bare thighs, causing licks of pleasure to race north.

His thumb stroked her jaw. "Maybe I just need to keep kissing you until your mind agrees with me."

Her heart thundered. She didn't want to have to decide. If he kissed her, the decision would be made.

Then he lowered his lips to hers. The kiss was slow but insistent. And she was *not* backing away.

Chapter Nine

Trevor tasted Callie until his entire body thrummed with anticipation. Her silky hair tickled his arm as he held her head. The scent of her perfume was warm on her skin. He nudged her legs apart to press closer to her body. His free hand trailed up her bare thigh as he kissed her jaw and then her neck. He sucked on her pulse point and sank his teeth into the tendon at the juncture of her shoulder and neck.

She placed her palms against his chest, but she didn't push. She gripped his T-shirt as if to anchor herself. When his teeth scraped the sensitive skin of her neck, she moaned. His hand on her thigh inched upward until he had a firm handful of ass cheek. He squeezed, and she arched forward, rubbing herself against his leg. His dick became a rod in his jeans.

Still stroking her soft skin, he pulled back a fraction. She followed with her mouth.

"Callie." Her eyes fluttered open, and lazy lust stared up at him. "Are you okay?" She nodded.

"I need to hear it, Callie. I don't want to fuck things up between us. But I want you. Right here. Right now. If you're not on board, say something."

She reached up and stroked his jaw. "I have just one thing to say."

His heart and his dick throbbed in unison, hoping for one answer, dreading the other. Another lonely night with his hand didn't appeal to him in the least after having a taste of her in his arms.

She smirked. "The bedroom's that way." She tapped his shoulder and pointed to the stairs leading to the loft.

He walked backward, pulling her with him. Although the new air conditioner was running, it was working hard to balance the temperature in the house. The air was still warm, but he didn't want to let go of her. He feared if they lost contact she might reconsider.

As they fumbled up the staircase, she tugged his shirt out of his jeans. Her cool fingers coasted across his stomach and up to his chest. He walked blindly toward her bed. Because it was at the back of the house, it was dark; little light filtered in from the alley.

As if reading his mind, Callie left him and flicked on the bedside lamp. The soft glow illuminated the room. He looked around, expecting to be surrounded by Callie's sunny personality, but the room was pretty utilitarian, almost as empty as a hotel room. Like maybe she hadn't planned to stay.

Except for the world map on one wall, different cities marked with bright colors, he wouldn't have guessed the room belonged to her. He bent and untied his work boots, loosening the laces enough to kick them off. She watched him as she stepped out of her sandals.

He yanked his shirt over his head, and she stepped close again, tracing her fingers up his stomach and across his chest. His muscles twitched under her touch. He reached around her and tugged the zipper down on her dress. The skinny straps stuck where her arms were still raised, stroking his chest hair, but the material gapped, and he glimpsed the bright blue satin underneath.

Pulling her arms away, he stripped the dress off. Her bra and underwear matched, and he was insanely jealous that she'd worn this for some other man. That she wanted to look good for that guy, maybe get naked for him, made Trevor want to rip the scraps of material away. But he held tight to his control, knowing the reaction was ridiculous.

Instead, he led her to the bed and gently pushed her to lie back. With her head on the pillow, she raised a hand and beckoned him to join her. He dropped his jeans and socks where he stood and crawled over her body. He kissed his way up her torso, causing her to giggle in response. Trevor made a mental note about her being ticklish.

He sucked her nipples through the bra before continuing his trail of kisses up her neck until he reached her mouth again. She spread her thighs and he settled between them, feeling her heat on his cock through the clothes they still had on. He pressed against her while kissing her, thrusting his tongue into her mouth, tangling with hers.

Callie bucked her hips up, circling them, making them both hotter. And wetter. But he had no reason to hurry. While he always wanted the woman he was with to have a good a time as he did, with Callie, he wanted to know everything. He wanted to know what drove her crazy, what made her scream, what would make her beg for more.

"Condom's in the drawer," she whispered.

"We'll get there." He reached under her, undid the clasp of the bra, and pulled it away. Then he went back to playing with her tits and her nipples.

She slid her hand between them and stroked him, giving the head a little squeeze. His breath caught, and he pinched her nipple lightly.

"Stop trying to rush me," he said against her mouth.

"Not rushing. Just moving along. We have all night. We can go slow later. I want you inside me now." She pushed past the elastic on his underwear and rubbed her thumb along the slit on his dick. "I'm ready."

Her words had him thrusting into her hand twice, but then he pulled away to remove her panties. Evidence of her arousal was plain. He stared for a moment, her scent calling to him. "I want to taste you. That okay?"

"So polite, Trevor. I never took you for a guy who would ask permission."

He lowered again so they were nose to nose. "This is our first time. Like I said downstairs, I don't want to screw this up. I want to know what you like so that I can take care of you. I won't always ask."

"Yes, you can go down on me. I love when a man can make me come with his mouth."

"Any specific directions? Fast? Slow? Hard? Soft?"

"Yes," she answered with a bright smile, and then she shoved his shoulder to get him moving. She threw her arms above her head and widened her legs even more.

Trevor's shoulders pressed into her thighs as he

lowered his mouth. He nuzzled her mound and then swiped his tongue along her slit. When the tip of his tongue flicked against her clit, her hips jumped, so he anchored his hands around them to hold her still.

Then he did everything she asked, listening to her body as he did so. As she rose up, she called to God and to him and when she came it was on a high-pitched moan, then utter stillness, except for her thighs trembling around his head. His cock ached, and he was dying to be inside her, but he waited for her to come back to him.

He wanted her to feel everything that he did. He slowly backed away, grabbed a condom from her drawer, and put it on. Settling between her legs again, he watched as she reopened her eyes and a smile crept across her face. Bracing a forearm near her head, he rubbed his dick on her, the head bumping her clit, making her jump again.

Then he slid in and never wanted to move again. Wet heat surrounded his dick, the aftershocks of her orgasm pulsating around him. He rested his forehead against her shoulder. Then he began a long, slow slide in and out.

But Callie wasn't having it. She began to thrust up to meet him, grinding against him. She dragged her nails sharply up and down his back, squeezing his ass to pull him close again.

"More, Trevor."

He pumped harder, faster. Her face was tight, her pussy clutching him, but she wasn't quite there, and he wanted to take her there again. He reared up and back, missing the warmth of her skin. But he positioned her legs on his shoulders, giving him deeper penetration.

Watching where their bodies joined, seeing his dick

slide into her made him move faster, seeking his own finish. Using his thumb, he pressed against her clit and then made circles like he had with his tongue.

Callie's entire body bowed up, pulling him deep. His balls tightened and the base of his spine tingled and he followed her orgasm with his own, growling as he fell forward and drove into her to drain himself.

They were both spent. Hot and sticky, but he didn't want to move.

She shoved his shoulder. "Move, you big lug. I can't breathe."

He rolled to the side. "Sure, use me and shove me aside."

She huffed, and he thought it was supposed to be a laugh.

"Give me a few minutes to catch my breath and I'll use you again."

Now it was his turn to laugh. "I'm not twenty anymore. It'll take me more than a few minutes." He removed the condom and wrapped it in a tissue before dropping it in her wastebasket. Then he flopped back on the bed. He really hoped she wasn't expecting him to go back home right now.

She turned and curled next to him. Toying with his chest hair, she asked, "Were you watching me earlier tonight when Craig came to pick me up?"

Busted. He weighed his options. He'd tried to be sneaky about it, but she obviously must've seen him. "Yeah. I wanted to see who you chose to spend your night with instead of having dinner with me."

He didn't need to admit that he'd been jealous.

"I'm sorry."

"For what?" he asked.

"For acting like nothing was going on between us." She levered up on an elbow and looked him in the eye. "I just thought that if I went on a date, found a spark with a guy, maybe I could forget about this."

"And yet you're in bed with me now."

"I spent the evening with Craig. He was boring. But even if he didn't spend the whole night talking about craft beer, there was no spark. You know that itch or chemistry when we're together. It wasn't there with him."

Trevor was glad to hear it. While he'd dated some women after Lisa had told him that they had zero chance of reconciling, he hadn't felt that spark Callie was talking about. Even when he'd slept with other women, the few that there had been, it was about getting off. He'd never considered a tomorrow with them.

He couldn't imagine a tomorrow without Callie anymore. He didn't know what to do with that. "I suppose it would be tacky for me to say that I'm happy about that."

She laughed, her shoulders shaking against him. "It might be tacky, but I like hearing it."

He rose and kissed the top of her head. "Then I'm epically happy that your date with Craig was a failure. I'm even happier that you're here with me now."

"I'm happy, too."

CALLIE LAY IN TREVOR'S ARMS AND WANTED TO PINCH herself. For all the times she'd fantasized about being here, getting naked with him, she'd never considered that it would really happen. And this...this postcoital joking and talking. When was the last time she'd shared this with a man? Even if a guy had spent the night, which was rare, it had been more out of exhaustion than a desire to be with her.

Neither of them made any move for him to leave. She didn't want him to, so she wrapped her arm around him. At some point, they both dozed off. In the middle of the night, Callie woke shivering because the air conditioner had been on full blast and there was a chill in the air. She pulled a blanket over them and rolled to her side.

Trevor moved toward her, pulling her back to his front, saying nothing. She wasn't sure he'd even woken up. She took a moment to enjoy the feel of his hairy chest against her back, his arm around her waist, just below her breasts. With a deep breath, she fell back to sleep.

Hours later, with the sun barely brightening the sky, Trevor moved behind her. The fuzzy, still-half-asleep part of her brain assumed he was leaving for work. But he began to stroke her skin softly. With her eyes closed, she simply enjoyed the sensation of him touching her.

He kissed her neck, played with her nipples until she was wiggling against the hard-on pressing into her backside. Trevor reached between her legs and stroked her, making her ready for him. Callie turned over to face him. His eyes were much more alert than she felt.

"How long have you been awake?" she asked, her voice scratchy from sleep.

"A while." His hands continued to explore her body.

"Were you watching me sleep?"

"Depends. Is it creepy if I was?"

"Maybe."

His palm pressed against her clit as his fingers thrust inside her. She sucked in a sharp breath.

"You looked beautiful lying there. But you're naked, so it didn't take long before I started thinking about being inside you again." His fingers were moving in and out, the pressure of his palm constant.

Feeling breathless, she said, "Okay. Not too creepy."

She wrapped her fingers around his dick and stroked him. He answered with a groan. They lay face-to-face, foreheads touching, sharing their breath, driving each other crazy with their hands until they couldn't take it anymore.

Trevor rolled her over and reached for another condom. He put it on and inched into her. He made slow love to her as the sun rose in the sky.

It was the laziest morning sex she'd had in years. It was glorious to just enjoy another person's body, learning what he wanted, what pushed him to the edge, what made him growl her name.

After they both came and he'd disposed of the condom, Trevor kissed her neck, her lips, and then her forehead.

"I have to get ready for work."

"Okay." She rolled over, pulling the blanket back over herself. "I think I'll go back to sleep."

But as he gathered his clothes and hastily put them on, she watched with her eyes half closed.

"Dinner tonight?" he asked.

"Sure. You want to order in or should I cook?"

"You pick. I don't care." He stepped into his boots and

didn't bother tying them. "I'll come here when I'm off work." He bent and kissed her again.

"Will you spend the night again?" She didn't know where they were headed and didn't want to presume anything, but she didn't think either of them thought last night was a one-night-only thing.

"I'd like that."

Then he left. She heard his heavy boots clomping down the stairs, and a moment later, her door opened and closed. Callie rolled over the other way and pulled the pillow into her arms. It smelled of Trevor, and it was enough to coax her back to sleep.

When she woke up hours later, she took a shower and got dressed. Then she planned to check out some job prospects. She'd been thinking more and more of looking for something permanent that would keep her close to home. But her career had been built on her willingness to go anywhere to get the job done.

She'd never had anyone to answer to or worry about in her personal life, so it had always been an easy choice to make. Lately, the choice had gotten harder. Even before Lisa died, Callie had started to grow tired of constantly being on the go. But now, with Hannah, Evan, and Trevor, it felt right to stay in Chicago.

While she drank coffee sitting at her kitchen counter, she looked for photography jobs in the area. The prospects were slim, but she had time. There was no crushing urgency for her to find something now. The few local freelance gigs she had would tide her over. She also went through her contacts on social media and spread the word that if anyone heard about a job that would be good for her, to pass it on.

By the time afternoon hit, her legs were numb and sore from sitting on her ass for too long. After a long stretch, she looked out her back window into the yard. Lisa's garden was torn up with nothing but a few weeds growing. Seeing that would break Lisa's heart. She'd loved that garden.

Callie was struck with what her afternoon project could be. She grabbed her keys and went to the gardening center. She bought the brightest, prettiest flowers she could find. Although the kids had never worked on the garden with Lisa, it had always been filled with flowers. The only help Callie had ever offered was company since she knew nothing about gardening, but now, with Lisa gone, it just seemed wrong to let the garden sit untouched.

Plugging in her earbuds to listen to some classic '80s music, Callie got to work. She turned over the soil like the guy at the garden center suggested, and she dug holes, putting the little plants in each spot. She spaced things according to the information on the tags, but as she worked, it didn't look like she remembered it looking when Lisa did this.

She'd totally lost track of time and suddenly a pair of worn-out boots were in her field of vision. Looking up, she saw Trevor talking to her, but her music drowned out his voice. Yanking out an earbud in the middle of Madonna's "Like a Virgin," she said, "Huh?"

Trevor pointed to the ground. "What are you doing?"

"Oh." She straightened and rubbed her dirty hands on her shorts. "I looked out the window this afternoon and it dawned on me that Lisa's garden was empty. I thought I'd fill it."

She turned off her music and stepped back. From this angle, the garden didn't look any better than it had when she was on the ground. Hmmm. Maybe once the flowers grew in some, it would look better.

"It's...interesting."

She nudged him. "Come on. It's not that bad." With another glance at her work, she added, "Okay, so I'm not a gardener. I was just trying to do something nice. And I needed a project to get me off my ass."

"Why?"

"I spent the day on my computer looking for a new job." She gathered the tools she'd been using and tossed them in the bucket to put back in the shed.

"A job?"

"I have some proposals out for more freelance work, but I've been thinking about seeing if I can find something local."

"To stay local?"

"Yeah." She turned toward her house, and he followed.

"You don't want to travel anymore?"

"I don't know." In her kitchen, she reached into the refrigerator and pulled out a couple bottles of water. "I've been traveling for twenty years. I've seen a lot of the world, and I love to travel, but now..."

"What?"

She didn't know what to say. Was it too early to talk about their relationship as a reason? "I told you I'd be here to help with the kids. That's hard to do from the other side of the world."

Something flashed on his face, stealing a bit of the brightness of his smile. "Oh. I guess you're right. But don't turn your life upside down because of the kids. I think I kind of have a handle on this parenting thing."

She drank some water to give herself a minute to gather her thoughts. The air was thick with awkwardness. "It's not just the kids," she started.

"No?"

Was that hope in his voice?

"Even before Lisa died, the travel was getting to me." She was still dancing around the situation.

He said nothing.

"Jeez. This is stupid," she announced. Slamming her bottle on the counter, she said, "What are we doing?"

"What do you mean?" he asked.

"As I said, I've been toying with the idea of slowing down on the travel, and Lisa's death and the kids are a convenient excuse, but part of why I'm looking for a local job is because of you. Because of us."

He continued to stare at her, and Callie began to think she'd fucked up again. "I know we only spent one night together, but it didn't feel like we were just scratching an itch. Correct me if I'm wrong about that."

"You're not."

"Then I shouldn't feel like an idiot taking us into consideration when I'm figuring out my life and my career. Should I?"

He took a deep breath and released it slowly. Setting his water bottle down beside hers, Trevor stepped closer. He took her hand and waited for her to make eye contact. "I'm glad I'm part of the equation of your life. But I don't expect you to give up what you love because of me."

"It's not because of you. I have no intention of taking a job I won't enjoy, but this feels important. My career has always taken first place on my list of priorities. Maybe it's time to switch things up."

"Do what you need to do. Leaving the career you built is something you might end up regretting. And if you do it because of us, you'd resent me." His thumb stroked across her knuckles. "I've wasted enough years dealing with disappointment and resentment. Whatever you choose, do it for you."

His words were right. They were diplomatic and what she should've wanted to hear, but she wondered if they were honest. Trevor had always teased her about her continent-hopping and not being around. Part of her even wished he'd asked her to stay. Wasn't that a kick? That was the main reason every other relationship she'd ever had fell apart. They'd asked her to stay, and she'd booked the first flight out of town. Ultimately, though, Trevor was right. She needed to figure out what she wanted.

"So what do you want to have for dinner?" he asked.

"I have stuff for sandwiches," she offered.

"Sure."

He put his arm around her shoulders and pulled her into a hug. Kissing the top of her head, he said, "I'll be here whatever you decide about work."

As far as commitments went, it wasn't too bad. She'd never had anyone willing to just be there for her. Except Lisa.

Trevor turned and began pulling food from the fridge. Callie watched him and thought of Lisa. If you're watching, *I hope you're okay with this, Lisa, because I think I'm falling for him.*

For the next three days, Trevor spent the night in Callie's bed and woke with her in his arms. The rest of their time together was much like it usually was: they ate dinner together, watched TV, and talked about their days. It had been so long since he'd had a partner in his life and in his bed that he'd forgotten how awesome it felt to have a woman in his arms.

He knew they needed to address their relationship in regard to the kids, but he didn't know how to bring it up. They'd spent four days in their own little bubble, but he knew it couldn't last. Hannah and Evan would be home in a few days.

He'd spent the day trying to figure out what to say. He was falling for Callie, but he didn't think he was ready for their relationship to be open to the kids. What if something happened between him and Callie? They'd already lost so much. He needed to be sure before they told Hannah and Evan about their relationship.

But he didn't know how Callie would take it. Or if she would agree. It seemed that when it came to the kids, they butted heads more than anything. He'd worked later than usual, something he often did when he needed to think. He liked being on the job site alone. The solitude gave him peace with his thoughts.

By the time he parked the truck in front of the house, the sun was setting. He'd texted Callie hours ago to let her know to eat dinner without him. Determined to talk about the kids tonight, he'd bought her a bouquet of flowers. He'd wanted to bring something to remind her that she was important to him.

At times like this, he wished he wasn't an alcoholic. A normal man would bring a bottle of wine to share and have a conversation. What was he supposed to do? Bring her a bottle of pop? Shaking his head, he grabbed the flowers and walked down the gangway straight to the backyard.

He passed the garden that Callie had worked on earlier in the week. It looked even sadder now. He didn't have the heart to tell her that he didn't think it would last. He knocked on the door and turned the knob without waiting for an answer. "Callie?"

She came running around the corner, her smile huge. "It's about time. I've been waiting forever."

The emphasis on "forever" made him smile.

Pointing at the flowers, she said, "What are those for?"

"You." He held them out, and when she grabbed them, he pulled her close for a kiss. Seeing her face was a stark reminder to him how she brightened his day. She filled all of his dark, lonely places with sunshine. Doubt about the necessary conversation crept into him.

When she pulled back from their kiss, she said, "Hello."

"Hi. What's up?"

"I have news. Let me put these in water. Go have a seat. Are you hungry?" She bustled around the small kitchen taking care of the flowers.

"No, I'm good." Instead of going to the couch, he watched her. Even her movements seemed happy. There was a lightness in her body. He had no idea how it felt to be that way, but being near her made him feel like a better person.

When she finished putting the flowers in a vase, she grabbed his hand and pulled him toward the living room. They settled on the couch.

Callie sat close enough for her legs to brush against his, which made it hard for him to focus. She took his hand. "I got a job offer."

"Already? That's excellent. Congratulations." He brushed hair off her shoulder.

"Well, don't congratulate me yet. It's not quite the kind of offer I thought I'd get."

Unease crawled over him. He'd seen this look on Callie's face before. When they were young, every time she planned to hit the road, she had a similar look. But he waited, hoping to hear something else.

"A travel agency reached out to me through some mutual acquaintances. They plan themed trips around the world. They want to hire me to go out for three weeks later this summer and bounce around taking pictures for a new tour they're setting up."

Three weeks? That wasn't so bad. He wasn't thrilled about it, but they'd survive. Something on her face told him that wasn't the worst of it, though—or maybe in her mind, it would be the best of it. "Okay," he said cautiously.

She took a deep breath and released it slowly. "The thing is, they want to use that trip as a test of sorts. If they decide they like my work, they want to hire me on for a longer project. Their goal is to update all of the photos for all of their tours."

"So more than three weeks."

"I don't know how long the whole project would last.

Easily a year or more. But the money is phenomenal. And I would get to literally travel the world, go to places I've never been." Her voice was no longer as eager as it had been when she started.

"I thought you wanted to find something local. Settle down." The words sat heavily between them. Their relationship was new, so new. They weren't at a place of committing to settling down. He knew in his gut that if he made demands of her, he would lose her. She'd run.

"I was looking for something here. But this fell into my lap. I don't know if I want to take it. I have a video call with the home office in Italy tomorrow morning. That's why I'm talking it over with you. We have this thing going on and there are the kids. But at the same time, this is an incredible opportunity." Her eyes studied his face, searching.

Unfortunately, he had no idea what she was searching for. He wasn't going to tell her to go, but he also knew he had no right to ask her to stay. "It does sound exciting."

His enthusiasm was nonexistent and his voice flat, but he wasn't trying to be an asshole. He'd just started trying to wrap his head around his relationship with Callie and now she was talking about leaving. Again.

She shoved his shoulder. "Yeah, that sounds like you're really happy for me."

"I *am* happy for you. They'd be stupid not to hire you. But I'm a selfish bastard, and you're talking about leaving me for three weeks." His conviction there was solid and true. He would miss her. Desperately.

"We could talk or FaceTime."

"That's not the same."

"We could be naked while we do it."

His dick perked up at the mention of her getting naked. "As much as I might enjoy seeing you naked on the screen, I'd rather have you sharing a bed with me."

"Ahh, Mr. Booth, you sure do know how to sweet-talk me." She rose up and straddled him, bringing her body flush against his.

He instinctively bucked his hips up, his dick like a heat-seeking missile. He reached up and threaded his fingers in her hair as he pulled her in for a kiss. All thoughts of her conversation and his intended one fled when her tongue touched his.

For now, they had each other, and nothing from the outside world could intrude. They had time to deal with it all later.

CALLIE'S HEAD WAS SPINNING AGAIN. THE LIFE THAT SHE'D been living for a couple of decades, one of regular travel and irregular sex, seemed like a distant memory. She and Trevor had spent every night for the past four nights together. Sometimes, they just talked until they fell asleep. But usually, they had sex. Not that she was complaining.

Having someone in her life on the regular was weird. She found herself consulting him on everything, from what to have for dinner to what she should do about her career. She wasn't even really sure why. She'd spent her entire life going it alone. Trevor was bothered by the job offer, even though he tried to be supportive. Kind of.

She knew he didn't like her traveling. He was the kind of guy who needed structure and routine. He hadn't always been that way. It was one of the side effects of being sober. Needing to control everything in his life. So while he didn't try to control her, she understood that her life and career made him uncomfortable.

Lying in bed, naked with Trevor, she stretched and thought about the job for Around the World Travels. It was an exciting opportunity. And three weeks wasn't that long to be gone. Her typical trips were two to three weeks anyway. But it was the extension of a long-term job that niggled at her. Would she want to travel nonstop for the next year or two?

Trevor was right. She'd said she wanted to dial it down and stay at home, but the travel bug had its teeth firmly in her whenever she thought about it. Ringing brought her fully awake. Her alarm. She rolled out of bed and scrounged for an appropriate shirt to wear while she talked to the rep from Around the World. They wanted to talk details.

Downstairs, she started a pot of coffee and set up her laptop. She had about a half hour before the call, so she organized her notes and questions. As she sat to drink her coffee, Trevor came downstairs wearing his clothes from yesterday, looking rumpled and sexy.

He set his phone on the counter beside her, kissed the side of her head, mumbled, "Morning," and trudged off to the bathroom to brush his teeth. While he was in the bathroom, she poured him a cup of coffee. If she'd learned nothing else about Trevor this week, it was that he was a man who absolutely needed his coffee in the morning.

As she put his cup down, his phone jingled with some crazy tune that told her it was Hannah. Every time Trevor turned his back, his daughter changed his ringtones.

"Hey, Hannah's calling. You want me to answer it?" she yelled.

"Sure."

Callie scooped up the phone and hit the accept button for a FaceTime call from Hannah.

"Hey, babe. What's up?"

Hannah filled the screen with a scrunched-up face. "Didn't I call Dad?"

Trevor came in and took the phone from Callie's hand. "You did. I was busy so Callie answered so I wouldn't miss your call."

Callie couldn't see Hannah anymore, but there was a pause. She slid his coffee over to him. He took a gulp.

"What are you doing at Callie's? It's like six in the morning there."

He set his coffee back down. "Uh." Rubbing a hand through his messy hair, he said, "I got her a new air conditioner."

Yeah, like four days ago. And he kind of had been there since.

"I'm heading to work in a few minutes," he continued.

Callie waited for him to tell the truth. She shot him a look that called him out on his bullshit. While she hadn't expected him to tell his daughter they'd just been rolling around naked, she didn't expect him to flat-out lie either.

His return look was semi-apologetic.

"I'm calling because we're coming home today."

"What? Why? I thought I was picking you up on Sunday."

"Yeah, well, it's way more boring here than we remembered."

Callie snickered. "Told you," she yelled loud enough for Hannah to hear.

"Whatever. Tell Callie she was right. Grandma said she'd drive us back today."

"Okay. Does she want me to meet her halfway?"

"Nah. She wants to spend as much time with us as she can." Hannah's voice dropped. "I think she wants to stay with us."

"Fuck," Callie said. She didn't think it was loud enough for Hannah to hear, but Trevor did. It was his turn to give a dirty look.

If Diane was here, Callie couldn't imagine what that would do to her relationship with Trevor. Hell, she couldn't imagine what it would do to Trevor. The woman wasn't exactly in his fan club.

"Can you talk her out of it?" he asked quietly.

"I'm trying, Dad. We'll be home in a few hours. See you for dinner?"

"Definitely."

"Bye."

Trevor clicked off and set down the phone.

"What was that?"

"What?" he asked. His face revealed that he had no clue.

"Why did you lie to Hannah?"

He took another gulp of coffee. "What was I supposed to say? I wasn't ready for her to ask about why I'm here."

"How about you tell the truth?"

"Yeah, I'm going to tell my teenage daughter that I spent the night with her mom's best friend."

"You don't need to make it sound sleazy. We're adults, Trevor. And they're not toddlers."

He dumped his coffee in the sink and rinsed his cup. "Look, I've been thinking about this. I don't know if now is a good time to tell them about us. They just lost their mom. You're an important part of their lives."

Anger bubbled up at the possible implications of what he was saying. "Let me get this straight. You don't want to tell the kids, why exactly? Because you're embarrassed that you slept with me? Or this is a fling that will end and you're afraid it'll get ugly?"

He shook his head with a clenched jaw. "Neither. This thing between us is new. They've had a shitload of adjustments in their lives over the last couple of months. Dumping another on them right now probably isn't the best thing for them. Besides that, I don't want them to start making assumptions about us."

"Assumptions like what? We're a couple? We're in a relationship?" Her voice rose every time she opened her mouth. Any minute now she'd sound like a hysterical banshee. "I'm sorry, Trevor. I guess I was already making those assumptions."

"I don't want them to get too attached to someone who might leave!" He was shouting now, too.

They stared at each other for a couple heartbeats.

He shook his head stiffly again. "I'm going to work."

Then he walked out the door without another word.

Callie closed her eyes and slowed her breathing. She wasn't even sure why she was so angry. So he wasn't ready to tell the kids. It wasn't like she was calling her friends and telling everyone she had a boyfriend. And these were his kids. Crap. She'd really stepped in it now.

She'd probably come off as a crazy girlfriend looking for a lifetime commitment after spending a week with a guy. Which she wasn't. Yeah, she assumed they were in a relationship, but she could admit that she'd gone off the rails with that argument. The pressure of job hunting and this amazing opportunity that she wasn't sure she wanted—that all depended on a call in a few minutes—made her come unhinged.

She pushed away the relationship craziness, finished her coffee, and prepped for her conference call.

Chapter Ten

Trevor's brain was shit for the day. He'd been stressed about the whole fight with Callie this morning, and he dreaded a confrontation with Diane. Evan called when they got home around lunchtime. He told Trevor that Diane was staying for dinner. Trevor really hoped that would be the end of the visit.

While he wanted the kids to have a relationship with their grandparents, especially since they were the only set they had, Trevor didn't want to revisit his relationship with them. No way in hell did he want to share a house with his ex-mother-in-law. Talk about awkward.

So he did the smart thing, and he begged for Callie's help. It might be horrible to say, but if anyone could drive Diane away, it was Callie. While Jerry and the boys rolled up tools and material from the basement job, he stood by his truck and thought about what to say to Callie. He texted:

> I know you're probably still pissed at me, but I need a favor.

> Your timing sucks, Booth. I am still pissed.

> We need to talk. I know that. But if you don't help me, I might go crazy.

She responded with a winky face. He could totally picture her laughing at him.

> Diane is still at the house. I don't want her to think she should stay.

> What am I supposed to do about it?

> I think if we show a united front, she'd take a hint. We don't need her. More importantly, the kids don't need her here.

> Oh. So now we can be together?

He groaned. He should've known that he couldn't escape that easily.

> Please, Callie. I can't live with Diane. I had a hard enough time with her visits when I was married to Lisa.

> Still not my problem. Why should I care if you suffer?

> Because you do.

She didn't respond, and he felt like an idiot staring at his screen waiting for a response.

> If you help me drive her away, I'll come over tonight with ice cream and we can talk.

> I still have ice cream in my freezer.

> Tell me what I have to do. Anything. It's yours for the asking.

> Oh, honey. You're gonna regret that.

> So that's a yes? I'm heading home now. Picking up dinner on the way.

> See you soon.

> Are you going to tell me what this is going to cost?

> I haven't decided yet. But rest assured I will get great pleasure out of it.

Although she probably wasn't referring to anything sexual, the thought of pleasure and Callie at the same time made him picture her naked.

When the guys were cleared out, he went back into the basement to make sure it looked good. He'd planned on putting in a long day tomorrow on the trim by himself. Now that the kids were back and he was saved a trip to Indiana, he could work Saturday and Sunday and have Evan help him. It would be a good introduction for Evan with no one else around.

Trevor locked up and stopped for Chinese food on the way home. When he parked the truck, he sat for a minute to brace himself for the evening. He'd barely taken a couple of breaths when his phone buzzed.

> I see you sitting there. If I have to suffer through small talk, so do you. Or it'll cost you more.

He smiled. It'd be worth anything to not have to go in.

But he knew he couldn't. If nothing else, he'd missed the kids. He grabbed the bags of food and shoved out of the truck. Hannah met him at the door to help.

As she took a bag she whispered, "Thank God you're here. Do you know how tense and awkward things are? Please make it stop. I want to just go to my room, but Grandma is all nosy."

He sighed. "It'll be fine."

"I'm afraid to leave Grandma and Callie alone. They're so polite to each other it's scary. Like the minute they're alone, they'll attack."

Trevor smiled. "It's not quite that bad."

They walked to the kitchen together. Diane and Callie were sitting at the table not saying much.

"Hi, Diane. How was the trip?"

"Good."

He nodded and unpacked dinner.

"Is this how you've been eating?" Diane asked.

"No, Grandma. I told you, we cook most nights. I've been trying out a lot of recipes. And Callie helps."

Diane didn't look convinced.

Evan sauntered into the room.

"Hey, man. Have a good time in Indiana?" Trevor asked.

"Sure."

"I have work for you tomorrow. Trim in that basement job. It's a good place for you to learn."

"Work? He's not old enough to be on a job site," Diane said.

"Sure he is. I started working construction at sixteen. He said he wants to learn."

"It'll be a good experience for him, Diane," Callie added. "Just think. Next time Evan comes to visit, you can make him a honey-do list."

Diane gave her a look that wasn't quite dirty but was far from friendly.

"Cool," Evan said, and plopped down in a chair next to Callie.

Hannah took the one on the other side, leaving no seat for Trevor. He dragged one in from the other room and set it beside Diane. It put him across from Callie, who was all smirks and smiles.

"How have things been going?" Diane asked.

"We had a learning curve, but we've been doing well. Right, guys?" Both of his children dutifully nodded.

"Callie's been a huge help."

"I'm sure," Diane said before taking a forkful of beef and broccoli.

"Did you know that you can't get a good pizza by Grandma's?" Hannah asked.

Callie pointed at her with her chopstick. "Tell me about it. I had no idea what good pizza was until I moved to Chicago. And hot dogs. Oooh, and Italian beef. That's not even a thing in other cities."

"Really?"

"Yup," Callie answered before scooping up some rice.

Trevor loved the easy way Callie had with Hannah.

"While we might not have the same fancy restaurants you find in a big city like Chicago, small-town life has its own perks. Like lower crime. Knowing your neighbors."

"Nothing to do after nine p.m.," Callie countered.

"Nothing good happens late at night."

Callie snorted. "All depends on how you define good."

"Are you going to let her talk like that in front of your children?" Diane set her fork down.

Trevor looked at Diane, confused. "Like what?"

"Putting ideas in their heads."

Trevor backtracked over the conversation. "She made a joke. I expect my kids to be able to think for themselves."

Diane pursed her lips and then wiped her mouth with a napkin. "I should head out now that rush-hour traffic is done."

"Don't you want to finish your dinner?"

"I'm not all that hungry." She stood. "Will you walk me out?"

Fuck. While Callie had managed to accomplish exactly what he wanted, he didn't need to hear a lecture. "Sure."

He put his napkin next to his plate and rose. He waved at Hannah and Evan to do the same. "Say goodbye to your grandma. Thank her for taking you for the week."

They came around the table and hugged Diane.

Callie stood. "Do you want me to pack some food for you to take home?"

"No. Thank you."

Trevor stepped back and followed Diane out the front

door. Once they were outside, she turned to him. "I know you're trying, but do you really think Callie is the best influence?"

"The kids love her. She's been there for me this whole time. She's family. I'm sorry you can't get along with her, because she's an amazing woman. I don't understand why you blame her for Lisa leaving. Lisa had a mind of her own."

"I don't blame Callie for Lisa moving here. I simply don't like the way she lives her life."

"Well, you'll have to accept her, because she's not going anywhere. Have a safe trip home."

"Thank you for letting me have the kids."

"I won't ever stop you from having a relationship with them. You can visit or call whenever you want."

"Thank you." She turned and walked to her car.

Trevor waited on the sidewalk until she drove away. Then he went back into the house to finish dinner with his family.

For the rest of dinner, and into the evening, Trevor's night felt normal, like the past week hadn't happened. He and Callie hung out with Hannah and Evan, listened to the details of the visit with their grandparents, and watched TV. The only thing that changed was the fact that Callie kept sending him heated looks whenever the kids weren't paying attention.

She managed to make him feel like her fingers were raking over his body, which made sitting on the couch a little uncomfortable. Their chemistry was there, but so was the tension from their fight this morning.

She rose and said, "I'm heading home, guys. I'm glad you're back."

Hannah gave her a hug, and Evan mumbled something like good night. When Trevor stood, she looked momentarily startled.

"Thanks for coming over. I appreciate it."

"I'm sure you do." Her smirk said so much more than her words.

At least she didn't hate him.

It was only ten thirty, but Trevor turned off the TV anyway. "You guys should unpack your stuff."

"We got home at lunch, Dad," Hannah said.

He looked pointedly at Evan. "Did you unpack?"

"Of course not. I will."

"We have an early morning."

"Okay." The boy rose from the chair, but his eyes never left his phone's screen. He moved past Trevor, Callie, and Hannah without looking up.

Trevor turned to Hannah.

"I think he might have a girlfriend," Hannah said.

"Oh." *What am I supposed to say to that? Way to go?*

"And on that note, I'm outta here. See you guys tomorrow," Callie said.

Hannah went to her room, and Trevor puttered around the house for a while, debating whether he should go talk to Callie now or wait. He still wasn't sure what to say. He needed to fix things between them, but when he'd kissed her, he hadn't been thinking about his kids. He'd only thought of himself.

After checking that the kids were at least settled in their rooms, he ventured across the yard to Callie's. He knocked and waited instead of just pushing the door open as he had for the past few days.

She opened the door wearing a skimpy tank top and loose shorts, her hair wet from a shower. The scent of her shampoo wafted over and called him close.

"What do you want?"

"To talk to you."

She stepped back from the door to allow him to come in. He walked slowly into the kitchen and leaned against the counter. The same counter where he'd kissed her. "How was your thing this morning?"

"What thing?"

"With the travel agency?"

She looked shocked that he asked. "It went well."

He nodded. She crossed her arms over her chest as she leaned against the opposite corner. He didn't like the distance she'd created.

"Look. After we slept together, I started thinking about what would happen when the kids came home. I planned to talk it over with you last night." He pointed to the flowers he'd brought her. "But then you had your news and...I didn't."

He stepped close to her and unfolded her arms so he could hold her hand. "I started something with you without thinking about the impact it would have on the kids. That was wrong on my part, but I don't regret it, Callie."

She still didn't say anything.

"I don't want it to end."

"Neither do I," she said quietly.

"But I'm not ready to tell Hannah and Evan. It has nothing to do with being embarrassed or thinking this is a fling. I want to take it slow and figure things out. All of our lives have been turned upside down over the past few months. I just want them to have a chance to settle in."

"I get that, and if you had said that to me this morning, I'm pretty sure I would've been fine with it, but hearing you lie to Hannah just rubbed me every wrong way."

"I'm sorry."

"So am I. I shouldn't have gotten so upset. I was worried about the video call and my whole career-change thing. And this...this is complicated." She brushed something from his shirt, or maybe she just wanted to touch his chest, because she followed with a soft pat over his heart. "Then you said that I might leave the kids and it hurt. I travel. A lot. But I come back. Whenever they've needed me. A call and I'll be here."

"I know. I'm worried about them. I don't want to screw them up."

She nodded and pressed her body against his in a tight hug.

"We're okay?" He automatically wrapped his arms around her.

"We're okay." She tilted her face up with a smile. "Except...you still owe me for coming to dinner with Diane."

"I know. Have you figured out your payment?"

"I think so." Giving his hand a tug, she turned toward the stairs. And her bed.

He'd love to repay her in bed. Repeatedly. Up the stairs they went and when she neared the bed, she flopped down on her back. Trevor followed, covering her body with his, and kissed her.

She softened against him as he deepened the kiss. His

hand skated up her side, pulling her tank up so he could feel her skin. She grabbed his wrist, stopping his progress.

"What?" he asked.

"I haven't told you my payment terms yet."

"I thought I was working toward that."

"Roll over."

He turned so he was on his back beside her. If she wanted to be on top and do the work, so be it. He personally didn't think she should have to work for her payment, but okay.

She didn't move, just stared at the ceiling. "So I was thinking a skylight would look awesome over my bed." She pointed up, making a box with her fingers. "To be able to see the moon and stars at night, the patter of rain in the spring..."

His brain scrambled to catch up. "You brought me up here to talk about a skylight?"

She turned her head to face him, one eyebrow up. "Of course. What did you think?"

"I thought I was paying you with sexual favors, not construction work."

She burst out laughing. She laughed so hard she curled up against him, throwing an arm over his torso. When she sobered, she said, "Who said it's not both? Seeing you in work boots and a tool belt is a turn-on."

"Really?"

"Mm-hmm."

He rolled to his side and began touching her again. If she wanted a skylight, he'd put one in for her, but right now, he wanted her. Bare, needy, moaning. Pulling her clothes off, he couldn't get close fast enough.

Callie must've felt the same, because she was yanking at his jeans and shoving her hand inside to stroke him. Everything became a blur. For as careful and cautious with each other as they had been this week while making love, tonight it was fast and hard. They came together in a flurry of kisses and bites, strokes and tugs.

They didn't talk. No murmured compliments. It was all about feeling. And when they were done, Trevor felt like he'd been turned inside out. Their clothes were thrown everywhere, the blankets hung off the bed and they lay sprawled in the middle of the mattress, panting. Every time with Callie was new and different. He couldn't imagine ever tiring of her.

She turned into him, curling her body around his, her cheek on his chest. "I know you have to go," she whispered.

"In a little bit." In truth, he didn't want to go. Spending his nights with Callie had been his best nights in a long time. But this was about doing what was right for the kids. He sat up, set the alarm on his phone for a couple of hours, and lay back down with the woman he was falling for.

A WEEK LATER, CALLIE WALKED INTO THE HOUSE AND tossed her purse on the kitchen counter. She'd spent the day trying to find a local job that would be interesting and lucrative. The Around the World Travels people had given her a couple of weeks to decide if she wanted the job. If something else didn't kick off soon, she'd have to take it. This time of year she normally planned a fun trip. Somewhere she could take photos for a job but still relax and have a good time. Lisa's death had put a kink in her entire life. It wasn't just the loss of her best friend, but now she was practically co-parenting Lisa's kids and trying to juggle a secret relationship with their dad.

Her life had never been so complicated. She loved her time with the kids, even if it was just driving Hannah to and from band camp. Having a family to have dinner with and talk to each night was something she didn't think she'd ever have.

But part of her was missing the adventure that came with travel. What if she wasn't cut out to be a stationary person?

Being with Trevor was amazing but frustrating. She understood his need to wait to tell the kids, but she felt like she was being dishonest, and she'd always been honest with Hannah and Evan.

Man, she really wanted a drink. That was another thing she hadn't considered with Trevor. While she wasn't a huge drinker, she definitely liked to indulge on occasion. Could she give up alcohol forever? Reaching into her fridge, she grabbed a bottle of water. She took a gulp and regretted it wasn't the wine she'd just been thinking about.

One thing at a time. If she managed to tackle one issue in her life, then she could move on to others. The job was the most important, but thinking about making that decision was depressing, so she decided to move on to something that made her happy: Trevor and the kids.

She crossed the yard and walked into the kitchen. As

soon as she did, she heard yelling. No, not quite yelling, but strained voices. She followed the sounds to the living room, where Trevor stood at the bottom of the stairs, glaring up at Evan.

"You said you wanted to work. This is the real world. You don't just decide not to work because something more interesting popped up."

"Why not? The job will still be there the next day."

"But your paycheck won't. If you don't work, you don't get paid."

"I know that. I've been working all week. One day isn't a big deal." He crossed his arms as if to dare Trevor to argue.

"Yeah, easy to say that when you live in my house, eat my food, and enjoy the water and electricity I pay for."

"It's one day. What's the big fucking deal?" Then he turned and stomped across the hall.

Trevor opened his mouth, but Callie laid a hand on his arm. He stopped and turned to her.

"Things are kind of heated. Maybe let it cool before continuing the conversation."

The muscle in his jaw twitched. "You're probably right."

"What's going on?"

"Tomorrow's supposed to be beautiful, and he wants to go to the beach with his friends."

"And?"

"He's supposed to work."

Callie licked her lips. "He's seventeen."

"I know."

"He wants to have fun. That's what teenagers do."

"I'm aware. But he said he wanted to work. This is

how he wants to spend his life. Having him work for me this summer was your idea, remember?"

"You don't have to snap at me. Having Evan work with you is a great idea. But you have to remember that he's still a kid. His summer is supposed to be about not doing anything important, hanging out with his friends, playing video games too late at night, sleeping in all morning. It's what we all did."

"That's not going to show him what real life is like, though. If I let him work whenever he wants, that's not going to give him a taste of adulthood without a college degree."

Callie crossed her arms. "You only want him to work with you to make him miserable so he'll decide to go to college?"

"Yeah."

The way he said it made her feel like she was stupid for even asking, as if there could be no other reason. "He might not ever want college. He obviously likes working with you. What would be so bad about him being a carpenter?"

"I don't want him to have to bust his ass the way I had to do. I want something better for him."

"It's already better for him because he has you to teach him and help him."

Trevor's face softened. His gaze darted up the stairs, then he leaned in and kissed her briefly. "Thanks for saying that."

"Are you going to let Evan spend the day at the beach?"

"Nope."

She tugged his hand. "Come on. Let him be a kid."

He studied her face for a minute and then said, "I'll think about it."

She smiled, knowing that was as good as she was going to get. She vividly remembered what it was like to be a teenager dying to get away from her family, to have fun, live her life. Her parents had never wanted her to have any fun, which had led to a whole lot of rebellion.

Walking backward into the kitchen, she asked, "What's for dinner?"

Trevor moved past her, a quick slide of his hand down her back. He did that a lot, she realized. A sneaky touch here and there. Innocent but not.

Callie looked back over her shoulder to make sure the kids were still upstairs. "As long as we're alone..." she started.

He peered around the refrigerator door. "Not here," he whispered.

She smacked his arm playfully. "Get your mind out of the gutter. I want to tell you about a conversation I had with Hannah."

He backed away from the fridge and shut the door.

"Just a heads-up. I told her to talk to you, but you know, she's a teenage girl and you're her dad."

Trevor's whole body stiffened as if he knew exactly where she was headed.

"There's a boy—"

"The hell there is."

Callie shook her head. "This is not the first boy. Surely you know that. She's fifteen."

"So?"

"This is a boy that she knows from band. They've been friends for a while. He asked her out on a date."

"No."

"First, you can't just say no. Second, this isn't her first date. Lisa let her date a guy last year."

"What?" His voice rose sharply.

Callie immediately wanted to defend her friend, but staying in the moment was more important. "The first girlfriend Evan had was when he was fourteen."

"So?"

"Whoa. Double standard much? Hannah is a smart girl. You need to trust her."

"I do trust her. It's the boys I don't trust."

Oh Lord. If she had a dime for every dad who'd ever said that. "Treat her like the responsible girl she is. We had a lengthy conversation this afternoon about safety."

"You talked to my daughter about sex?"

Callie nodded. "Among other things. Not just being safe for sex. I talked about not taking a drink from anyone at a party and not going to deserted places with a guy unless she's sure about who he is and what she wants."

"What?" Just when Callie didn't think he could get louder, Trevor did.

"Calm down."

"Do not tell me to calm down. You had no business giving my fifteen-year-old the green light to party and fuck around."

Callie slapped her hand on the counter. "I did no such thing. This was a review of conversations she'd already had with Lisa, her *mother*. I was simply providing a refresher. In case your brain is too old to remember, teenagers rarely wait for a green light. They just do shit. I want to make sure she knows how to handle herself."

"She's fifteen."

"Open your eyes, Trevor. She's not a baby. What were you doing at fifteen?"

"Don't go there."

"Someone has to. You're being unreasonable. No wonder she came to me instead of talking to you."

His face reddened, and Callie knew it was time to go. She stepped back. He didn't scare her, not physically, but she didn't want them to say things that would get out of hand. "I think I'm going to go out to dinner. Think about what I said. You keep this up and you'll lose her."

When she turned around to leave, she caught sight of Hannah standing at the bottom of the stairs, eyes wide. Callie shrugged an apology. She'd tried.

Now she was going to go out and have a good strong drink. She didn't have to worry about offending Trevor tonight. She doubted they'd be hanging out.

Chapter Eleven

Trevor watched Callie stomp out of the kitchen and through the backyard. Hannah came up behind him.

"That was mean."

"What?"

"Everything you said to her. I don't know why she likes you. You're kind of a jerk."

At least his little girl didn't call him an asshole, which he'd both been expecting and deserved. Everything Callie said had made sense. He just wasn't ready to hear it. He looked at Hannah. He wasn't ready to talk to her, either. He put cash on the counter and said, "Order a pizza for dinner. We'll talk later."

Trevor went for a drive. He thought about going to a meeting, but alcohol wasn't what his restlessness and poor attitude were about. Instead, he called Tess to see if she was free for coffee. As a fellow parent of a teenage girl, she would be able to relate to what he was going through. She was on her way home from work and since her boyfriend, Miles, was with her kids, she could stop to meet him.

He drove to the El stop where he knew Tess would get off. No need for her to walk or catch a bus to the coffee shop when he was driving there. When she emerged with the crowd, he honked his horn.

Tess jogged over to the truck and opened the door. "I thought we were meeting at Sunny's."

"I knew this was your stop, so it didn't make sense for you to walk." He pulled back into traffic and drove toward Sunny's Diner.

"What's up?"

"I need to talk."

"Everything okay?"

"Fuck if I know." He parked in Sunny's lot and they got out.

When she walked around the front of the truck, she took a minute to study him. He knew that look. It was the one people gave when they were trying to figure out if he'd fallen off the wagon.

"Don't worry. I'm sober." They walked into the diner and grabbed a small booth instead of the large corner one they usually took in the mornings. As soon as the waitress poured them each a cup, he blurted, "Callie and I have been sleeping together."

If Tess hadn't paused with her cup halfway to her mouth, he might've thought she didn't hear him. She said nothing.

"It was simmering there, you know. We both wanted it but didn't think we should want it. Then we kissed."

"Is that the problem?"

"Maybe. I don't know." He toyed with his cup, not

drinking anything. "The whole week the kids were with their grandparents, we were a couple. I spent every night in her bed. Woke with her in the morning. But then the kids came home."

The corner of Tess's mouth lifted. "And you were back in the real world."

He knew if anyone could understand his relationship with Callie, it would be Tess. She'd had to struggle with how and when to bring Miles into her kids' lives. "Yup. I don't think the kids are ready for that. We talked and agreed to keep our relationship under wraps for now."

"How's that working out?"

He blew out a heavy breath. "It's rough."

"I would think it would be harder. Miles and I dated during the day. It was easier to sneak around because he wasn't literally living in my backyard."

"That's not the problem. I don't think. Tonight, she told me that Hannah talked to her about some guy that asked her out. Callie talked to her about sex and safety and I lost it."

Tess snorted. "Such a dude." She set her cup down. "If you're smart, you'll go home and kiss Callie's feet. She had a difficult conversation with your daughter. One you sure as hell don't want to have."

"Of course I don't want to have those conversations. Hannah's too young."

"No, she's not. You need to have those conversations early and often. If she's not prepared, things might go bad. You can't disseminate the information and advice after the fact."

"I know. But she's fifteen."

"Zoe is almost there and we've been talking for a

couple of years now. If you don't raise your daughter to have expectations and high standards, she'll be lost." She took a sip of coffee. "I have a feeling that coming to terms with the fact that Hannah is growing up is only part of the problem."

"She went to Callie. Not me."

"Callie's a woman she trusts. She lost her mom. Would you be bothered if she talked to Lisa?"

"Of course not."

"I'm sure Callie knows that she's not Lisa's replacement, but she's someone you want in your kids' lives. You can't pick and choose when you want her to have a role. If your relationship with Callie is serious, you can't get mad at her for being involved."

Trevor didn't know what he'd wanted from this conversation with Tess, but it wasn't a verbal slap-down. "Does it ever get any easier?"

"Being a parent or starting a new relationship while being a parent?"

"Both." He drained his cup.

"Parenting alone sucks. Having someone to lean on helps. The relationship part gets easier. You'll fight and make up, but if it's worth holding on to, you will." She, too, finished her coffee.

"You want a refill?"

"Nah. I'm going home to my family."

"I'll drop you off." It would give him time to think. He needed to deal with Hannah. Then Callie.

After dropping Tess off at home, Trevor stopped at a drugstore and then went home to have one of the most difficult conversations he'd ever have to have. At least he hoped it was the worst of it.

In his kitchen, the remains of a pizza sat on the table. He trudged upstairs with the box of condoms in hand. Knocking on Hannah's door, he said, "Can I come in?"

"Yeah."

She sat at her desk doing something on the computer and twisted in her chair to face him.

"We need to talk."

"About what?"

"Callie told me you talked to her."

"Oh God." She hung her head.

"I just...I want you to know that it's okay to talk to me about stuff. I'm not going to pretend to be cool with it, but I don't want you to run away, either." He reached into the plastic bag and held the box of condoms. "I want you to be safe. Do you need to go to the doctor—"

"Oh my God. I am not talking to you about condoms and sex. You're my dad! Leave. Please." She jumped out of her chair, face red.

Trevor stood, still totally confused. How had he made this worse? "Hannah, if you're thinking about sex, you should be able to talk about it."

"Not with you!" She flung her door open and stood at the threshold, hugging her middle.

He set the box on her desk and left. Downstairs, he put away the leftover pizza and figured he'd go try to fix things with the other female in his life. He couldn't screw that up, too, right?

He knocked on Callie's door, but she didn't answer. She'd said she was going out to dinner, so he sat down and leaned against her door. The sun was sinking, sending a glow across the garden.

About three plants were thriving. The rest were struggling. He sat there as the air cooled. He didn't know how much time passed, but the sky darkened. He just enjoyed the silence and peace.

When the gate creaked open, he sat up.

"Stalking me now?" Callie asked.

"If I were stalking you, I would've figured out where you were instead of waiting here. Technically, I'm just sitting in my yard."

"I'm not in the mood, Trevor. Go home."

He rose and waited for her to near. "I'm sorry I overreacted."

She completed a slow eye roll.

"I tried talking with Hannah. I bought her a box of condoms with the intention of talking to her about everything."

Callie's eyes narrowed. "You gave your daughter a box of condoms."

He nodded.

She burst out laughing. She laughed so hard, she doubled over and stumbled. Trevor caught her shoulders and a whiff of alcohol.

"You were right in that I do treat Evan and Hannah differently. But she's my little girl."

Callie stepped away from his grip. "How did that conversation go?"

"She shrieked and told me to leave her room."

Callie fell into another bout of laughter. Maybe waiting for Callie to get home wasn't such a great idea. She'd obviously been drinking, and she found every difficult thing he'd experienced hilarious.

"Are you done?" he asked when she regained composure. She inhaled deeply, and he watched the rise and fall of her chest. He reached for her hand. "You were right. She wanted to talk, and you handled it. I want her to come to me, but at least she's talking to someone."

Callie was still distant, not moving toward him or responding to his touch.

"Callie?"

She pulled from his grasp. "So happy I can be someone for your daughter." She waved a hand. "Now can you move so I can go to bed?"

"But—" He closed in again.

Her hand flattened against his chest. "I wasn't kidding. Not in the mood."

Her face showed no sign of the woman who was laughing like crazy moments ago. "I don't want you to go to bed mad at me."

"I'm not mad, Trevor. Just tired."

He held still for a moment and looked into her eyes. "If you're not mad, why can't I come in?"

"Because I've been drinking."

"So?"

She tilted her head and stared at him. He had no idea what she expected.

"Callie, I've been sober for seven years, three months. I've been around people who drink. I'm not going to run off to a bar because I see that you're buzzed."

"But what happens when you kiss me and taste the alcohol?"

He hadn't thought about that. Every date he'd been on and every woman he'd slept with since his divorce had been sober. Alcohol hadn't been part of his relationship with Callie. She was painfully aware of his past, both the successes and failures.

The fact that she worried about causing him to relapse touched him. She didn't want to risk what they had. She cared so much about his well-being and peace of mind.

Man, if he hadn't already figured out how awesome she was, he'd totally fall for her right now. He slid an arm around her waist and pulled her into a hug, kissing her temple.

"Good night, Callie. See you tomorrow." Then he released her and went to his own bed alone.

CALLIE HAD A FITFUL NIGHT'S SLEEP. SHE'D GROWN USED to falling asleep with Trevor, even though he got up in the middle of the night and left. She liked having him here. Dehydration hadn't helped matters. She lay in bed, trying to convince herself that she should get up, when there was a sharp knock on her door downstairs.

Was she supposed to drive Hannah to camp today? She scanned her memory, and as she did, the door swung open.

Trevor called, "Callie, you up?"

She sank back against her pillow. "More or less."

The thudding of his boots on the stairs was a comforting sound. She'd never lived with anyone, but small things like that had become not only normal for her, but welcome.

When he came to her bedside, she opened her eyes.

He set a large cup of coffee on the nightstand and held out a hand.

Pushing herself up, she asked, "What?"

"Ibuprofen in case you have a headache. Gatorade." He put a bottle next to the coffee. Pointing, he added, "And your morning fix."

Taking the coffee, she said, "I thought it wasn't cool for addicts to make jokes like that."

He sat on the edge of the bed. "Shh. Don't tell."

After a sip of coffee, which was heavenly, she said, "Thanks for this. About yesterday…"

"I told you, I'm sorry. I'm not mad about Hannah."

She clenched her jaw before speaking. "I didn't do anything worthy of you being pissed off at me. I meant last night. When I didn't want you to come in."

"What about it?"

"It's something we need to discuss, don't you think? If we're a couple, does that mean I have to live a life of sobriety, too? It's not a big deal, but sometimes I like a glass of wine when I'm out."

"I see no reason why you can't do that."

"But what if that triggers you?"

"Then I'll go to a meeting. I know how to handle this. You don't have to treat me like I might fall apart."

She scooted farther up in bed and set her cup back down. "This is big, Trevor. It's not like before. If you fuck up this time, the kids will be ruined. Diane will be here to snatch them up in a minute."

"Where is all of this coming from?" His voice was soft, his eyes filled with concern.

Callie knew that look. She'd seen it on his face numerous times—when Lisa had separated from him, when she'd said she wanted a divorce. It was a look of despair, like he was losing everything. "I'm worried. I was on the sidelines during your recovery, but Lisa talked to me a lot. I don't know how she lasted as long as she did. She had this never-ending hope that you would fix yourself."

"I did."

"After it was too late."

He got off the bed. "I know."

"I'm not Lisa."

Rubbing a hand over his short hair, he said, "I don't want you to be. I don't need you to be."

"What I mean is, I'm not as strong as she was. I won't keep giving you chances. I can't ride that roller coaster."

"Are you saying you want this to be done? You're not even going to give us a shot?"

She swung her legs over the side of the bed and stood in front of him. "No. I'm saying that you need to be sure. Your whole life has changed. Right after Lisa died, I thought you might start drinking again. I watched and I waited. I lived with the fear that if you drank, I'd lose the only family I have left."

"I wish I could tell you that I'll never drink again. I'd love nothing more than to give you that reassurance. But it would be a lie. That's not how addiction works. I have a support system, and I know what to do if I feel like I might relapse. It's something I have to live with for the rest of my life. You were right last night. I don't know if kissing you would've triggered something in me. I hadn't considered it because I've surrounded myself with sober people." He stepped close and touched her hand, not quite holding it. "If you can't sign on for that, I get it."

He walked away but paused at the top of the stairs. Looking over his shoulder, he said, "But before you decide, think about why. If you're doing it because you're afraid, keep in mind that we're all afraid, Callie. You talk about flying to the other side of the planet, and that freaks me out. Not knowing where you are or if you're safe. But I wouldn't want to lose out on us because of that fear."

Then his boots were clomping down the steps again. Only this time, instead of comforting, the sound left her feeling at a loss.

She didn't want to give up on them. She believed they had a chance to have something amazing. But she was afraid. If being with her risked his sobriety, she'd never be able to live with herself. Returning to bed, she finished her coffee and took the ibuprofen Trevor had brought her.

With the exception of last night, she hadn't had a drink since before Lisa's death. She hadn't missed it. Why was she so worried about not drinking?

She knew the reason. It was the lack of freedom. She didn't like having choices taken from her. It was instinct for her to rebel. She was old enough that the need to rebel should've been exhausted. She'd been living her life on her terms for decades. Maybe she didn't know how to compromise.

Or maybe she just didn't really want to.

Rolling over, she closed her eyes and went back to sleep. Life was simpler in her dreams, where she and Trevor shared a bed without any disruptions from the real world.

Trevor didn't know how he'd been suckered into hosting a barbecue for the Fourth of July. He'd never been much of a party host. Okay, maybe in his twenties when it was all about getting drunk and all he had to do was buy a keg and some bags of chips.

But this year, Tess and Evelyn had decided to make it a family outing, and they suggested his house. When he'd mentioned it to Callie, she'd practically jumped in excitement, so he couldn't say no. So here they were—Tess and Miles and her kids, Callie and his kids, and Evelyn and Owen—sitting in his backyard, snacking on watermelon, and playing Frisbee and bags. It was everything Lisa had imagined when she'd bought the patio furniture. It didn't seem fair that he was living the life she'd always wanted.

Trevor had already gone a round with water guns and the kids, so he took off his shirt and leaned back on a towel in the grass. Maybe if he closed his eyes and pretended to be asleep, everyone would leave him alone. He couldn't focus with Callie running around in shorts and a tank top. Her clothes weren't skimpy, but he kept picturing her naked. Maybe because he hadn't seen her so in about a week.

He didn't know where they stood, but he couldn't help but think that alcohol had cost him another woman. Even with his eyes closed, he felt a shadow pass over him. Squinting behind his sunglasses, he watched as Callie plopped down next to him.

She nudged his leg with hers. "I know you're not asleep."

"How?"

"Your body isn't relaxed."

Pushing his glasses up, he gave her a once-over. "You're too much of a distraction for me to relax."

"Why, thank you, Mr. Booth. You do have a way with words."

"I have a way with other things as well."

"Such promises."

"Let me come over tonight and I'll deliver on those promises."

"Okay." She slid lazily down until she was lying next to him.

"Did you say okay?"

"Yep."

"Just like that?" He rose up on an elbow and turned to look at her face. "What about everything you said the other day?"

"About drinking?" She lifted a shoulder. "There are things I enjoy a lot more than a glass of wine. Many of them involve you being naked. So if I have to pick, I choose you."

Her declaration was a little silly, but his heart suddenly filled his whole chest. "I'll be sure to make it up to you."

"You better," she said. "I also expect to tell Hannah and Evan soon. Sneaking around was a rush when I was a teen. No so much anymore."

"I get it. We'll tell them soon. I promise." He lay back down with the back of his hand brushing hers. Not quite the touch he wanted, but he could wait until tonight.

After a few minutes, Tess gave up on the beanbag game and sat down on his other side. "What's going on with Evelyn and Owen?"

"Huh?" Trevor asked.

"Evelyn and Owen. Don't you see it?"

"Oh, yeah," Callie said. "There's some hotness simmering there."

Trevor sat up and looked to where Evelyn and Owen stood side by side at the bags platform. "What are you talking about? They're just talking."

"Yeah, like I talk with Miles or you talk with Callie."

Heat rose on his neck and into his face, and Trevor was grateful for the blazing sun. "They're friends."

"Please tell me you aren't that dense," Callie said.

"What are you seeing?"

She sat up, putting her shoulder to shoulder with him, the soft skin of her arm warm against his. "Look. Right there." She pointed to where Owen brushed Evelyn's hair back from her face. "If we were watching a movie, we'd all expect the long-awaited kiss right about now."

"I don't get it."

Callie sighed.

Tess touched his arm. "Would you move Callie's hair like that?"

He shrugged. "Maybe."

"Bullshit," Callie answered. "You've actually done it."

In his defense, her hair was soft and silky, and he liked to touch it. But he wasn't about to admit that now. "Okay."

Tess said, "But would you make the same move on me?"

He looked at his friend. "I don't know." Now they'd

put the idea in his head, so he thought about it. While he and Tess were close, there had never been anything other than friendship between them. They hugged on occasion, but in general, he wouldn't be standing close enough to play with her hair.

He turned back to Owen and Evelyn, who had slipped her arm around Owen's elbow as she laughed after he threw a beanbag and missed by a mile. "Point taken. But if they're not addressing it, they probably don't want you guys talking about them."

"You're no fun," Callie said.

"Tell me about it," Tess added. "He's such a grumpy Gus most of the time. I will admit, though, that since you've been back in his life, he's had a sunnier disposition."

"Christ. That's my cue to leave this chick talk." He walked away from Tess and Callie. "Time for me to start the grill."

He turned the grill on and went into the kitchen to get the meat. While he should be happy that Tess and Callie got along, it made him nervous. They each knew him from different points in his life. Seen him at various levels of his worst—because every time he didn't think things could get worse, they did. Callie was the first woman he'd introduced to his group of friends, but he wasn't sure he was ready for her to be comparing notes.

It made him glad that Nina had a party to manage for a client. She'd be all over his relationship with Callie. And he was sure she'd have input about Owen and Evelyn. The women in his life were too nosy.

He pulled the steaks and chicken from the fridge and seasoned them. The back door opened, and Callie came in. She slid her sunglasses to the top of her head, pushing her hair back in the process. Setting her camera on the counter, she smiled as she neared and rose up to kiss him.

It was a quick kiss, but he loved the naturalness of it. Like she belonged right here with him.

When she backed away, he asked, "What's with the camera?"

"I'm just snapping some shots."

He'd watched her throughout the party. Her camera was like an extension of her body. It amazed him that she could do that, take pictures like a job, but still interact, converse, and make friends.

She picked up the camera and turned the screen so he could see it. Pressing a button, she scrolled and pictures flashed on the small screen. It was like watching a movie of their day.

"This is my favorite." She stopped and handed him the camera.

It was a picture of him with Evan and Hannah. The kids had ganged up on him with their water guns to soak him. Callie had captured the looks of pure joy on their faces. Even his.

"Can I get a copy of that?"

"Sure." She took the camera back and set it on the counter.

"The only thing missing in that picture is you."

"I was taking it. Some other time I'll insert myself into a family photo." She pointed at the food he'd taken out. "What can I help with?"

"Make the salad and see what we have for vegetables. I think Tess brought corn on the cob."

Callie moved around the kitchen as if it were her own.

He suddenly wondered if she would feel weird living here, like he'd worried when he first moved in. It had been Lisa's house, and while he felt like he'd more or less made it his own, he hadn't considered what he and Callie would do. What about when their relationship progressed? Would she be willing to move in here?

Fuck. He hated having to worry about every little freaking thing. He went back outside and put the meat on the grill. Moments later, Tess walked past him saying something about helping Callie.

Callie joined him at the grill, handing him a can of pop. "Everything okay?"

"Yeah," he said, a little rougher than he'd wanted.

"That was totally believable. Want to try again?"

He sighed and shook his head to clear it. "I was just thinking about us and this damn house. Where do we go as a couple?"

"What are you asking?"

"At some point, we'll live together. Where does that happen?"

"Whoa." She raised her hands and took a step back. "Moving a little fast there, don't you think? You haven't even told the kids about us."

"Just thinking ahead."

"Borrowing trouble."

"What?"

She came close again and held his hand. "You're worrying about something that isn't happening yet."

"But—"

"But what? We're not in a position to talk about living together. We're still figuring out how to be a couple. Let's just enjoy that."

He looked at her smiling face and decided that she had a pretty good plan. He spent a lot of time worrying about things—things that might happen, things he had no control over, things that scared the shit out of him. Maybe she could teach him how to step back and just enjoy, because that was something that Callie was really good at.

Trevor had fun hosting a party in his backyard. Most of his closest friends spent the day. His kids laughed and had fun. Callie and Tess had formed a friendship. By the time night had fallen and everyone was exhausted, Trevor told Tess to leave with her family. She offered to stay and help clean up, but he insisted he could handle it.

Callie went inside to wash dishes with Evan, and he and Hannah tackled the mess in the backyard. Through the screen door, he heard Callie's laughter, and it made him smile.

Hannah scooped up the beanbags and shoved them into a plastic container. "Callie makes you happy."

The remark caught him off guard. "She's a good friend."

"Yeah, right."

He stopped gathering cups and glasses to take inside. "What's that supposed to mean?"

"Dad, do you really think we don't know?"

"Know what?"

She groaned and rolled her eyes. "That you wait until we're in our rooms so you can sneak over to Callie's house to spend the night?"

He froze. He had thought they didn't know. He'd tried

to shield them. Being caught now, though, he decided to take it head-on. "Okay. You're nosier than I thought. How do you feel about it?"

"About you and Callie? It's awesome."

He sighed. This was what he'd been afraid of. "It's still really new. We're figuring things out. So don't..." He didn't know where to go with that. Don't what? Get your hopes up? Think it's going to be forever? He'd been cautious, but part of him had already bypassed all of that. He was falling hard for her. The only thing that held him back was his fear that it wouldn't last.

"Don't what? Plan the wedding?" She burst out laughing. "That might kill Callie."

Hmm. Hannah thought Callie would be the problem in moving their relationship forward. "Does Evan know about us, too?"

"Of course. We're not blind. Anyone with half a brain can see it. Every time you guys look at each other, you're all googly-eyed." She set the tub of bags down. "You think you're being sneaky touching each other and holding hands, but you're not that good."

That would teach him to try to hide things from his kids. He should've known better. For her entire life, Hannah had always managed to figure out where they'd hidden birthday and Christmas presents. The girl was like a bloodhound once she caught a scent.

"I'm not making a big deal about it. I just wanted you to know that we know." Then she turned and finished cleaning up the games.

Trevor carried the glasses into the kitchen and put them in the dishwasher. Callie had the rest of the dishes done and was wiping down the counter. "Where's Evan?"

"Went upstairs to talk to his girlfriend."

"I just had an interesting conversation with Hannah."

Callie tossed the sponge in the sink. "Whatever it was, I didn't do it."

He chuckled. "She let me know that we're not as sneaky as we think we are. She knows I've been spending the night at your place."

"Yeah?" she asked with hesitation.

"Yeah. She's good with us being together. She sees you make me happy."

A smile brightened Callie's face. "I've been known to have that effect on people."

He moved in and wrapped an arm around her waist, pulling her close. "How about I walk you home?"

"Will you spend the night? Like all night?"

"I could probably arrange that." He kissed her then, taking a small taste because he couldn't do what he really wanted to here in the kitchen.

From the side of them, he heard, "Gross," and the same time from behind he heard, "Just because we know it happens doesn't mean we want to see that."

He and Callie separated and looked at the kids. "Time for bed."

Evan groaned. "Nothing I want to think about my dad doing."

"I meant you. See you in the morning."

"Good night," Hannah said. She gave him and Callie a hug.

"Hey," Evan said. "If you're spending the night at Callie's, that means I could sneak out and you wouldn't know."

Hannah smacked her brother's arm. "You probably shouldn't announce your plan if you want it to work."

Evan laughed, but Trevor made a mental note to install an alarm that would let him know when the doors opened.

Then, holding Callie's hand, he went across the yard to take her to bed.

For the first summer in years, Callie enjoyed time in Chicago. She'd always had a good time in the short term—a few weeks here and there—but she'd forgotten how much fun the city was. Festivals in every neighborhood. Crowded beaches. Walks at the zoo. Concerts at outdoor venues. She loved it all, but she had no luck finding a steady job. She'd spent every day taking in the sights and sounds of the city, taking pictures of everything so she could at least add to her portfolio. Some of those shots she'd be able to sell online.

But she'd had no offers for permanent work. Definitely nothing that could compete with the offer from Around the World Travels. As much as it stung, she began to think her options were limited and she'd have no choice but to take the job.

Look at me, borderline whining about having someone pay me to travel all over the world. Twenty years ago—hell, ten years ago—this would've been a dream job. In many ways, it still was. She'd had a few more email conversations with the tour company about their vision and where they wanted to send her. She'd get the chance to visit places she'd never been. She'd be able to visit the best beaches, places of spiritual or historical significance. The chance to see the Wonders of the World was reason enough.

If she timed her trips well, she could probably bring Trevor and the kids with her to some locations. By the time she did one run, she'd have enough flyer miles to cover tickets for everyone. She started to get excited at the thought of hopping on a plane again.

Then she thought about Trevor and the fact that he never traveled. He didn't even take a nearby vacation. He had a business to run, and it was rare for him to take a day off.

She liked the life she had here. She and Trevor shared a bed most nights. They stayed in his room the other night because he'd started to think that the kids would take advantage of his not being in the house. As a person who had routinely sneaked out of her parents' house, she couldn't argue. Being in his bed, in his room, wasn't as weird as she thought it would be.

Even though Lisa had bought the house, it was no longer hers. Trevor had stamped his mark on it pretty quickly. Of course, her reaction might be different if he had used Lisa's bedroom, but since he was downstairs, she hadn't been as squicked out as she'd expected to be.

Sitting in her living room, she felt restless. Trevor was at a meeting and said he'd be late tonight. So she used her free evening to play on her computer, scrolling through some of the locations she would be able to travel to. She made a list of requirements that she would expect for this job to happen. She needed to be able to come home often. They would have to cover the bill for decent accommodations. She was done spending the night in tents and not sleeping because she feared her equipment would be stolen.

As she filled a sheet of paper with ideas to gather her thoughts, her phone rang. She answered without looking because she assumed it was Trevor letting her know he was home. "Hello."

"Callie?" Evan sounded weird, but there was so much background noise, it was distracting.

"Evan? Where are you?"

"At a party."

Trevor hadn't said anything about that. "Does your dad know?"

"Nuh-uh. I'm not okay to drive. Can you come get me?"

Before he finished his sentence, she was already sliding into her flip-flops and grabbing her keys. "Text me the address right now. Then sit on the front porch so I can find you."

"'Kay."

She ran through the yard and looked for Trevor's truck out front. He was still at his meeting, so she couldn't call him. As she started the engine in her car, her phone buzzed with a text. She plugged the address into her GPS and took off.

She was happy that Evan was smart enough to call for a ride instead of trying to drive himself after partying, but fear niggled at her as she drove. It was still early. What time had they started for him to be drunk before ten o'clock? Or had something happened that made him want to leave the party?

As she neared the address Evan sent, the street was

filled with cars. There was little doubt which house was having a party. Every light was blazing; thumping music could be heard down the block. Her car crawled closer, and she called Evan since she didn't see him on the porch. She really didn't want to have to go into the house to get him.

The phone rang in her hand, and she saw a shadow emerge from the side of the house. Evan wove crookedly toward her car. He opened the passenger door and fell onto the seat.

Eyeing him, she asked, "Want to talk about it?"

"No." He leaned against the window and closed his eyes.

"Thank you for calling instead of driving drunk."

One eye eased open. "Can we not tell Dad about this?"

She shook her head. "Sorry, honey. I can't keep this from him."

Evan groaned.

"Are you gonna be sick?"

"Don't think so."

"Must've been a good party, huh?"

"It sucked."

Not quite the answer she expected. At seventeen, sneaking out and getting drunk at a party came with bragging rights, usually claiming to have done a lot more than you actually did. "You didn't have a good time?"

He looked at her with watery eyes filled with sadness. Her heart lurched, and her fear became reality. Something was seriously wrong.

"What happened, Evan? Are you okay?"

"My girlfriend broke up with me this afternoon, and she showed up at the party with some other guy."

"Ouch."

Evan closed his eyes again.

Callie left him alone. He was going to feel like crap physically and emotionally. Heartbreak was no joke, especially for a teenager. "When we get home, make sure you drink a bunch of water even if you're not thirsty. It'll help you feel better."

"Doubt it."

"I know." She reached over and patted his leg.

Part of her wanted to go find this girl and yell at her for being cruel, but she knew it would be pointless. There was nothing Callie could do to fix this for Evan, but she wanted to.

Chapter Twelve

Trevor got home and saw that Callie's car was gone. Inside, the house was silent. "Hannah? Evan?"

"In my room," Hannah called.

"How about your brother?"

"Went out with friends."

Oh yeah. Evan had texted him earlier that he was going out. Trevor realized he wasn't great at keeping track of his kids. If they were still toddlers, he probably would've lost one by now.

He put away the dinner dishes and made a mental list of invoices and proposals he needed to get out to clients. He'd lived for years on his own, without having the kids underfoot, but the house was so quiet, it was unnerving. He thought of texting Callie to see when she'd be home, but that felt needy or controlling, and he didn't want to be either.

A *thump* at the front door caught his attention. By the

time he got to the living room, the door swung open, and Evan stumbled in.

The boy could barely keep himself upright. Callie was at his back, holding his shoulders to guide him.

"What the fuck?"

"Hey," Evan said.

"You're drunk." A swarm of emotions attacked at once. Fear. Panic. Hurt. Anger.

Evan smiled. "I was at a party."

"You're seventeen!" He was yelling, but he didn't care.

"Didn't drive, though." Then he winked. At least Trevor thought it was supposed to be a wink. It was more of a spastic blink.

"Did you do this?" he asked Callie.

"Did I do what?"

"Get him drunk."

She reared back. "Hell no. How could you even think that?" Her eyes were wide with what might've been hurt, but Trevor couldn't stop to think about that.

"You're always telling them about your partying youth. It was so cool, right?"

Whatever hurt he'd thought was there was quickly replaced with a flash of anger. "Don't be an asshole, Trevor. He got drunk and called me to pick him up. It's no big deal."

Something about the way she said it, the way she tossed the comment out, made him see red. "It *is* a big fucking deal. He's a minor and he's drunk. Not a beer. Not trying something. Totally fucking blitzed."

"Don't yell at her," Evan said. "What's the big deal?"

"The big deal is that this is a path you can't afford to go down."

Evan scoffed. "So I got drunk. I'm not you." Then he pushed past Trevor and climbed the stairs.

It took every ounce of patience he'd ever had to lock his muscles and not grab that boy and drag him back.

"Remember what I said about water," Callie called after him.

Evan waved over his shoulder.

Callie crossed her arms and stared at Trevor.

"What?" he asked.

"I'm waiting for an apology."

"You'll be waiting a hell of a long time." He pointed in the general direction of Evan.

"How is this my fault?" Callie asked. "I was at home, minding my own business, and he called me. He's a teenager. They screw up. He had a rough night and got drunk. We've all been there."

He jabbed a finger in the air at her. "That right there is the goddamn problem. You act like it's all okay. No big deal. It is a *huge* fucking deal. He's seventeen. If he's solving his problems by getting drunk now, where's he going to be in five years? Ten? Are you going to continue to enable him? Run out to get his next six-pack?"

Callie took a long, slow inhale through flared nostrils. "I'm trying to remember that you have tunnel vision on this topic because of your issues. But you're crossing a line here."

"No, Callie. You're the one who keeps crossing the line. You make decisions without consulting me. I'm their dad. *I* decide what's important."

She dropped her arms to her sides. Her head angled, and her eyes filled with sadness. "You're right, Trevor.

You get to decide everything. I hope you can live with those choices."

She walked around him, the sound of her sandals slapping against the floor urging him to do something.

But he was pissed. They'd been around and around when it came to the kids. He was their father, and she couldn't just make decisions on their behalf. It wasn't up to her to tell Evan that getting drunk wasn't a big deal. Having Trevor as a father meant that it might be a slippery slope for him. Trevor wasn't willing to take that chance with his kids. That's why he took such a hard line.

Of all people, Callie should understand that.

She'd been standing beside Lisa when his wife had enforced that hard line for him. And he'd failed time and again. No way was he going to watch his son make the same mistakes he'd made.

When he turned to go to bed, he saw Hannah standing at the top of the stairs, arms crossed, eyes filled. "Why do you do that to her?"

"Not now, Hannah."

"Then when, Dad? How many times do you think she's going to let you treat her like that before she leaves?"

"I didn't do anything to Callie. If you heard all of it, then you know your brother went out and got drunk." The words were glass in his throat. So many things could've gone wrong for Evan. He scrubbed a hand over his head. "I know you guys think I'm being an asshole. But getting drunk isn't a way to solve anything. It's my job to protect you. Sometimes Callie makes that hard."

"Callie has never done anything to hurt us. She never would. If you think that, then you don't know her at all.

You don't deserve her." She turned on her heel and disappeared into her room.

Trevor felt the rage bubbling up, and he wanted to hit something. No, what he really wanted was a fucking drink. He needed to call Karl. But first, he needed to pummel something to release the frustration and anger. He went to the basement and taped his hands before going at the heavy bag that he kept for just this purpose.

He punched the bag until his hands were sore, his muscles exhausted and trembling, and his body was coated in sweat. It was all he could do to avoid going out and doing something stupid that he'd regret.

When he had nothing left, he sank to the floor and pulled out his phone. It was late, but Karl would always answer. It was why Trevor considered him more than a sponsor. He'd been a great friend over the years.

The ringing sounded hollow in his ears as he tugged at the tape on his knuckles.

"Trevor, what happened?"

Of course Karl would assume the worst. "I think I've fucked up."

"Where are you?"

"In my basement. I haven't had anything to drink. But I want to. Bad." *Wasn't that fucking ironic?*

Rustling on the other end told Trevor that he probably woke Karl up. "I'm sorry I called so late. This'll keep."

"I'm up now. You might as well tell me."

Trevor recounted the evening.

"You didn't mention you were involved with someone," Karl said.

"It's still pretty new."

"But she's living with you?"

Trevor huffed a laugh. Yeah, his life was weird. "She was my ex-wife's best friend. We were friends years ago. With Lisa's death, we reconnected. She's not really living with me. She rents the coach house out back."

"Son, the woman is living with you."

Trevor laughed again. "I guess you're right."

"Let's take this step by step. For your son, is this the first time this has happened?"

"As far as I know."

"Then your girl is right. He's a dumb kid. I'm not saying you should ignore it. He needs to be aware there's a possibility of predisposition. You should also be honest with him about how it makes you feel."

"What do you mean?"

"Come on. Be honest. How did you feel seeing him stumbling drunk? Why are you calling me?"

"Seeing him, I was pissed. As for calling you, I'm beginning to question that."

"I'm being serious. After the anger, what?"

"I'm scared for him. And yeah, I called you because I want a drink."

"That's all normal. He's old enough to handle the truth. Tell him how hard it is."

Trevor hadn't addressed his alcoholism with the kids in years. He'd always been up-front and didn't hide his recovery from them, but in recent years, he hadn't felt the need to discuss it. And if he was being honest with himself, he didn't want to be that honest with them. Alcoholism was an ugly disease.

As usual, though, Karl was right. It was time for him to face it with Evan and Hannah.

"Now, about Callie," Karl went on. "I know why you

took your anger out on her even though she didn't deserve it. We all do that to the ones we love. But the question is, what are you going to do about it?"

Love? They hadn't talked about it. They hadn't exchanged the words, but in his heart, he knew. He'd known for a while. He loved Callie. Yet he treated her like crap.

"I have no fucking clue what I'm going to do. I feel like we're always fighting and apologizing. That can't be healthy."

"Fighting about what?"

Trevor thought about every time they walked away from each other. "Mostly the kids."

"You mean like you fought tonight?"

"Yeah."

"Then you have a lot of decisions to make. Your so-called fight tonight was about you exerting control over your family. You want to be in charge of everything. If you can't back off and let her in, that vicious cycle will be all you ever know."

"You're all sunshine and rainbows, aren't you?"

"If you wanted that you would've called someone else. You reach out to me because you know you'll get honesty."

Trevor pushed up off the floor. "You don't have to be brutal about it."

"Some people don't listen and learn until they're beaten upside the head."

Trevor sighed. "I know. Thanks, man."

"Any time. You need to meet?"

"No. I'm going to bed. Looks like I have a lot to think about."

"Before you go to her again, make sure your head is on straight. Know what you're willing to do. Don't make promises you can't keep."

"I won't."

"And go to a meeting."

"That's where I was while my son was out getting drunk."

"Ain't that a bitch."

"You know it. I'll talk to you later." Trevor disconnected and peeled the tape from his knuckles, which were still red. His whole body ached from the late-night workout. When he got upstairs, he looked out the kitchen window and saw Callie's lights on. He wanted to go over and apologize, but Karl was right. He needed to figure out where they were going, what he wanted.

He wanted Callie. That much was clear. But he wasn't sure he could do what he needed to keep her.

CALLIE ROLLED HER LUGGAGE THROUGH THE AIRPORT, BUT it all seemed so unfamiliar. Not this particular airport, but the whole process, which made no sense. She'd been traveling for her career for twenty years. She'd been in more airports than she'd been in homes. She found herself checking her bags ten times to make sure she hadn't forgotten to pack something. Packing had been automatic. She never forgot anything.

Then again, she was usually well-rested before a flight. She hadn't slept at all last night after booking her flight.

She kept telling herself it was because she was worried about Evan, but it was more than that. Outside the airport, a car waited for her to take her to the hotel.

The tour company had been so thrilled to hear from her last night, their early morning, that they'd arranged everything. She should be exhausted with jet lag hitting her, but she just felt like a zombie. After putting her bag in the trunk, she sank into the back seat and called Hannah.

"Hey, Callie. Where are you? I stopped by because your car is out front, but you're not home."

"I just landed in Italy."

"What?"

"Remember the job offer I told you about? I agreed to take an in-person meeting with the travel company and take some local shots to see how well we work together."

"Wow."

She couldn't interpret the single word, so she forged ahead. "How are things there?"

"Same as always."

"How's Evan?"

Hannah laughed. "He was hurting so bad this morning. Every noise made him cringe. So you know I had to be extra loud. And of course, I *needed* to practice my sax."

Callie smiled. "Of course, you *had* to practice."

"It was my duty. When are you coming home?"

Home. That word was one she had no problem interpreting. In years past, Hannah would ask when she'd be coming back. Never home. Then again, she hadn't treated it much like home. Until recently. "I'm not sure. A couple weeks?"

Unless they wanted to hire her for an extended

project. They'd originally wanted to book her for a three-week tour, and last night she'd convinced them that photos from their home city of Rome could be enough of a test.

"Hey, do you think if you're going to be longer than that I could come meet you? I could be your assistant or something."

"Oh, I don't know about that. I don't think your dad would go for it."

"That's just because he worries. I bet you could talk him into it."

Callie's heart sank. If only Hannah knew how little sway Callie held with her father. She swallowed against the lump in her throat. "I don't think he wants to hear anything from me right now."

"He's dumb," Hannah said sadly.

"No, he's not."

"Yeah, he is. I heard what he said to you. I told him he doesn't deserve you."

Callie's eyes filled. "Thanks for standing up for me, but I don't want you to do that. It'll drive a wedge between you and your dad. I don't want to be the cause of that."

"You're not. He is being dumb."

Callie knew when an argument wasn't going to move. "I'm almost to my hotel. I just wanted to call and let you know where I am. I'll call you later in the week, okay?"

"Okay. Be safe and have fun."

"Good night."

"Don't forget my postcard."

"Do I ever?" Ever since Hannah was old enough to look at a map to see where Callie was traveling, Callie had sent her postcards. Hannah had a wall in her room decorated with the cards. It had become their thing. She wondered if Trevor was aware of his daughter's desire to travel. She'd probably get the blame for that, too. "Bye," she said before disconnecting.

At the hotel, Callie checked in and fell into bed. Her eyes were gritty and her throat sore. She wanted to blame it on the long flight, but she knew her emotions were tearing her apart. Tomorrow would be better.

The following morning, Callie didn't feel any better. She'd tossed and turned as her mind raced. Trevor hadn't made any attempt to contact her. He might not even know she was gone. That hurt almost as much as his accusations last night. Two nights ago? Damn. She was a mess.

She readied herself for her meeting. Victoria, who was her point of contact at the company, planned to give her a small tour, and then they'd meet with the heads of all the departments to discuss what they were looking for. Callie certainly hoped they had more specifics than wanting pictures for each tour.

Armed with her small camera and a notebook, she left the hotel. She should've stopped for breakfast, but food held no appeal. Coffee, on the other hand, was a necessity, so she walked down the block, sure she'd find somewhere to get her morning caffeine. The hotel Victoria had booked for her was within walking distance of the office, so Callie had time to wander a little before her meeting.

She'd been to Rome before, but not often enough that she knew her way around. The first time she'd come, she'd stumbled through the streets with a paper map in hand that had gotten her lost more often than not. Callie laughed at the memory as she typed the address of the office into her phone's GPS. Life was so different than it had been back then.

At twenty-five, the thought of landing in one place and staying forever had freaked her out. She'd watched Lisa fall in love and create a family, and while Callie could appreciate Lisa's life, she couldn't wait to escape. Standing on the corner, enjoying the extra strong coffee, Callie thought back over her trips.

Some of the longest trips she'd ever taken away from Chicago had coincided with major events in Lisa's life: marriage, kids, divorce. It hadn't been that Callie had avoided her friend's life. She thought she'd been there for Lisa, but something about the reality—no, the finality—of what Lisa was signing on for had driven Callie out of town. Every time.

The realization turned the bitter coffee sour in her stomach. Had she been a bad friend? Lisa had never said anything.

Pinching the bridge of her nose to stop tears from forming, she whispered to no one, "I wish you were here. You'd tell me what the hell is going on with me."

Then Callie laughed. She was talking to her dead best friend. Lisa was probably looking at her like she was nuts. She'd fallen for Lisa's ex-husband. Like in deep love. How the hell had that happened?

Laughter echoed behind her, and Callie could've sworn it was Lisa's laugh, but when she turned, she saw no one. *Great. Now I'm going crazy.* Insane or not, given her situation, she could totally see Lisa laughing at her. Dumping her cup into a trash can, she turned to head to the tour company. Time to see if this was a job she really wanted.

Trevor had risen early and gone to work without waking Evan. He knew better than to even try. As far as he knew, this was the first time Evan had gotten drunk. The hangover might be harsh, and Trevor knew enough about himself to know he might not be kind.

He'd worked hard all day but checked in with Hannah to see how Evan was doing. Based on the texts she'd sent, Evan might've been better off coming to work. Trevor enjoyed Hannah's torment a little too much. Hopefully, Evan would learn his lesson.

He picked up a pizza for dinner. As he parked his truck, he saw Evan's crappy car across the street. Then he eyed Callie's car. He knew he needed to talk to her. He'd spent the night and the entire day thinking about her. Thinking about her and the kids and all of them together. He came to the conclusion that what he wanted was for them to be a family.

But Karl's words stuck in his head. Trevor didn't know exactly what he was willing to do. He wasn't trying to be a tyrant controlling everything. He had no idea what he was doing with Hannah and Evan. He was so afraid of screwing them up that he had to be in charge.

With pizza in hand, he climbed the steps to the house, feeling the weight of everything in his life. He set the pizza on the table and went upstairs. He knocked on

Hannah's door and told her pizza was downstairs. Then he went to Evan's room and knocked.

"Come in."

Trevor pushed through the door and strode in. He sat on the edge of the bed, and Evan paused the video game he was playing without even being asked. Looked like the kid had a brain in his head.

"How'd your car get back here?"

"I took the bus and brought it home." His son looked at the floor and said, "I'm sorry about last night. But at least I didn't drive. I know better than that."

"That's the only reason you still have a car." Trevor's voice was stiff, another reminder of his discomfort and knowledge that he was clueless. "Was it the first time?"

Evan's eyes met his. "What?"

"Drinking? Getting drunk?"

Evan shook his head, and Trevor's muscles tightened. "How many times?"

Evan lifted a shoulder.

Trevor closed his eyes and thought. "This isn't about getting in trouble with me. I'm trying to wrap my head around this. How often have you been drinking?"

"Just at parties and stuff. Not a lot."

He asked the question he didn't really want the answer to. "Did your mom know?"

"She caught me a couple times, noticed when I'd been drinking after hanging out with friends. She grounded me. I figured you knew."

Trevor shook his head. "She never told me." He sighed. "Probably because of the way I reacted last night." He leaned forward and braced his elbows on his knees. "I need you to understand where I'm coming from."

"I know, Dad. You can't drink. But..."

"You're not me," Trevor finished for him. "The thing is, that's the same thing I said when I was your age. I know you don't remember my dad. He died when you were too young. But he was an alcoholic, too. Drank pretty much every day of my life. I convinced myself that I would never be him."

Trevor's throat was tight. With the exception of Lisa and Karl, he'd never talked to anyone about this. "When I was a little older than you, I played in a band. Our gigs were mostly in bars. It was a natural thing to stay after our sets and have a few drinks. That's where I met your mom. She came to one of our shows. And then another."

Evan leaned forward, his full attention on Trevor. "What happened?"

"Everything. Things were good, except when they weren't. I drank as a crutch. Didn't get a gig we wanted? Got drunk. Stressed-out wife at home? Got drunk. Lost a job? Got drunk."

Evan nodded. "Got dumped by a girl and watched her with another guy at a party? Got drunk."

Trevor stared at his son. Callie had said Evan had a hard night, but he hadn't listened. "I didn't know. Why didn't you say something?"

"What was I gonna say? We broke up."

"If something's bothering you, you should be able to talk to me. It helps."

Evan smiled. "Like you talk?"

Trevor straightened. "I'll have you know that I have people I talk to when something's bothering me. Last night I talked to Karl, my sponsor. Other times, I talk to

Nina, Tess, Gabe, Evelyn, or Owen. And there's Jerry at work."

"And Callie," Evan added.

Since he wasn't sure where he stood with Callie, he felt guilty even thinking about her as someone he could count on. "The point is I have a lot of people to lean on. You're my kid, so I'm not supposed to confide in you. But you should talk to me."

"Okay."

"As far as the drinking goes, I can't allow it. You know that. Besides the fact that it's illegal because you're underage, it makes things too hard for me. I'm not saying that you'll cause me to fall off the wagon, but I'd rather not take any chances. When I go out and I know I'll be around people who are drinking, I mentally prepare myself. I go to an extra meeting. I have a plan in place. You stumbling in drunk isn't something I can plan for."

"Why can't you just stop?" Evan looked straight into his eyes, and Trevor saw he wanted honesty.

"I wish I could. I know you know it's a disease, but saying that doesn't help. Alcohol is something that pulls me in with lies. There's no such thing as a taste or a drink. It hits my body, and then I'm telling myself if one was good, two will be better. In the moment, that's all that matters." He stood and walked across the room, toying with the crap Evan kept on his dresser.

He wasn't very good at explaining what the addiction was like. His muscles were tight, and his stomach rolled over. But he knew giving Evan this might save them all a lot of grief later. "Alcohol lies. Your body craves it, but your mind believes it's doing good. It takes away the pain."

Evan scoffed. "Yeah, till the next morning."

"Even then, there are excuses. You'll tell yourself anything just to make it okay to drink again." He turned back to Evan. "I've been sober for years, but there are still days that I want a beer. Want it so bad I can taste it."

"What do you do?"

"Find something to occupy myself until it passes. Sometimes it's a meeting. Sometimes it's the heavy bag in the basement. It took a long time for me to realize it would pass. That I could find a better outlet."

Evan leaned back in his chair and studied him. Trevor didn't know what else to say. He desperately wanted his son to agree to never drink again, but he knew it was an unrealistic wish.

"Thanks for being honest."

"All that being said, you're still grounded."

"What?"

Evan's indignant posturing was for show. Trevor knew he was doing it because it was expected.

"A week. No friends. Extra chores."

"I did what I'm supposed to do. I called for a ride instead of driving."

"Like I said, it's the only reason you still have that car. What you were supposed to do was not drink. For the record, I'm the one you should've called."

"I called Callie because I knew she wouldn't give me a hard time and you would. I already felt like shit. I didn't want it to get worse."

Trevor's heart sank. "I'm trying. I'm going to get mad when you do stupid shit. But we have to be able to count on each other."

Evan sank back in his chair. "I was counting on Callie to not rat me out."

Trevor smiled and patted Evan's shoulder. "It might've worked if I hadn't been home."

"Nah. I tried. She told me she couldn't keep it from you."

The admission made Trevor feel worse. Callie did have his back. "Pizza's downstairs if you're hungry."

"Be there in a few." He returned to his game, and Trevor watched him play for a minute. Then he went downstairs.

His conversation with Evan had been difficult, but not nearly as bad as he'd imagined. Evan had made him pay attention to a couple things he'd been ignoring: one, he did lean on Callie, and two, he loved the fact that his kids knew she was on their side. He wanted his kids to have as many people in their corner as possible. He'd been an ass for the way he'd treated Callie.

She'd been putting the kids first. His kids. It wasn't something she had to do. She did it because she loved them. Not once had she kept anything from him. She'd done things to help lighten his load, and she'd asked for nothing in return.

Man, he'd truly fucked this up. He just hoped he wasn't too late to fix it. He had his answer for Karl's questions. He'd do whatever he needed to keep Callie in his life.

As he crossed through the kitchen, he saw Hannah at the table chomping on a slice of pizza and scrolling through her phone. Trevor didn't bother to interrupt her. He continued walking out the back door and across the yard. He needed to talk to Callie.

He knocked on her door and waited. He'd left his keys in the kitchen by the pizza. She wouldn't want him using his key to barge in anyway. He knocked again, louder, in case she was working. He'd seen her get so lost in thought while studying pictures that the rest of the world ceased to exist. The back door of the house opened. "She's not home," Hannah called.

"Her car's out front."

"She's in Italy. Didn't you know?"

Italy? Fuck. She took the travel agency job. The one that would keep her away for a year. His heart raced and his vision clouded. He closed his eyes and focused. He couldn't fall apart. Hannah was watching. He sucked in enough air to fill his chest and reopened his eyes.

Then he turned to go back into the house.

"She's in Rome, but she said she might be back in a couple weeks."

"Oh," was all he could say. He wanted to rage and scream, mostly at his own stupidity, but it wouldn't help. "When did you talk to her?"

"Earlier today. She's there for a job."

He climbed the steps and joined Hannah on the porch.

"It sounds like a really cool job."

He slid his arm around his daughter's shoulders and turned her to go back in. "I'm sure it is."

He couldn't muster even fake enthusiasm for the job that might take Callie away for good. His entire body felt raw and exposed, irritated. He mumbled good night to Hannah and went to his room, trying to figure out the time difference between Chicago and Italy.

Chapter Thirteen

Italy was beautiful. Everywhere Callie turned, it was impossible to take a bad picture. Who wouldn't want to come here on vacation? The downside to negotiating a trial run in the same city as the home office of the agency was that they kept calling her in to various meetings.

The CFO wanted to talk budget. The marketing team always had another question or idea. She'd been in town for four days. Four days, ten hours, and thirty-two minutes. Not that she was counting. Right now, she was trying to enjoy a quiet evening at an outdoor café away from the suits and charts and wheeled office chairs.

Her phone buzzed, and she glanced at the screen without picking it up. Trevor. Again. He'd called eleventy billion times but had yet to leave a voicemail. It had been more than five days since they'd spoken. Five days since he'd accused her of getting Evan drunk, or at least allowing it. Five days since he'd reminded her, again, that she continuously crossed the line with his kids. She still didn't have a clue what that meant.

Her heart hurt every time she thought about it. About him. About home. She knew she hadn't done anything wrong, so she should feel angry. But the ache of loneliness washed away everything else. What did that say about her?

The worst part was that she didn't know what to do. She'd always been sure of herself and her path. She saw what she wanted and went after it. This job was everything she'd ever looked for as a travel photographer, but her brain was preoccupied with thoughts of Trevor and the kids.

She missed having dinner and watching TV with them. She missed hearing about Hannah's day at band camp and what silly things the cute boy said to her. She missed listening to Trevor and Evan tease each other over something that had happened at work. It had only been five days. What would she be like if she took this job and traveled for months at a time?

But if she walked away from this fabulous opportunity, what was she giving it up for? A guy who wanted to only share his bed with her but not his whole life? She could find a guy for a casual relationship; it wasn't hard. For the first time in forever, she'd believed she was building something more. Trevor seemed to block every path of progress, though, so maybe he didn't want this relationship.

She finished her coffee and went back to her hotel room. Her clothes still sat in her suitcase. Her camera equipment covered every available surface. She looked at her laptop. She wanted to video chat with Hannah, to see a smiling, friendly face.

And yeah, maybe she wanted to get a feel for what was going on with Trevor. Looking at the time, she did some quick calculating. Trevor must've called on his lunch break. She wasn't sure if Hannah would be home from camp because the time varied each day, but now would be a good time to try.

She sat in front of her laptop and dialed Hannah. The ringing echoed in the room as bubbles circled the screen waiting for connection. A moment later, Hannah's beautiful face filled the screen.

"Oh my God. Why haven't you called? It's been like forever."

Callie's throat tightened. She missed her so much. She forced a smile. "Don't be a drama queen. It's been a couple of days. It's not like you've been sitting around waiting for me to call."

"I know, but I have so much news!" she squealed in excitement.

Callie would've given anything to wrap her arms around Hannah to enjoy whatever was making her happy. Luckily, Callie didn't need to talk. Hannah had plenty to say. Sam, the cute boy from band, had taken her out on a date, with Trevor's knowledge, she pointed out. Trevor even drove them and hadn't acted like a dork. It was the best. Date. Ever.

And Callie was missing all of it.

When Hannah wound down, she asked, "So how's the job? Is it awesome? I bet it is."

"It is pretty awesome. Except for all of the stupid meetings I've been to. I don't care about projections and demographics. But they insist, so I sit there and doodle while pretending to pay attention." Hannah giggled.

"So how are things there? With...Evan?" She couldn't even bring herself to say Trevor's name. She was a sad case.

"Fine. I mean, Evan's grounded for like a week. And he has to do extra chores." She laughed again. "Dad has him working on that pitiful garden you left."

"What? My garden was cute."

"The flowers are all dying. Your thumb isn't exactly green."

One more thing that she'd tried and failed at.

"Anyway, Dad spent a lot of time talking to both of us."

"About?"

"Lots of stuff. Him drinking, why he got so mad at Evan, how hard it is for him. I never really knew, you know? I don't remember the bad stuff. I knew what Mom told us when they divorced, but he's always just been my dad. I didn't know how hard being sober is for him."

Callie didn't really know, either. She'd met alcoholics of course, but no one really close to her. No one she would get that personal with. Except Trevor. She swallowed hard. "Did he drink?"

"No." Hannah's eyes widened.

Relief eased through Callie's body. She wanted to ask how Trevor was doing. Was he as messed up as she felt? But asking Hannah seemed creepy.

"He misses you."

Callie's stomach flipped, and another lump formed in her throat. She couldn't speak.

"The day you left, after he talked to Evan, he went to

your house. He didn't know you were gone." Her eyes narrowed on Callie. "Why didn't you tell him?"

She forced some words out. "He was mad. We needed space."

"Thousands of miles." Hannah waited a beat. "You should call him."

She should, but she didn't know what she was supposed to say. She nodded. "I will."

"When?"

Leave it to Trevor's kid to close all loopholes.

She didn't want to lie to Hannah, but she also wasn't going to confide all of her insecurities to a teenager, either. "I'm not sure. I have some thinking to do."

Hannah leaned closer to the camera and stared at Callie. "What's there to think about? You guys love each other, and when someone matters to you, you talk to them."

Heavy words coming from a kid. Definitely Lisa's kid. Lisa had always laid the facts out to her. Especially the facts Callie wanted to avoid. "It's more complicated than that."

"That's what adults always say." She huffed.

While she was right, it didn't make it less true. "One day, you'll be an adult, and you'll understand exactly how complicated life can get."

"Whatever. Just call him soon, okay? He's all mopey. He tries to hide it, but he sucks at that."

Callie smiled. She loved this girl. Hell, she loved all of them, but she wasn't sure love was enough to make things work. "Soon."

They said their goodbyes, and Callie flopped back on the bed. She scrolled through her laptop to see if there was a movie or something to watch. But her mind kept going back to Chicago. In all the years she'd been traveling, everything had felt like a way station. Nothing had ever felt permanent. Until she'd moved into that little coach house behind Lisa.

Now when she thought of home, she imagined the house and yard and Trevor and the kids. The pictures were all intermingled in her mind. The worry about losing all of it ate at her. If she and Trevor couldn't fix their relationship, get to a point where they were equals —partners—she wouldn't have any home at all.

And that was the worst feeling she'd ever had.

TREVOR BUSIED HIMSELF WITH EVERYTHING HE COULD possibly think of. He worked all day, teaching Evan what he could. As it turned out, his son had natural ability, and he loved working construction. Trevor was trying to wrap his head around the idea that maybe college wasn't the path for Evan. He attempted to be more open-minded, but he wasn't very good at it.

After they ate dinner at night, Trevor found some other project to occupy himself. If he did nothing, he felt the world close in on him. Thoughts of Callie and the fact that he'd fucked up so bad that he'd driven her away consumed him. Although he didn't know how to fix it, he focused on what he could do, what he had to offer. He would be ready when she came home. He had to believe she would return to him.

She wouldn't even answer the phone when he called. Hannah had spoken to her, so he knew she was alive. He called every day, and she never answered. When he heard the voicemail pick up, he disconnected. He needed to talk to her.

He repainted the basement, which was unfinished and didn't need to be painted, but he couldn't figure out what else needed to be fixed. After the brushes were cleaned and the slate-gray paint tucked under the stairs, he went out to the back deck and sat on the steps.

The temperature was still warm, but a cool breeze kicked up. Cicadas chirped and fireflies flickered. When he was younger, this had been his favorite time of year. It was perfect for festivals and barbecues, music and laughter. He'd gotten away from all of that with sobriety, which was sad. His life had become stagnant. All he had was work.

Until Callie. She'd broken the monotony of his life. She was the brilliant sunrise after a long night. Her laughter lifted him no matter how bad things felt.

He needed to get her back.

The screen door opened behind him. Hannah leaned out. "She's coming back."

"Huh?"

She came all the way out, and the door slammed behind her. That would be his next project—adjust the closer so the door didn't slam.

Hannah sat next to him. "Callie. She goes away, but she always comes back. Always."

"Maybe not this time."

"You're wrong."

"How can you be sure?"

"Because she told me she's coming back. And Callie doesn't lie."

"Did she say *when* she was coming back?"

"Sheesh. Do I gotta do everything? And you guys say teenagers are bad. Talk to her."

Trevor shook his head. "Tried. She won't answer."

"Mom never taught you anything about being tricky." She pulled out her phone. "Callie won't answer for you, but she always does for me."

His daughter was brilliant. It hadn't occurred to him to call from a different phone. He took the cell. "Thanks."

Hannah went back inside, leaving him with the sounds of the bugs and his hammering heart. He'd gotten used to calling Callie, knowing she wouldn't answer. He had the solution in his hand. After all those failed calls, he should know what he wanted to say, but his mind blanked.

He stood and paced the yard. What words could he say? Of course, he owed her an apology, but it wasn't enough. He'd apologized every time he screwed up, but he kept making the same mistakes. He had to convince her that he could change.

The more he procrastinated, the more likely it was he wouldn't call. He scrolled through the phone and hit send. On the third ring, he was ready to hang up, his stomach already in knots.

"Hey, hon. What's up? Miss me already?"

God, her voice. It was the warm sunshine he'd been missing for days. "Actually, yeah."

Silence.

"It's me, not Hannah. Don't hang up."

"Trevor? What's wrong? Are the kids okay?" She went from sunny to frightened in a breath.

"The kids are fine."

"Then why are you using Hannah's phone?"

"Because you wouldn't answer when I called from mine." He inhaled deeply, totally at a loss for words. "It was Hannah's idea. She knew you'd answer."

"Why are you calling?" So many reasons. He needed to organize his thoughts so he wouldn't sound like a rambling lunatic. He should've written this down. Made a list. Something.

"I'm going to hang up if you don't say something."

"How was your flight?"

"It was five days ago."

"Yeah." Man, he sounded stupid. "How's Italy?"

"Beautiful."

Crap. Was she going to offer anything other than one-word responses?

"If you're looking for small talk, I'm done."

"Don't." Another deep breath. "I miss you. I'm calling because I miss you more than I ever thought possible. I've been calling you every day, but you don't answer. I should've figured out by now what to say, but I don't know."

She sighed, and her breath whistled across thousands of miles.

"I screwed up, Callie. I know I did. I'm sorry. I also know that giving you an apology isn't enough. But I don't know what else I can do or say when you're on the other side of the world."

"I don't know what you could say, either. What you said the other night hurt. I would never do anything to hurt you or the kids. I know I'm not their mom, but I love them."

"I know." His heart sank. She loved the kids. No mention of how she felt about him. "I was scared for Evan. I lashed out at you, and it wasn't fair. But you ran away again. And not just for a day or a weekend. You flew to Italy for a job that would take you away from us for at least a year. That scares me."

"I didn't run away. It's not like I fabricated a reason for leaving. You knew this job offer was on the table."

"But you said you wanted to stay in Chicago." *To build a life here.* He almost said it, but he didn't want to start a fight or pressure her.

"I needed to get away."

"Why?"

"Because I don't know how to deal with you. With us. It's so freaking complicated. When I need to figure things out, I need space."

Her words made him feel like he was losing her all over again. "We can make it work."

"I'm not so sure about that. You say you want me there, to have a life with you, but you also want to keep me separate from the most important part of your life. It's okay for me to be the fun aunt or chauffeur for the kids, but I have no voice in anything that matters."

He opened his mouth to argue but clamped his jaw shut.

"I don't need to be their mom. I just want to feel like I matter."

"You do matter, Callie. You matter to all of us."

"Words are easy, Trevor."

"Tell me what you need from me."

"That's just it. I'm not sure. I wish I could give you a road map for this, but I don't think one exists."

They sat in silence for a few moments. Trevor was afraid to say anything and more afraid to hang up.

"I think we both need to take this time while I'm away to figure out what we want and need."

"That's easy. I need you. Here with me."

"And what if I can't give you that?" More silence. "I'll be home in a couple weeks. We'll talk then."

"Can I call you before then?"

"Why?"

"To talk to you. To make sure you're okay. To hear your voice."

"I won't promise to answer. This is hard for me."

He hated knowing she was torn up over him. He wished he could pull her into his arms and kiss her, because in those moments, nothing else mattered. They could do anything. "Okay. Be careful. I'll be waiting for you when you get home."

"Goodbye," she whispered before disconnecting. Trevor stayed out in the yard, holding the phone as if it were a way to hold on to Callie.

For another week, Callie thought long and hard about what she wanted and expected from Trevor. He continued to call every day, but she didn't pick up. She hadn't figured out what to say. But now he always left a message. Mostly short things to let her know he was thinking of her.

Her productivity suffered. By the end of her second week in Italy, she'd had enough. She wasn't happy with the photos she'd submitted. Something was missing.

Her personal life had never taken a toll on her professional life like this. Then again, she'd never been in love like this before. The more time she spent in Italy, the more she missed Chicago.

She missed home.

That was the deciding factor. Even if she and Trevor couldn't make anything work, she wanted to be in Chicago, part of the kids' lives, building a place for herself.

She had a lengthy conversation with Victoria, offered them a cut-rate price on the shots she'd taken in Rome, and gave them the names of some of her acquaintances who she thought would be interested in the job. She agreed to do a Great Britain tour in a few weeks. She also left the door open to do other tours in the future if they wanted. But she couldn't commit to the full long-term project.

Such was the story of her life.

Long-term wasn't her thing. It was a niggling fear that settled into the pit of her stomach. Maybe Trevor was right. She routinely ran away because she didn't know how to stick it out. She said she needed space because that's what she thought worked. Looking back, it never had. She took off, and people gave up on her.

But she'd never had anyone like Trevor, someone who believed in her. Someone who would wait for her, who knew she would come back. She wanted to try to stick it out.

She flew back to Chicago without telling anyone. Hannah wasn't expecting her for at least a few more days. Unfortunately, it wasn't like she could hide out at home and go unnoticed.

Her flight landed at nearly ten at night. By the time she got her luggage and a car to go home, she was exhausted. When the car dropped her off in front of the house, she saw the lamps glowing in the kids' rooms. The blue light of the TV flickered in the living room. As much as she felt like she was home, she couldn't just walk in, so she sneaked into the backyard as silently as possible.

Unlocking her door, she pushed in and met a wall of muggy air. This was the price she paid for not telling anyone she was coming back. In the past, she'd call Lisa, who then came over and turned on the AC so the house wasn't miserable. She dragged her suitcases into the living room and turned on the unit.

While the air began to blow, she shoved her equipment bags into her darkroom and opened her suitcase full of clothes. She took the pile of dirty laundry and put it in the washing machine. Then she tucked her suitcase in the closet and took her toiletries to the bathroom. She accomplished all of this with minimal light because she wasn't ready to draw attention to her arrival.

She took a cool shower, happy to be in her own space with her soap and quality water pressure. Whenever she traveled, it was the little things like this that she missed.

Until now, a nagging voice sounded in her head. This time, hot water had been the least of her concerns.

Trudging upstairs, she walked to her bed, feeling like something was off. She looked around her room. Everything seemed to be in its place. Sinking to the mattress, she flopped back. That was when she saw it—a beautiful clear skylight right over her bed.

The recurring lump in her throat was back. While she'd been avoiding him, Trevor had installed the skylight she'd joked about wanting. It was amazingly clear, giving her a little slice of evening sky to stare at.

It would've been easier to appreciate if her eyes hadn't filled with tears. She was turning into such a sap.

She sat up in bed. So he put in a window for her. He was a carpenter, for Pete's sake. It wasn't like he'd carved her a sculpture out of marble. This was what he did for a living. She didn't cry over a man. She was the kind of woman who took huge bites out of life, content to go it alone.

Swiping at the tears, she took a deep breath. Time for her to figure out what she wanted and needed. Life was too short to waffle.

Just then, a noise outside caught her attention. She stood and looked out the window from her loft, which offered a full view of the back of the house and most of the yard. Trevor had come through the back door.

He stood there and looked up at her house. Callie's heart thudded. He couldn't see her. At least she didn't think so. Watching from the edge of her stairs, she saw a man who looked tired. Defeated. Sad. But he still hadn't asked for help. It was as if he didn't trust her to be there for him, as if she couldn't be counted on. Unless he didn't want to face conflict with his ex-mother-in-law. Then he was happy to ask for her help.

He went back into the house, and she returned to her bed and stared up at the skylight. At some point, she'd have to face him, make some decisions about what they were and where they were going. She loved him. That was the only thing she was sure of. Whistling in the yard caught her attention. Sharp and clear with a melody, the sound was not someone calling in a dog.

The calming tune soothed her, and she closed her eyes to listen. A guitar joined the whistling. She knew the song but couldn't place it. Somewhere in the back of her mind, like a long-ago memory. She hummed along trying to recall the words.

Then Trevor's voice began singing, and it all came rushing back to her. Trevor in the band, the first time they'd met. The band had performed "Patience" by Guns N' Roses. The iconic whistle should've been enough to trigger the memory. She'd swooned over him that night, and she'd nudged Lisa to pay attention to the band.

She slid from bed again and slunk to the window to watch. He stared at her window, undeterred by her lack of acknowledgment. He just kept performing. Except she knew this show was just for her. Moving into view, she made eye contact and felt his gaze deep in her soul. She opened the window to hear him more clearly as he sang about having patience and being willing to wait because they had what it would take to make it.

He was telling her that he wanted to make them work, no matter what. He believed in them.

She licked her lips. History made her look like a bad bet. She did have a habit of taking off at a moment's notice. She wanted to be here for him, though. She wanted to be the one he leaned on.

Could it be that simple?

Swallowing hard, she straightened and did what her heart demanded. She went to get what she wanted.

Chapter Fourteen

Trevor stared up at Callie's window. When he'd come up with this crazy idea, he hadn't considered how stupid he would feel carrying it out. Luckily, none of his neighbors had yelled at him yet. He should've chosen another song. Something more upbeat. Something shorter.

Being in a band had been easy. He'd never sung solo, except when he was screwing around at home. Pouring his heart into a song for the woman he loved was no joke.

When she disappeared from the window, he almost stopped—gave up—but the musician in him continued, despite the worry and fear.

Her door opened as he finished the final chords of the song. She leaned against the doorjamb, arms crossed, wearing a pair of shorts and an old T-shirt that had been one of his. Her wet hair clung to the front of the shirt, covering the name of the band whose concert he'd attended years ago. That shirt had never looked so good.

He stood and set his guitar on the patio chair. She said nothing.

He wanted to go to her, but his feet were stuck, his legs frozen in place. "Why didn't you tell us you were coming home?"

"My flight was late, and you're usually in bed early."

"I would've picked you up."

"How'd you know I was here?"

"I saw some lights on and heard the air conditioner." Should he admit that he came out every night and looked for signs of her being home?

She hitched a thumb toward her second floor. "Thanks for the skylight. I wasn't serious about that, you know."

"Don't you like it?"

"I love it."

Silence stretched between them for a moment, hanging on the weight of the words she'd spoken. Love. He'd installed the skylight because of love. He hoped she knew that.

"The song was pretty damn good, too."

"Words don't always work for me, but music and building are things I'm good at."

"You express yourself differently. I get it."

Did she? Did she understand how it was killing him to not rush to her and hold her?

"Why didn't you come over when you got home?" he asked.

"I was still sorting things out." She pushed away from the door and walked barefoot across the grass toward him.

"Did you figure it out?"

She nodded slowly. "I think so."

Air whooshed from his lungs. He couldn't read her expression, didn't know if she planned on dumping his dumb ass for good, but he wouldn't go down without a fight.

She stopped about a foot away from him. Close enough to touch, and he wanted to reach for her.

"Did you mean it?" she asked.

"Mean what?"

"The lyrics. The song. Do you believe in us? That we have what it takes to last as long as we have patience?"

"I do. For the first time in a lot of years, I'm able to picture a future with someone. You."

"I want us to work, Trevor. We're not kids anymore. When things get tough, we should be able to turn to each other, to have someone to count on. I thought we could be that for each other."

"That's what I want, too."

"But you're not showing that. You keep everything bottled up and under such tight control, I don't know what to expect. I want you to trust me enough to lean on me, to let me help."

"You already do so much—"

"The small, meaningless stuff. You hang on to every ounce of control, and I can't live like that."

"I'm afraid to dump too much on you. I did that to Lisa. She took care of everything, and I thought I knew, but I didn't. Not until it was too late. I don't want to make that mistake again. I don't want to be a burden."

Callie stepped closer and sat on the step, tugging his hand so he would join her. The small contact set his skin on fire. He wanted to touch her and not stop. But once he sat, she released his fingers and tucked her hands between her knees.

"You have to trust that I'll tell you if it's too much. Lisa loved being in charge. She lived for being a mom and running everyone's lives. She thrived on it." Callie turned to face him. "On the weekends when you had the kids, she was lost. We used to do movie night, but she spent most of the time doing laundry and trying to feed me."

"She shouldn't have had to shoulder it all."

"She chose to, Trevor. She could've asked you to step up and do more, but she didn't. And now you're doing the same thing."

"I'm just trying to be a good father."

"But you don't have to do it alone."

"I don't want to."

She took his hand, and for the first time in this conversation, he felt hopeful. "Then let me in. Trust me to take on some of the burden, to be your partner."

"It seems unfair."

"It's not. If you ask too much, I'll tell you to back off."

"I want to try. I've missed you so much for the past two weeks." With his free hand, he ran fingers through her hair. "What do you get out of this deal? It seems a little one-sided."

"I get a partner, someone to count on, just like you do. More importantly, I get family and a place to call home. I haven't had either in a really long time."

Trevor couldn't wait any longer. He leaned over and brushed his lips against hers, needing to taste her, show her how much he'd missed her. When his tongue touched hers, he vibrated with need. He wanted to scoop her up, strip her bare, and slide into her forever.

Forever. The word buzzed through his mind, and a new need took over. He pulled back and waited for her eyes to reopen. Cradling her face, he said, "I love you, Callie. I don't want you to run away anymore. You belong here—with us, your family."

Her eyes filled, and his heart lurched again. He'd only considered his need to say the words, not whether she was prepared to hear them.

"I love you, too," she whispered. "But I don't run away."

A laugh burst from his chest, and he held her close. "Oh, honey, yeah you do. You've been running almost as long as I've known you. The first time you ran was when I proposed to Lisa."

"I thought I was losing my best friend."

"I'm no shrink, but I can see that you always run when you think you're going to be left. Like you want to be the one to do the leaving."

She slid away and looked at him. "And yet you want to be with me?"

He wrapped an arm around her waist, drawing her close again. He had no intention of ever letting her go. "Well, since I don't plan on leaving, it seems safe. Besides, something Hannah said the other day reminded me of Lisa's words years ago. 'Callie runs, but she always comes home.'" He kissed her temple. "I'm patient. I'm strong enough to stand and wait, as long as you always come back to me."

"I think I'm done running."

"Yeah?"

She nodded against his chest. "Pretty sure. I was kind of miserable in Italy, which is a travesty." After another tight squeeze, she slid away again. "I didn't take the job. At least not what they offered. I'm going to go to Great Britain for a couple weeks. I might do some tours later, but I won't be traveling all the time."

Trevor's heart lifted. She planned to stay with them, plant some roots.

A noise behind them caught Trevor's attention. "Hey, is that Callie?" Evan called from the kitchen.

"Yeah," she answered, taking Trevor's hand. "Making out with your kids as an audience probably isn't a good idea, huh?"

He smiled, and Evan came out onto the deck. "Why are you guys sitting out here in the dark?"

"We were thinking about running naked in the yard to celebrate summer," Callie answered.

"Ew. Not an image I need to have."

Callie doubled over with laughter. When she straightened, she said, "Sometimes you guys are so easy."

Evan came to the top of the steps. "I'm sorry for the trouble I caused between you and Dad."

Callie's forehead wrinkled. "That wasn't your fault."

"Felt like it was."

"It wasn't. You have nothing to apologize to me for."

"Thanks for getting me that night. Not sure if I said it before you left."

"It's okay. Part of the job."

Warmth spread through Trevor because she was right. She'd been acting as a parent to his children, but he kept trying to draw boundary lines. It was time to erase those lines.

"Why don't you go tell Hannah that Callie is back?

She'll be excited." Evan nodded and took off into the house. They heard his yell from where they sat.

Trevor groaned as he pulled Callie to stand. "Not quite what I had in mind." He put an arm around her and led her up the stairs. "I owe you another apology."

"What for?"

"You've been taking care of the kids for a long time. From what I can tell, even before Lisa died, and I dismissed it. I'm sorry. In my effort to try to do it all, I neglected to notice—really pay attention to—how much you do and how much they already count on you. Bad news for you, though."

"Why?"

He held the back door open for her. "Because now we're never going to let you go."

She stretched up and kissed his cheek. "That's good, because I love you. All of you."

He'd never tire of hearing that.

TREVOR DRAGGED HIMSELF IN FROM A LONG DAY AT WORK. Evan trudged behind him. He gave his son credit. He'd been working every day, keeping up with Trevor and paying attention to almost everything Trevor tried to teach him. Of course, there were times when Evan acted as if he knew what he was doing, or maybe he thought he could figure it out on his own, and it inevitably blew up in his face. Trevor remembered what it was like to be an apprentice, to want to prove yourself. But for the most part, the boy worked hard.

In the kitchen, he poured them both a cold glass of water. "I'm proud of you. You've been doing a great job."

"Thanks." His son ducked his head at the praise. Trevor gulped the water. "I'll admit you lasted way longer than I thought you would."

Evan lifted his head and looked at him with narrowed eyes. "Nice to know you had so little faith in me."

"It's not that. I brought you to the job because I hoped to scare you off. Your mother and I always expected you would go to college. To be better than me."

Evan lifted a shoulder. "I like working construction."

Trevor sighed. He believed Evan, because he saw the eagerness on his son's face when they were challenged on the job and he was really invested in learning. He expressed way more interest there than he ever did in school.

"I guess college doesn't have to be a requirement. You can always decide to go later, right?"

Evan huffed. "Yeah, sure."

"I'm serious. I'm not going to pressure you now, but I want you to keep your options open."

"I guess I can do that."

"Good. Now go shower. I have a meeting to get to." Evan set his glass in the sink. "Do you even need meetings anymore?"

Trevor was still getting used to his kids asking about his addiction openly. "Maybe not *need*. But if you keep in touch with the things that are important, you're not out of practice when you do need them."

Evan nodded, satisfied with the answer, and left the room.

Less than an hour later, he was heading to his AA meeting, and Hannah sidelined him at the door.

"Can we talk for a minute?"

"One minute. I'm on my way to a meeting."

"I'll talk fast." She took a deep breath. "I've been thinking about school, and I want to do a semester abroad next semester. The deadline to apply is in like a week, so I know I should've started sooner, but I just found out about it."

"A semester? Like six months? Where?"

"There are a lot of options, but I'm thinking about maybe Korea?" The hesitation in her voice told him she knew the likelihood of him agreeing was slim.

"No."

"But, Dad. You didn't even consider it."

"I'm not sending my daughter halfway around the world to a place that might start a war with its other half."

She huffed. "How about Spain, then? Spain is totally safe."

"Nothing is totally safe when you're on your own, thousands of miles away."

"I wouldn't be alone. I'd be with a host family."

"Oh yeah. I'm going to send you to live with strangers in a strange place. Not gonna happen."

"But—"

"I have to go to my meeting." He kissed the top of her head, even as she pulled away with crossed arms. He'd gotten hip to how Hannah played things. She often tried to ask for permission when he was distracted or leaving.

Asking for money to hang out with friends didn't hold a candle to asking to move to the other side of the planet.

But maybe when she was done being mad at him, they could talk about options for traveling for school when she was older, like in college. As he climbed into his truck, he thought that maybe he was getting a handle on this parenting thing.

CALLIE HAD A GREAT DAY TAKING PHOTOS IN THE CITY OF people and places. She'd begun to think about maybe putting together a gallery show of her pictures. She hadn't done one in years
—more years than she'd like to consider—since before she began doing travel photography regularly. She'd taken them on film and figured tonight might be a good time to give Hannah a lesson in developing.

She didn't know how interested Hannah was in photography or if her interest was mostly in spending extra alone time with Callie, but she'd take it. When she pulled up to the house, Trevor's truck was already gone. Damn. She'd hoped to catch him before his meeting. They'd missed each other this morning, and she wanted to talk to him about her upcoming trip to Great Britain. She'd meant to talk to him last night, but as usual, Trevor had distracted her with other things.

Gathering her camera bag, she climbed from her car and went into the house. "Hannah?" she called.

Hannah came flying down the stairs. "Good. You're here."

"What's going on?" Callie tamped down her worry. If it was something bad, they would've called her.

"I need your help with Dad. He's being so...overbearing. He won't listen. He didn't even pretend to consider it."

Callie shook her head to try to follow. "Consider what?"

Evan passed behind his sister. "She wants to go live in Korea for a year."

"What?" Callie asked.

Hannah huffed. "I want to do a semester abroad next semester. The deadline to apply is in a week. I mentioned Korea, but when he talked about me going someplace unsafe, I suggested Spain. He still wouldn't listen." She tugged Callie's hand. "You have to talk him."

"I don't know, Hannah. You're young to be that far from home for so long. It's a huge decision to make with less than a week's notice."

"But you travel all the time. You can tell him it's safe."

"I can't say that. I don't know anything about the program you're interested in. I have no idea what kind of oversight there is. I didn't start traveling around the world until I was an adult. And if that travel has taught me nothing else, it's that the world is a very unsafe place."

"Seriously? You're not going to help?"

"I agree with your dad on this one. Especially since we don't have time to check out the program. Maybe another year after we've investigated all the options."

"I can't believe this! You're supposed to be on my side." Hannah turned and stomped off.

Callie was flabbergasted. Hannah's barb shot right through her. She *was* on Hannah's side.

Evan came from the kitchen with an apple in his hand. "Looks like you're more of a mom than our friend now, huh? That sucks."

Then he walked away.

Callie had no idea what to do. She was trying to be a role model for them, an adult they could count on, someone Trevor could lean on. But she was going to make them hate her. And that was something she couldn't handle.

She slipped out the back door to her place. Every time she tried to make a decision in the best interest of the kids, she screwed it up. She had no idea what she was doing. There was a reason she wasn't a mother.

Leaving her camera bag on the counter, she went upstairs, sat on her bed, and stared at her closet. Her suitcase was right there. It would take her less than thirty minutes to pack and get a ticket to London. She could just go early. By the time she finished the job, things here would be settled. All decisions would be firmly up to Trevor and she wouldn't have to take the heat for anything.

She grabbed her bag and flipped it open on her bed. As soon as she turned back to the closet to pick out clothes, Trevor's words rang in her head: *you always run when you think you're going to be left.*

Damn it. She hated when he was right. She did run. But she'd also told him she was done running. Time to follow through.

"Callie?" Trevor called from the stairs.

"Up here," she answered as she scooped her suitcase back up.

He stopped abruptly when he reached her room. "What's going on?"

"Nothing." She tucked her bag back in the closet.

"Callie."

Turning to face him, she took a deep breath. "Just a little freak-out. Old habits, you know."

Concern filled his face. "What happened?"

"Nothing really."

"It must've been something to make you want to run."

She sighed and sank onto her bed. "Hannah came to me all like, 'Dad won't listen. You have to talk to him.' Then she told me it was about going to the other side of the world and I was like, 'No way.' She got mad and stomped off. That was bad enough, but then Evan looked at me and said I'm not their friend anymore."

Trevor sat beside her and laughed. Actually laughed.

"I don't see what's so funny."

"Welcome to the world of parenting. Hannah tried a workaround and got mad because it didn't get her what she wanted. Do you have any idea how often she tried to play me and Lisa against each other? As far as what Evan said, he's probably right, but I don't think that's necessarily a bad thing. If you're friends with them, it's harder to parent."

There was that word again. *Parent*. He was right. She had wanted to be all in on this family thing, including the tough parts of parenting.

She laced her fingers in his and leaned her head on his shoulder. "Thanks. I needed to hear that."

"What do you think about Hannah? Do you really

think it's a bad idea for her to study abroad for a year, or did you just say that to have my back?"

"Do you think I'd not give my honest opinion?" She chuckled.

"I guess not."

"She's so young. The world is a scary place. I did tell her maybe later, after we have a chance to investigate the program and check out all the options. She didn't want to hear that, either."

"I don't know if I'll ever be okay with sending her that far away." A sudden thought struck Callie. "What about if you didn't have to send her alone?"

"I'm pretty sure most places would frown on a dad tagging along for her semester."

Callie straightened. "No, I'm talking about taking her with me to England when I go. It'll be for a few weeks, and she might miss the beginning of the school year, but the experience would be good for her. It would give her the taste of traveling she wants. You wouldn't have to worry about her safety because she'd be with me."

Trevor studied her a minute. The silence nearly broke her. Maybe he didn't trust her to be alone with Hannah out of the country.

"I'd still worry. About both of you. But we can talk about it."

Callie wrapped her arms around him. Every time she thought she knew what to expect from him, he surprised her. "I love you," she whispered.

"I love you, too."

Three weeks later, Callie was once again packing her suitcases. It was time for her trip to Great Britain, but this time, she looked forward to the work because she had her very own assistant. Hannah was joining her for the two-week tour. Callie had been surprised when Trevor agreed, because Hannah would miss the first day of school orientation.

She'd never seen Hannah so excited, though. She'd done nothing but talk about all the places she wanted to visit. Luckily, since Callie was there to take tourist photos, she was getting paid to take Hannah on a tour. It was the best of both worlds.

Trevor was tense at the thought of Hannah being so far away, but Callie understood that was normal parental worry. The important thing was that he trusted Callie to take his daughter.

Callie hauled her bags over to the house. They were all going to have dinner together tonight. Then Trevor would drive them to the airport in the morning. Evan would drive himself to the job site to get to work. Callie smiled. Trevor had been true to his word. Over the last few weeks, he'd really worked on being less controlling.

Their family wasn't perfect, but they fit together well. Callie was insanely happy.

At least until she walked through the back door of the house and heard the one voice that had the ability to always ruin her good mood. *What the hell is Diane doing here?*

Callie froze and although it was juvenile, she eavesdropped.

"How can you trust that woman to take Hannah thousands of miles away? She's not her mother."

"Hannah is well aware of who her mother was. We all are, including Callie. But she's part of their lives. She's not going anywhere."

"You don't understand the influence she can have, Trevor."

Callie's stomach turned. God, why would Diane do this to her? She knew Diane didn't like her, but to try to ruin her relationship with Trevor and the kids... Straightening her shoulders, she rolled her bags through the kitchen and into the living room. Diane and Trevor sat across from each other. Both of them shut their mouths at her entrance.

"Hi," she said, cautiously.

"Hey," Trevor said. He rose and took her bags from her, leaving her with nothing to cling to. He tucked them in the corner and came back to her. Taking her hand, he pulled her to the couch.

"What's going on?"

"Diane drove here to talk to me about Hannah going on the trip with you."

Callie pressed her lips together. She didn't want to spend her last night in Chicago fighting with Diane. Plus, why the hell should she have to?

Diane glared at her.

"Forgive me for being rude, Diane, but it's none of

your business. Trevor has given Hannah permission to take this trip, and that's all that matters."

Trevor laid a hand on Callie's thigh, and her entire body tensed. *Please don't change your mind to appease this woman.*

"Actually, Diane, this was a decision Callie and I made together. I told you weeks ago that we're a couple."

He had? He hadn't said anything to Callie about it.

"So she gets more of a vote on my grandchildren's lives than I do?"

"Callie and I are in love. We're a couple. We're raising the kids together. If you can't accept that, I don't know what to tell you. I don't want to keep the kids from you, but I won't have you bad-mouthing Callie to them. They love her. So do I. She's not going anywhere."

Diane sniffed. "Except to Europe."

"It's a two-week trip, Diane. It's work for me, but it will be a great experience for Hannah," Callie said. She hoped simple logic would help.

"This time it's two weeks. What about the next trip? What about when you go to dangerous locations and Hannah thinks it will be fun?"

Callie clenched her jaw. Logic wasn't helping. She should've known better.

Trevor took her hand and interlaced his fingers with hers. "I trust Callie to make positive, safe decisions for the kids. We talk through things together. If there's another trip Hannah wants to take with Callie, we'll discuss it."

Callie was stunned. Words completely left her. Trevor was not only standing his ground with Diane, but he was defending Callie to her.

Diane's face grew pink. "It seems as though she

already has her hooks in you, and no matter what I say, you won't listen."

"Not when it comes to my relationship or what I allow the kids to do."

Diane stood. "Would it be all right for me to say goodbye to the children?"

"Of course. Like I said before, I want you to be part of their lives, but if you want a relationship with them, you'll have to accept Callie. We're a package deal."

Diane simply looked from Trevor to her and then turned to go upstairs to see the kids.

Callie's stomach flipped. As much as she didn't like Diane, she didn't want to cause a rift between the kids and their grandparents. They sat in silence until Diane came back. Callie still wasn't sure what to say. Trevor walked Diane to the door and locked up. Callie stood and waited for him to come back. Simply having Diane out of the house eased the tension in her. When he neared, she wrapped her arms around his neck. "So I have my hooks in you, huh?"

"Oh, yeah. Stuck deep, too."

She laughed and pressed closer to him. "Thank you for that."

"For what?"

"For standing up to Diane. For making me and the kids a priority. For explaining that we're a team, even if she doesn't want to accept it."

"I know I avoided fighting with her before, mostly because I want the kids to know their grandparents, but they don't get to make rules for my life. This is our family."

Those were the best words to hear. Callie loved having a family of her own.

Also by Shannyn Schroeder

The O'Leary Family
More Than This (The O'Leary Family #1)
A Good Time (The O'Leary Family #2)
Something to Prove (The O'Leary Family #3)
Catch Your Breath (The O'Leary Family #4)
Just a Taste (The O'Leary Family #5)
Hold Me Close (The O'Leary Family #6)

The O'Malley Family
Under Your Skin (The O'Malley Family #1)
In Your Arms (The O'Malley Family #2)
Through Your Eyes (The O'Malley Family #3)
From Your Heart (The O'Malley Family #4)

The Doyle Family
In Too Deep (The Doyle Family #1)
In Fine Form (The Doyle Family #2)

Daring Divorcees Series
One Night with a Millionaire
My Best Friend's Ex
My Forever Plus-One

Stand Alones
Between Love and Loyalty

Meeting His Match

Hot & Nerdy

Her Best Shot

Her Perfect Game

Her Winning Formula

His Work of Art

His New Jam

His Dream Role

Sloane Steele's Books

The Counterfeit Capers

Origin of a Thief (The Counterfeit Capers 0)

It Takes a Thief (The Counterfeit Capers #1)

Between Two Thieves (The Counterfeit Capers #2)

To Catch a Thief (The Counterfeit Capers #3)

The Thief Before Christmas (The Counterfeit Capers #4)

Milton Keynes UK
Ingram Content Group UK Ltd.
UKHW021522080824
446708UK00031B/453

9 781950 640539